IT HAD TO BE YOU

A CHANCES INLET NOVEL

TRACY SOLHEIM

Sun Home Productions

This one is for BAGO. Love you, man.

PROLOGUE

PAIGE HOLLISTER STOOD in the shadows of the crowded ballroom, looking on as her father toasted his new family. *As he toasted about love.* Apparently, all the love he needed was right here in this little backwater town. A town that didn't even boast its own Starbucks. She swallowed the disappointment clogging her throat and made her way out of the mansion as quickly as her stupid knock-off Jimmy Choo heels would allow.

Coming to Chances Inlet had been a colossal mistake. Not to mention a waste of frequent flyer miles and a black Marc Jacobs dress that was well above her schoolteacher's budget. Twenty-eight years old, and she still couldn't outrun her pathetic daddy issues.

Her plan was to surprise him. To accept the olive branch he was offering, but on her terms. That was before she'd gotten a glimpse of him in his new element. One where he seemed sickeningly happy with a family that didn't include her.

Well, she didn't need a father she barely knew to fill any holes in her life. He could take his shiny new family and stick it where the sun didn't shine. Paige had a great career at one of the most prestigious private schools in Chicago. She had a tight-knit circle of friends who supported her. And a new man in her life who just might turn out to be "the one."

Sheriff Lamar Hollister didn't know what he was missing.

She hurried through the mansion's heavy front door, only to crash into the back of someone waiting at the valet stand.

"Oh my gosh! I'm so sorry." She patted his wool suit jacket much like she would soothe one of her kindergartners who'd suffered a similar fate. "I wasn't looking where I was going."

"No worries, sweetheart," he said as he turned, his Australian accent melting some of the thickness in her throat.

Was there a woman alive who wasn't a sucker for that accent?

A slow smile of what looked like appreciation tugged up the corners of his mouth, revealing even white teeth and a perfect set of dimples. Laugh lines fanned out beside his eyes. Long sable lashes and the dark night made it impossible to make out their color, but she'd bet money they sparkled, whatever their shade. He had that devil-may-care way about him.

"I hope you're not in a hurry." He gestured to the empty valet stand. "It seems they've vanished."

Paige groaned dramatically. She needed to make her escape before her father discovered her here. Down Under Dude propped a shoulder against one of the pillars supporting the mansion's portico, crossing his feet at the ankles. He shoved his hands in his pockets.

"My thoughts exactly." Except he didn't seem as exasperated as she was. He studied her with a lazy grin. "I take it you're headed somewhere special for midnight?"

Ugh. Midnight on New Year's Eve. Every single woman's annual lament.

She should have stayed in Chicago. So what if Jon had a business event he had to attend tonight? At least she could have spent the evening with her friends.

Except all her friends were neatly paired up. She would

have been the seventh wheel in a group of couples. Most likely, her New Year's Eve would have involved a bottle of Prosecco and Netflix. Of course, that very scenario had been the catalyst for her making tonight's absurd trip.

I should have stuck with the Prosecco.

He chuckled, making Paige suspect she might have mumbled that last part out loud. *Oh well.* She didn't care how nutty she looked or sounded. It wasn't like she was ever going to see the guy or this little town again. Ignoring him, she pulled her cashmere wrap tighter around her bare shoulders.

"If you'd prefer to wait inside, I'm happy to pop in and let you know when the valet returns."

"I'm fine." No way was she going back in there. She softened her tone. There was no reason to be rude when he was acting like a gentleman. "Thank you, though."

"My lucky night, then."

Her knees nearly buckled at the potency of those damn dimples of his.

"You aren't escaping for a midnight rendezvous?"

For crying out loud! What in God's name made her ask him that? She was supposed to be slipping away unobtrusively, not flirting with a dark, handsome stranger who likely could rat her out to everyone inside.

He shook his head, his knowing smile never dimming. "No such luck. I'm headed home to bed. Alone."

Her nerve endings sparked to life at the word "alone." She was playing with fire here, and she knew better because she was always the one to get burned.

"Early flight," he explained as if to excuse the fact that a man as potently sexy as he would be companionless on New Year's Eve.

Welcome to the party, buster, cried single women everywhere.

Paige was saved from embarrassing herself more by the sudden arrival of another man. One dressed in a uniform typical of someone who worked in law enforcement. She swiftly stepped back into the shadows.

"Evening, deputy," Down Under Dude said. "You didn't happen to see the valets out there, did you?"

The deputy removed his brimmed hat, the lights from the party inside illuminating his classic features of broad shoulders, square jaw, sleek nose and close-cropped light hair.

"They're helping with a dead battery," he said. "One of them should be back shortly."

He glanced intently through the glass door.

"Are you looking for the sheriff?" the Australian asked.

"No." The deputy shook his head. "This is a big night for his family. I don't want to disturb him for anything."

The bile was back in her throat. Paige must have made a sound because she could feel Down Under Dude's gaze homing in on her. For his part, the deputy ignored them both, seemingly transfixed by something inside.

"Excuse me. I need to check on someone," he said before pulling the door open and disappearing into the mansion just as one of the valets sprinted up to the portico.

"So sorry to keep you waiting, sir," he said breathlessly. "I'll bring your car around right away."

The kid nearly fell over himself in deference to the Australian, making Paige wonder who the guy was.

"I can wait," Down Under Dude said. "Please fetch this lady's car first."

The valet shot a surprised look in Paige's direction, his eyes squinting into the darkness she was hovering in. Clearly, he did not realize there was anyone else besides the chivalrous stranger waiting. She stepped out of the shadow and gave the valet her parking stub.

"But you just got here," the valet protested.

Paige narrowed her eyes at him. "And now I'm leaving."

Mumbling something she couldn't quite make out, the valet disappeared into the parking lot again.

"That wasn't necessary. You were here first," she said to the man beside her. "But thank you."

He stepped a little closer, lowering his voice. "I must admit that my imagination is working overtime. Why do I get the feeling you're running from the law?"

A very unladylike snort escaped her lips. *If he only knew.*

"Nothing quite so dramatic," she replied.

"Did your date stand you up? Tell me his name, and I'll take care of him for you. He has no excuse."

She couldn't hold back the ridiculous grin his teasing brought to her face.

He stilled beside her. "I doubt there's a man alive who could resist that smile."

Her throat grew tight once again. He'd be surprised how wrong he was. There was one man. A man who had no trouble resisting her. And he was inside. With his newly acquired family.

Paige swayed slightly in her heels. Her companion of the past few minutes instantly wrapped warm fingers around her elbow to steady her. Her entire arm sizzled beneath his touch. His sharp intake of breath told her he felt it too.

The tires of her rental car squealed on the pavement as the valet brought it to a halt in front of them. She hesitated a long moment before attempting to pull away, but he tightened his grip slightly.

"Allow me," he said softly. "We can't have you falling down the steps."

A stronger woman would have asserted her independence, but the truth was, it was nice not having to stand on her own for once. She allowed him to guide her to the driver's side of her car, where the valet stood holding the door open. Paige fumbled for her bag to grab a tip, but her Dark Knight had already pulled some bills from his pocket and was handing them to the teenager.

"Have a good night, ma'am," the valet said. "I'll just go get your car now, Mr. Gillette."

Paige drew in a calming breath as she slid into the driver's seat. She turned her head to the side and nearly collided with the mysterious Mr. Gillette's lips. Not that she would have complained. They looked as sinful as the rest of him. But this could never be one of those nights that ended that way. Not when she needed to put as much distance between her and the North Carolina coast as quickly as possible.

He hesitated for a long beat, seeming to have his own internal debate about whether to pursue her or not. She quickly made the decision for him.

"I really need to be going," she whispered, confused by the regret she heard in her words.

He nodded and slowly pulled away.

"I hope the new year brings you everything you wish for," he said, then gently closed her door.

Paige didn't dare hesitate. She put the car in drive and hurried away before she could do a second foolish thing tonight.

CHAPTER ONE

THREE MONTHS LATER...

"YOU HAVE ARRIVED AT YOUR DESTINATION."

Paige Hollister snorted at the navigation app's announcement. She most certainly was *not* at her destination. Nowhere near it, in fact. When she'd left Chicago seventeen hours earlier, her destination was home: Ames, Iowa. Where her mother no doubt waited with a stern "I-told-you-so." And as if that weren't enough, Mother Nature planned to follow up that not-so-warm welcome with a bone-chilling snowstorm.

Something came over Paige when she neared the on-ramp for I-80 west, however. Rather than take her exit, she did what every unemployed, heartbroken woman staring thirty in the face would do. She hopped on the southbound lanes and headed toward sunshine, margaritas, and sand.

Going home felt like giving up for good. As angry and hurt as she was, she wasn't ready to throw in the towel. To admit her mom was right and she should never have left the farm for the big, bad city.

Paige may be down, but she was not out. Besides, she'd spent the bulk of the impromptu road trip giving herself a stern come-to-Jesus lecture. No more foolishly trusting a man with her heart. Did she learn her lesson when Jackson Miller asked her to prom only to ditch her for Chelsea Sorkin, whose unofficial senior class superlative was "most likely to smother a man with her double D's?" Nope. Did she learn her lesson when, sophomore year in college, Kurt Wallace wined and dined her, taking the gift of her virginity, only to dump her after she'd single-handedly spent all semester completing their project for advanced marketing? Apparently not.

They say "the third time is the charm." Except in this case, the third time was the kick in the ass Paige needed. Instead of wallowing in the misery of rejection, she was going to pick herself up, dust herself off, and live life her way.

On her own.

A sign nestled among the pine trees caught Paige's eye. Not that anyone could miss it. It was large enough that it was likely visible from space. The townspeople obviously wanted to suck in as many tourists as possible.

"Welcome to Chances Inlet, North Carolina, the home of second chances," it read.

Paige snorted again. "Second chances, my ass. If people weren't so quick to screw me over, they wouldn't need a second chance. Not that I'm giving anybody one. Ever," she practically shouted.

Her cellphone began to buzz as soon as the words left her mouth, causing her to nearly steer the car into the thick berm lining the road. She glanced at the screen, despite knowing exactly who was calling. Summer Pearson's face smiled back at her. Her best friend was likely tracking Paige's every movement on the friend locator app. Paige clicked the button on her dash to answer.

"Thank goodness you made it. Now tell me everything. What's it like?" Summer demanded immediately.

"You're worse than having a toddler in the car with me constantly asking 'are we there yet?' And I haven't even reached the actual town." She stopped at a red light. The gas station on the corner advertised worms and coffee on a placard beneath its sign. Paige shook her head with equal parts humor and disgust.

"But this time you'll get to see the town in the daylight at least." Summer's subtle reminder of the last time she'd been in Chances Inlet made Paige tighten her grip on the steering wheel. Three months ago, she'd vowed never to return to the sleepy coastal hamlet. Ironically, it was the only New Year's resolution she'd ever made that lasted more than a week.

Her estranged father had invited her to the double wedding of two of his new wife's sons. On New Year's Eve, no less. Paige initially refused. How dare he assume she didn't have better plans for the big night? But when her douchebag ex claimed to have to work that weekend, curiosity got the better of her and she decided to surprise her dad.

She wasn't sure if she wanted a relationship with a man who had barely been a blip in her life. But she did want to show him that she was a mature, independent woman who no longer needed his acceptance. Even if her heart never fully recovered from his abandonment.

In the end, though, she never got the chance to show off her new and improved self. Seeing him in his new element stirred up emotions she thought she'd gotten control of a long time ago. All it took was a few moments observing the warm gaze he showered on his beautiful wife and listening to his heartfelt toast about family to send her scurrying from the reception before she'd even made her presence known.

Maturity was a funny thing. Apparently, it came and went at will.

"I'll bet the town is adorable." Summer sounded like one of Paige's kindergartners—*make that former kindergarteners*—waxing on about some fairy garden. "With quaint little shops and people who actually say hi when you pass them on the sidewalk. I'll bet there's even a gazebo."

"You do know that Stars Hollow is not a real place?" Paige asked. "'The Gilmore Girls' was a television show filmed on the Warner Brothers lot."

"But there are real towns like it out there," Summer argued.

Didn't Paige know it. Ten years ago, she'd escaped the small town where she grew up and never looked back. Summer, on the other hand, was born and raised in a Chicago suburb. Her idea of life outside a major metropolis consisted of the idyllic small towns depicted on television or in movies.

"And who says Chances Inlet can't be like Stars Hollow," Summer insisted. "Who knows? They may even have a kitschy diner where everyone goes to gossip. You'll go in for a cup of joe and meet the man of your dreams. He'll be sitting right there at the counter next to you."

If only Summer could see how hard Paige was rolling her eyes. She'd been the subject of gossip enough to know she'd rather be just one in a million living in a large city. And as for men…

"Not gonna happen. I'm finished with guys, remember? Forever. I'm just passing through this rinky-dink town on my way to a two-week rent-free vacation at my stepbrother's Myrtle Beach timeshare."

"Yet you added an extra hour to your trip by getting off the highway and cruising through said 'rinky-dink town,'" Summer said. "Why is that I wonder?"

It was a question Paige had been asking herself for the past forty minutes.

"Morbid curiosity, I guess."

"Wanna know what I think?" Summer asked.

"Not really."

Not surprisingly, her friend ignored her. "I think you regret not sticking around New Year's Eve and getting to know your dad and his new family. I mean, he married a woman whose kids are celebrities. One of her sons is a United States congressman, for crying out loud. Another son is a professional baseball player. And don't forget the cute one who was *Cosmo's* Bachelor of the Month before he married a soap star. And he had that home improvement show. What was it called?"

"I have no idea," Paige lied. She'd binged the entire season of "Historical Restorations" in a single sitting last month while she was hiding out in her apartment trying to figure out what do with all of her empty days.

"Ooo, maybe you could stay at the gorgeous B & B your dad's wife owns. The Tide Me Over Inn, I think it's called. The pictures online look amazing," Summer gushed. "It supposedly books up a year in advance. I'll bet they have a room reserved for family, though."

"You're forgetting that I'm not family," Paige all but snapped.

She passed several chain hotels, grocery stores and beach shops as she made her way into the more historic part of the town. The sun was warm overhead, and her car was getting stuffy. She pressed the button to open her sunroof, allowing some fresh air in.

"Who says you can't be? Your dad clearly wants that. Or else he wouldn't keep inviting you to family events." Summer softened her tone. "Paige, you're not betraying your mom by getting to know your dad."

Was that what she was doing?

"Honestly, Sum, I don't have the emotional capacity to deal with my dad and his overachieving family right now. There was no other reason for me to divert off the highway other than I needed a change of scenery. I'm driving straight through to the beach where I'm going to put my toes in the sand, open a couple of bottles of wine, and spend a few weeks someplace where nobody knows my shame."

"Stop talking like that," Summer said. "You have absolutely nothing to be ashamed of."

"Tell that to the board of directors at Preston. They fired me for cause. Six years of exemplary work and suddenly my character is not appropriate for young minds."

"They are a bunch of hoity-toity pompous assholes," Summer argued. "They based their decision on rumors spread by a coven of bitchy moms with nothing better to do than tear people down. I agree with my brother. Sterling says you should sue them for defamation of character."

"Did your brother even pay attention during law school? Everyone knows the defense for defamation is truth. The truth is, I had an affair with a married man. The uncle of one of my students."

"Who never told you he was married!" Summer practically shouted. "The slimebag used you."

Of course he had. And yet, Paige was the one who paid the price. Her career was cancelled all because she trusted the wrong man. The unfairness of it still made her sick to her stomach.

It also made her question herself. How could she have been so blindsided by a sexy smile and complimentary words? Well, it wasn't happening again. She had a new life plan. It was a simple one. Never let anyone close enough to hurt her again.

"It's all going to work out," Summer said softly. "Sterling is putting together a case to get you your job back."

"He's wasting his time. My reputation is shot. If I want a coffee, I have to drive to the next suburb to avoid the angry glares of the parents staked out at our shop."

She didn't dare mention the ugly anonymous letters she received each week. Or the vicious DMs attacking her character. There was no point in stressing Summer out, too. Instead, Paige had shut down her social media, packed up her favorite books, and headed toward the sunshine. She would spend the next two weeks pulling on her big girl panties and figuring out her next move.

Whatever that might be.

"Then we will find you another job," Summer insisted.

Easy for Summer to say. Teaching was a side hustle for her friend while she pursued her dream of becoming a concert cellist. For Paige, teaching was more than a job. It was her calling. Her identity. Without it, she wasn't sure who she was anymore. And that scared her more than the attacks on her character.

She breathed through her nose to keep the tears at bay. Summer thought Paige was long past the days of crying jags on the sofa. Paige wanted her friend to believe she'd rounded a corner. Heck, *Paige* wanted to believe she'd rounded a corner.

"Sum, I can't even get a nannying gig. Apparently, moms don't want the 'other woman' near their husbands. Go figure."

Paige's car seemed to sense her precarious mood. It grew more and more sluggish as she made her way into the historic downtown area. Eclectic looking shops and restaurants surrounded a lush, green town square complete with a sprawling live oak tree and, *damn it,* a large white gazebo. Not that she was mentioning that little tidbit to Summer.

The sound of kids squealing flowed from the phone.

"I've gotta go," Summer said. "The kids are arriving for rehearsal. Don't forget you're coming to Milwaukee for my conducting debut with the children's symphony next month."

Her friend was finally living her dream. She'd found the love of her life—the last decent bachelor on earth—and she was performing again. Something that only a few months ago seemed impossible. Summer came out of the other side of her quarter life crisis with a picture-perfect life.

Paige forced herself not to be jealous. Instead, she told herself that if her friend could survive her most embarrassing moment, so could Paige. Except without the guy, thank you very much. She didn't need a man to complete her.

"I'm not making any promises," Paige teased. There was no way she'd miss Summer's return to the stage. "I might decide to take up swimming again and look for a lifeguarding gig."

"You would stay in Myrtle Beach? Forever?" The hurt in Summer's voice was unmistakable.

"Kidding. You know I'll be in the front row cheering you on. I'm the president of your fan club, remember?"

"And I'm the president of yours," Summer said. "Text me when you get to the condo so I know you arrived safe. Love ya, girlfriend."

No sooner had Paige ended the call when her car misfired, the sound echoing loudly down the town's main street. From the corner of her eye, she watched as a woman walking her dog put her hand to her chest before glancing around as if someone had fired the Civil War cannon in the town's square. Several heads peeked out from the open doorways of the shops lining the quiet street.

So much for passing through town unnoticed.

"Shh," she hissed at her misbehaving car.

The car responded with a jerk.

"No! No, no, no. Not now. Not here. Please," Paige begged.

But her normally reliable late model SUV wasn't listening. The engine began to rattle. Paige pressed down on the accelerator, but instead of speeding up, the car slowed down. She managed to steer it into a parking spot before it shuddered to a stop and the engine died, a solemn puff of black smoke wafting from the tailpipe as its epitaph.

With a groan, Paige pressed her forehead to the steering wheel. "This can't be happening."

"Oh, it's happening, sweetie," a woman announced from outside the driver's side window.

Paige nearly jumped through the open sunroof. She turned to glance out the window, still grimy with salt and sand from winter in Chicago. A petite lady with blue-gray hair framing her chubby, smiling face stood beside the car. Paige swallowed a panicked breath before waving her fingers at her. The woman adjusted her fuchsia cat-eyed glasses as if that would help her see through the dirty window more clearly. Thank goodness, before leaving Chicago, Paige wiped off the "slut" someone had traced into the grime.

She sighed. There was no way to avoid the woman without being rude. As angry as she was at life right now, it wasn't in her character to take it out on a stranger. Besides, if she stayed in her car, she'd likely pass out from the nasty smell seeping in from the front end. She gestured for the woman to back up—hopefully way the hell back into the next county—and opened her door.

Gulls squawked in the distance as Paige inhaled a lungful of the salty sea air. Her lower back complained about the long drive, causing her to wobble slightly when her feet hit the ground. The other woman reached out a hand to steady her, but Paige waved it away.

"I'm fine." She gave the woman a shaky smile.

Her companion arched an eyebrow as if to disagree. Paige glanced down at her rumpled appearance, hastily swiping at the orange cheese puff crumbs stuck to her sweatshirt. Her leggings sported two tiny holes in the thigh. So much for dressing for comfort. Of course, the woman in front of her was a walking Chicos ad, smartly dressed in an oversized linen blouse draped with a floral scarf and cropped pants to match her bright pink flats.

Paige tucked several wayward strands of her stringy blonde hair behind her ear before lifting her shoulders. At five foot ten and a half, she towered over most women. Her farm girl physique of big bones and broad shoulders, coupled with her height, made her appear menacing to some. Of course, this had to be a good Samaritan who refused to be intimidated. Her expression implied she was hell-bent on helping Paige, whether her assistance was wanted or not.

"Bless your heart," the woman said. "Your ride isn't fine." She wrinkled her nose at the pungent rotten egg smell the car was giving off and pulled a heavily bedazzled phone from her pocket. "Lucky for you, we've got a fabulous garage right here in town. I'll just give Chet a ring, and he'll be right over to sort this out."

"No!"

The woman started at Paige's harsh tone. But the last thing Paige wanted was to linger in Chances Inlet. If she used the local garage, she'd be a sitting duck all day. No doubt the busybody standing in front of her would have everyone in town knowing her business by dinnertime. The longer she stuck around, the greater the odds of her coming face-to-face with the father she didn't want to see.

"Thank you, though. You're very kind." Paige gave the woman the smile she used when she needed to placate a parent. Firm but kind. "I have Triple A. I'll just call them for a tow. That way, the expense will be covered."

Covering the cost of whatever was wrong with her car would be a whole different matter, however. Her credit cards were already feeling the pinch of the lack of a paycheck these past three months. But she'd have to worry about that later. Right now, her priority was to get the heck out of Dodge. She reached back into the car to grab her phone.

The woman tsked. "If you say so." She pulled a business card from her phone case and handed it to Paige. "But if you find yourself still in a pickle, call me. I know everyone in this town."

Precisely the reason Paige wanted to put some distance

between herself and—she glanced down at the card—Bernice Reed.

"Thank you, Ms. Reed. I'll certainly look you up if I need help," she lied.

"Call me Bernice. Everyone does." With a jaunty wave, she trotted off like a woman on a mission to butt into someone else's business.

Paige released a slow breath of relief. No way was she sticking around Chances Inlet. She patted the hood of her car. It probably just needed a rest after the long drive. She'd go find a place to grab a drink and use the restroom. By the time she returned, her car would be ready to go again. With any luck, she'd be at Myrtle Beach in an hour. Once she got there, she'd give her car the rest of the weekend off.

She glanced around the square for anything resembling a Starbucks. Summer would be delighted to know there was a diner. Paige's stomach rumbled when she spied The Queen of Hearts Bakery. Right next door was the Java Jolt coffee shop.

"When in Rome," she mumbled to herself as she headed in the direction of sustenance.

Halfway across the square, the unmistakable sound of a child sobbing stopped Paige in her tracks. She immediately went into teacher-mode, following the sounds to a picnic table located behind, of all things, the cannon. The crying grew more muffled the closer Paige got, almost as if the child heard her approaching and didn't want to be found.

Paige crouched down to peek beneath the table. A little girl with the most gorgeous eyes Paige had ever seen stared back at her. Wide and wary, they were a lovely mix of green and brown, sitting above cheek bones that likely already had modeling agents clamoring. Her tear-streaked skin looked to be a soft brown. Wavy black hair formed a wild corona around her face, but her clothing looked clean and very similar to the expensive designer duds most of the students at Preston donned every day.

"Hi," Paige said gently.

The little girl's lips trembled but remained firmly shut. She pulled her knees up to her chest and wrapped her arms around the stuffed bunny she was clutching onto for dear life.

Paige forged on. "Is everything okay in there?"

No response. Paige studied her as closely as she could from four feet away. There weren't any outward signs of harm. Everything about the little girl screamed pampered princess. Mom or Dad had to be around here somewhere. Still, small towns weren't immune to child predators. Paige sank down onto her bottom, crossing her legs in front of her to wait until a family member came to collect the little girl.

"My name is Paige. Is it okay if I hang out with you until your mommy gets back?"

The child gulped a sob at the mention of her mother. Paige had seen that look before on many of her young students. Usually when they'd done something wrong, and they didn't want their parents to know. Maybe she was upset she couldn't get a cookie at the bakery. Or something from the toy store on the corner with all the colorful kites fluttering out front.

Paige glanced around at the nearby shops. The Whale of a Tale Bookstore was the closest. "Is your mommy in the bookstore?"

The little girl's chin moved side-to-side ever so slightly.

No, then. "Maybe she's in the bakery or the coffee shop?"

Paige hoped the child said yes because this day was already hella-long and she was growing desperate for a ladies' room.

This time, the chin shake was a bit firmer.

"Do you have any idea where your mommy is?"

The question was met with a gulping sob before the girl buried her face in her bunny's neck.

So that was it. She was lost. Paige huffed out a sigh. There was no telling how long the girl had been here. And no sign of a search party. Her bladder let her know she couldn't sit here all day. She scanned the square for somewhere safe she could leave the little girl until her family realized she was missing. Given how fate was screwing with her, the one place in Chances Inlet Paige intended to avoid at all costs was less than fifty yards away. It was also the best place where she could bring the child for help.

She glanced back over at the anxious little girl. There was no way Paige could sit here all day.

Fate is definitely male.

"You know you are never supposed to go anywhere with a stranger, right?"

The girl nodded swiftly.

"I'm a stranger," Paige explained. "But I'm a teacher, which means I'm a helper. And I'm going to take you to where the other helpers are so we can find your mommy. Okay?"

Her bladder did a happy dance when the little girl nodded solemnly before crawling out from under the table. Paige gingerly got to her feet.

"This way."

She said a silent prayer that someone—anyone—in the child's family would intercept them before they reached their destination, but no such luck. When they arrived at the steps of the weathered brick building, the girl slipped her small hand into Paige's. Those gorgeous eyes were full of trust as they looked up from beneath damp eyelashes.

"Right," Paige said with a nod before leading the way into the Chances Inlet Sheriff's Department.

CHAPTER TWO

PAIGE WASN'T sure what she expected to see once she ventured inside, but the twenty-by-twenty portrait of her father hanging in the entrance hallway wasn't exactly the first thing she would have imagined. Yet, there he was, looking as handsome and taciturn as he did in the photos she had from his days in the Army. He'd aged, yeah, but he'd aged well. With his sandy brown hair now mostly gray and his alert blue eyes, he was what women would call a Silver Fox. Not for the first time, Paige lamented the fact she had not inherited his perfect bone structure.

"Our sheriff is a handsome devil, isn't he?"

Paige jerked her head around. A woman with kind eyes but a don't-mess-with-me expression pointed at the portrait. "He's recently off the market, though. Blissfully happy, in fact."

Tell me something I don't know, Chica.

The woman glanced down at the girl beside Paige and then back up again. "Public restrooms are located next door in the visitor's center."

"Good to know," Paige replied. "But I'm actually here

because I found this child. She was hiding behind the cannon. She seems to have lost her mother."

The other woman immediately sprang into action, opening the swinging gate that allowed visitors to pass into the main room of the building. She motioned for them to come through. "Oh, you poor dear. Don't you worry. We are going to find your mommy."

Paige ushered the child toward one of the empty desks in the squad room. Several men and one woman dressed in uniforms were seated in glass cubicles, tapping away at keyboards while others were on the phone. The mood seemed relaxed and jovial for a law enforcement office. Dramatically different from the frantic and loud tenor of the Chicago police station she took her class to visit every year.

"Deputy Lovell, can you help these two?" The woman waved over one of the uniformed men. Of course it had to be the same guy Paige crossed paths with on New Year's Eve. She'd been in the shadows then, however. Not to mention showered and dressed in something other than her rattiest sweatshirt and stretched-out leggings. There was no possible way he would remember her.

But that didn't mean her father wouldn't recognize her if he walked in right now. He'd been following her on social media for years. Paige wasn't exactly living her best life at the moment. She was in no condition to come face-to-face with her dad. As much as she hated to abandon the lost young girl, she needed to hightail it out of this building and this town, pronto.

Deputy Lovell greeted them both with a potently charming smile. His blue eyes softened as he took in the girl. She detected a slight limp in his gait, but otherwise, he appeared to be perfectly fit judging by the way his uniform accentuated his sculpted chest and thighs.

Was there a requirement that every guy who worked in the Sheriff's department had to be eye-candy?

He sat down on a desk chair bringing him eye-level with the child. Points to him for not talking down to her. Most macho guys wouldn't have bothered.

"Hello. My name is Hayden." He had one of those smooth, bedroom voices that made Paige want to put on his handcuffs and reveal all her secrets to him.

Except she was done revealing her secrets to men.

"That's a cute bunny you've got there. Does it have a name?"

If it did, the little girl wasn't telling. Instead, she buried her face between the stuffed animal's long ears.

"A secret, huh? How about your name," the deputy asked. "Is that a secret, too?"

Still no response. At this rate, this interrogation would take all day. Paige had other pressing matters to take care of. Her bladder, for starters.

"Okay. Looks like you've got this under control." She backpedaled toward the door. "I'll just be on my way now."

The rest of the room had other ideas, however. The girl nearly dropped her bunny when she latched onto Paige's leg. Deputy Lovell's chill demeanor evaporated. His gaze was suddenly laser-focused on her. The receptionist who had let them in moved to block the swinging exit gate. A charged silence fell over the room.

"Not until you've answered some questions," the deputy said.

"I've already told you everything I know. I found her near the cannon. She was crying. I brought her here. End of story."

She was beginning to lose feeling in her leg. The little girl was strong for her size.

"Still, I'm going to need you to fill out some paperwork." The deputy's voice wasn't so sexy now. In fact, it was downright steely. The eyes of everyone else in the squad room were trained on her. She didn't dare move a muscle for fear guns might be drawn.

"Paperwork? What kind of paperwork?"

"Let's start with your name," Deputy Lovell demanded.

Oh, no, no, no. No way was she telling these people who she was.

"Paige?"

Seconds from a clean getaway.

She pivoted as best as one could with a child attached to one's leg and locked eyes with her father. His expression was one of surprised disbelief. Then his mouth relaxed into a broad smile.

"It is you." He said it as though he was trying to convince himself she wasn't an apparition. "You're here."

This was too much. She didn't have the bandwidth for a reunion with her dad right now. Not until she found a restroom, at least. Paige glanced down into the worried eyes of the little girl. Gently, she pulled the fingers from her leg, pointing to a chair as she did so.

"Sit here and don't move until I come back."

The frightened, abandoned look on the child's face threatened to rip what remained of Paige's heart to shreds. There was no way she could desert her. She wouldn't. Even if it meant she had to make nice with her father.

"I'm not going to leave you. I promise." She brushed a kiss onto the girl's forehead and turned toward the receptionist. "The restroom is at the visitor's center, correct?"

The woman nodded as she silently pushed the gate open, only to snap it closed once again when the sheriff cleared his throat. He stepped in front of Paige.

"Restroom's down the hall." The wonder she'd heard in his voice moments earlier was long gone. He was in full, aloof sheriff mode now.

Great.

Paige nodded as she hurried in the direction he indicated. Locking the door behind her, she tried not to focus on the fact she'd already lost the upper hand in this little father-daughter reunion. Or the fact she'd just promised a child she'd never seen before that she wouldn't leave her.

"I SWEAR. I only took my eyes off her for thirty seconds. I was texting the clubhouse to check your tee time."

Tanner Gillette slowed his panicked jog to a racewalk so he could level a death glare at the man huffing and puffing beside him. Sonny Amoroso, Tanner's caddy for the past seven years, nodded contritely. The man rarely made excuses and always owned up to his mistakes. It was the reason Tanner paid him so well. That and he was damn good at reading a golf course.

Looking after slippery four-year-old girls, however, wasn't exactly in the caddy's wheelhouse. Sonny's own three kids lived with his ex-wives. Tanner suspected everyone was probably better off that way.

"Take a pass through the art gallery," he instructed the caddy. "I'll check the bookstore. They've got a lot of colorful children's books in the window. They would be tempting to a little kid. Meet me right back here."

Sonny nodded and hustled off.

Bells tinkled overhead when Tanner pulled open the door to the Whale of a Tale Bookstore. Two women looked up from the counter where they were arguing over how to solve that day's Wordle puzzle.

"Well, hello." One of the women greeted him with a wide smile. "What brings you in on this fine day?"

"I'm looking for a little girl." He gestured with his hands. "About yay high. Black hair. Light brown skin. Probably carrying a stuffed bunny. She was wearing—"

Shit. What was she wearing? Almeda, his housekeeper, was the one who got her dressed each day. Tanner was already at physical therapy when the kid woke up this morning. Soon after, Almeda got an urgent call from her daughter in Charlotte. She was in labor—four weeks early. Almeda had no choice but to leave the little girl with Sonny. His caddy had the brilliant idea she'd enjoy a walk around the downtown while they waited for Tanner to finish PT.

"It's nobody's fault," he mumbled to himself as he zigzagged among the stacks of books.

No sign of her.

He raced back to the front of the store where the two women stared at him with matching perplexed expressions.

"Is everything okay, sir?" the other women asked.

Hell, no he wanted to shout. Nothing had been okay since Tristan fucked everything up by dying. Except Tanner was finally getting a handle on the pain of that loss. He was back at the top of his game. Ranked number one in the world thanks to his recent victory at the Players. He was poised to win the cup. Either in spite of or in honor of his brother. He hadn't decided that part yet.

Except fate had other plans. Screwing up his life again by dropping a mute little girl off at his country club five days ago with nothing but a stuffed rabbit, a suitcase and a note from her mother begging him to keep her safe until she could return. He didn't recognize the name on the note. But he damn sure recognized his name listed as the father on the child's birth certificate.

Black spots danced before his eyes foreshadowing an impending panic attack. Tanner hadn't had one in months. They'd been a frequent occurrence after Tristan's death though, keeping him off the tour. He was all too familiar with what happened next. He needed to get out of the store before he passed out and everyone discovered his weakness. With a half-hearted wave at the women, he rushed out the door.

Tanner gulped in a few lungfuls of the ocean air, blowing them back out slowly in an effort to get his heart rate back under control.

"Not in there, either?" Sonny asked when he arrived at Tanner's side.

Tanner could only manage a shake of his head in response. He peered around the square for what felt like the hundredth time until his gaze landed on the sheriff's office at the end of the block. When he looked over at Sonny, the caddy nodded in defeat.

They hurried up the steps. As soon as they entered the foyer, Tanner spied the little girl sitting in the squad room, surrounded by a group of deputies staring questioningly at Sheriff Hollister.

"Whitney," Tanner managed to gasp before he bent at the knees and heaved out several deep breaths to calm his racing heart.

She's safe.

Sonny patted his back. "Thank, God," he murmured.

"She's fine, Tanner," Sheriff Hollister assured him.

Tanner pushed through the swinging gate and rushed toward Whitney. He had to see for himself. Squatting down on his haunches to get a closer look, he ignored the child's slight recoil. Somehow, he'd become the bad guy in this scenario and that pissed him off even more than the situation. But he would never take it out on an innocent child.

"Whitney, you can't just run away like that." He did his best to keep his tone even and soft despite the fact that he still felt like he was going to pass out. "You had us all scared."

Of course, she didn't respond. It had been five days, and the child hadn't uttered one word. If he didn't hear her crying out for her mother in her sleep at night, he'd worry there was something wrong with her. Alden Bryant, the town's pediatrician, diagnosed it as selective mutism. She'll talk when she's ready, the doctor reassured Tanner.

Dammit, that wasn't good enough. He needed her to talk now. He needed to know where her mother had seemingly vanished to. He needed to know why she'd left Whitney with him. Because he was for damn sure not the little girl's father. That was the only thing he knew for certain right now.

"I apologize for any disruption to your day," Tanner announced to the room as he got to his feet.

The stilted silence continued. Everyone's attention was still focused on the sheriff. Perhaps they were annoyed their boss hadn't shared with them the gossip about Whitney and her supposed relationship to Tanner. Too bad. Tanner had done everything he could to keep the circumstances under wraps. His reputation, not to mention his family, had suffered enough these last eighteen months. None of them needed another scandal.

Thanks to his military service, Sheriff Hollister had connections throughout the country. He was working with his sources trying to locate Whitney's mother. But the search was slow going. And he doubted they'd locate the woman before tomorrow when Tanner needed to head to Charleston for a tournament.

"Almeda's daughter went into labor," he announced by way of explanation. "We're doing the best we can."

Sheriff Hollister nodded. "The option of Child Protective Services is still on the table."

"No!" Tanner replied sharply.

"No!" A female voice shouted just as vehemently at the same time.

A bedraggled woman emerged from behind the sheriff. Strands of her dishwater blonde hair had escaped her ponytail holder, some sticking to her pink cheeks, while others brushed her broad shoulders. She was tall enough to look Tanner in the eye. And she was doing just that. He thought he saw recognition flare in her pale blue eyes—eerily similar to Sheriff Hollister's—before she notched her chin up and shuttered her expression.

"You can't put this child into the system," she said.

The sheriff let out a resigned sigh. "Paige, this isn't your concern. Why don't you wait in my office."

You could hear a pin drop in the room, the silence was so tense. Tanner noticed everyone else's gazes were ping-ponging between whoever Paige was and the sheriff.

"I will not."

She stomped past the sheriff and over to where Whitney sat wide-eyed, taking in the proceedings. Apparently sensing this woman was her champion, Whitney launched herself into Paige's arms.

"I promised her I'd help her find her mom," Paige declared. "And that's what I'm going to do."

"Well, what the hell do you think I'm trying to do?" Tanner snapped.

Paige's surprised gaze collided with his. Whitney pressed herself against the woman.

"Enough!" Sheriff Hollister commanded. "Let's take this discussion into my office."

No one moved.

"Now!"

The deputies returned to whatever it was they were doing. The receptionist answered a ringing phone. Paige remained still as a statue until she tore her eyes away from Tanner's and trudged down the hall, Whitney's bunny slapping her in the back as they went. Tanner and Sonny followed.

Deputy Lovell opened the door to a conference room beside the sheriff's office. They all filed in silently. Paige sank down into one of the conference chairs with Whitney still clinging to her. Sonny took the seat across from them. Tanner was too keyed up to settle into a chair. He leaned a shoulder against the wall instead. If the sheriff wanted him to sit, he was going to have to shoot him.

The receptionist came into the room, some crayons and a coloring book in her hand.

"Whitney, honey, we've got some donuts in the break room," she said. "They've got sprinkles on them. Why don't you come with me, and we'll go get ourselves one."

Whitney snuggled in closer against Paige. Her protector smoothed the child's hair down with her hand before gifting her with a soothing smile and nodding. Whitney unfurled herself from Paige and, without protest, left the room with the receptionist.

What the hell kind of magical powers was this woman wielding? And why was there something vaguely familiar about that smile of hers? One that had Tanner suddenly focusing in on her very full, very lush lips.

"Paige found Whitney in the square earlier," the sheriff explained, interrupting Tanner's wayward thoughts.

Tanner pulled his gaze away from the vexing woman to focus on the sheriff who was leaning against the opposite wall mirroring his pose.

"Whitney was crying and uncommunicative, so Paige brought her here," Sheriff Hollister continued. He turned his attention to Paige. "Whitney was delivered to Mr. Gillette's club last week with a note from her mother asking him to care for her until she returns."

Paige's eyes widened. "Seriously?"

The three men in the room nodded. Tanner was grateful to the sheriff for leaving out the part about his name being on Whitney's birth certificate. He was waiting on the results of the paternity test Alden performed a few days ago to clear up that little misconception.

"That's awful," Paige said. "I hope she's not in some kind of trouble."

Oh, she was in trouble, all right. He was pretty sure abandoning one's child was a felony. He didn't bother pointing that out to Paige, though. She was clearly on the side of Team Mum.

"We are doing our best to locate her." The sheriff pressed his back against the wall, crossing his arms over his chest before leveling a flinty look at Paige. "In the meantime, Mr. Gillette is doing his best to care for Whitney."

She had the nerve to chuckle. "Clearly, he's doing a bang-up job."

Tanner pulled away from the wall. He didn't have time for this woman's snark. "Sheriff, if that's all, I have a tee time for a practice round I need to get to."

"And who is going to watch Whitney?" Paige demanded.

"Paige," the sheriff admonished her.

"Our housekeeper has a friend who is going to come stay with her for the week," Tanner managed to grind out through his tight jaw. What the hell was it to this woman, anyway?

"For the *week*?!" Paige jerked from her chair. "Do you even know this—" she made air quotes with her fingers "friend? Have you run a background check on her? Does she know CPR? You're just going to leave a perfect stranger with a kid who is clearly already traumatized?"

Sheriff Hollister shoved away from the wall to stand between Tanner and the annoying shrew. "That's enough, Paige."

Tanner was clenching his teeth so hard he feared he might have cracked one. How dare she make him feel guilty for his choices? Whitney landed in his lap during the busiest stretch of the golf season. The first of the tour's four majors loomed before him. He had no choice but to leave her with someone until they located her mother and sorted this ridiculous mess out.

Besides, he had no idea what to do with a four-year-old. Kids weren't his thing. Sure, he enjoyed being around his nephews, but only for a few hours at a time. With his golf game peaking, Tanner wasn't the least bit interested in fatherhood. Especially instant fatherhood.

Paige should be grateful he refused to use the nuclear option of Child Protective Services. Even he knew it would exacerbate Whitney's issues. Fortunately, Tanner was a wealthy man. He could afford to provide Whitney with whatever care she needed. It just wouldn't be him caring for her. He had a cup to win.

"We're going to be late," Tanner snapped. "Let's go, Sonny."

His caddy followed him out the door. Paige moved as if to follow them, but the sheriff blocked her path, thankfully. Tanner stepped into the break room where Whitney was quietly coloring under the watchful eye of the sheriff's receptionist.

"Time to go, Whit."

Her eyes darted past him into the hallway, presumably looking for Paige. Something sharp slammed into his ribs at the crestfallen expression on the little girl's face. She quietly stacked the crayons on top of the coloring book and picked up her bunny. With a wave to the receptionist, she followed Sonny out of the building. Tanner ought to be thankful that Whitney was such a sweetheart. Instead, he was seething at Paige for making him second guess his decisions.

CHAPTER THREE

"Not so fast."

Her father still had Paige cornered in the conference room. Clearly, she wasn't leaving until he'd gotten his pound of flesh. She sank back down into the chair in defeat. The only point in her favor was that Mr. Gillette, her handsome Aussie stranger from New Year's Eve, hadn't put two and two together and mentioned her presence at the wedding. She didn't want to have to explain that to the sheriff.

Tanner Gillette's accent still had the power to twist her stomach in knots. He didn't need a tailored suit and tie to exude potent vitality and sex appeal. Even dressed in shorts and a sweaty T-shirt, with his mahogany hair disheveled from anxiously combing his fingers through it, he'd have women fawning at his feet. His eyes were amber, but they weren't as welcoming as they had been a few months ago. The dimples were in hiding today, too. His distress over Whitney's disappearance was palatable. The fact that he didn't want to put the little girl into foster care endeared him just a little bit to Paige.

But it could also be a huge red flag.

"You're just going to let that guy leave with that little girl?" she said. "How do you know he's not some sort of perv?"

He pinched the bridge of his nose with his fingers. "There's no evidence that he is a 'perv.' And the child is legally in his care."

Legally in his care. That could only mean that the arrogant Mr. Gillette was related to the child in some way. *Of course.* More than likely, he was the little girl's father. He probably refused to acknowledge Whitney—right up until mom forced him to.

If that were the case, shame on the mom, too. She should know better than to use her own daughter as a pawn. Whitney couldn't be more than four or five. A child that age wouldn't fully comprehend what was going on around her. She'd only be scared at being left with a stranger.

"Except that I found her hiding beneath a picnic table. Crying," she argued. "She's afraid of him."

"She told you that?"

Of course she hadn't. Whitney wasn't much of a talker, apparently.

Her father arched an eyebrow at her. "Years in this business have taught me the facts can be interpreted a multitude of ways, Paige. For instance, what if Whitney was in a new, exciting place, and she got distracted by something, then she became separated from her guardian? Might that be a reason for her to be crying beneath a picnic table?"

Well, when he put it that way. "But—"

Her father held up a hand. "Enough. There are lots of extenuating circumstances to this situation. All of them private. Rest assured, however, that Whitney's welfare is first and foremost for everyone involved."

Paige crossed her arms over her chest. She was just going to have to take his word for it. But that didn't mean she wouldn't spend the next few weeks worrying about Whitney's well-being. It was in her DNA to care about kids.

"Are you out of school for spring break?" he asked, steering the conversation to a path Paige didn't want to go down.

"Something like that," she muttered.

Her father's eyes brightened. "And you decided to spend it in Chances Inlet?" The unmistakable delight in his voice punched Paige's guilt button. *Huh. Go figure.* She thought her mom was the only one who had access to that particular part of her psyche.

Paige could only imagine the man's reaction when he discovered the real reason for her sudden beach trip. And he would find out. No doubt he'd call her mother as soon as Paige left. Her mom would have no compunction about spilling the tea. Heather Franks never resisted an opportunity to prove she was right.

Time to end this meet and greet before things got even more humiliating.

"Just passing through, actually. I'm on my way to Myrtle Beach." Her father's face dimmed. "But I figured while I was in the area, I'd pop in and say hi." She waved a hand. "Hi."

He made a sound deep in his throat. "Well, Myrtle Beach is barely an hour away. Perhaps you can make some time to come up for dinner one evening. Meet Tricia and her kids. I know she'd like that very much."

She'd like that very much.

Somehow Paige doubted that. She couldn't hold a candle to his wife's star-studded progeny. It stung, too, that he only wanted her to come to dinner to please his new wife. His tune would change when he found out the truth about Paige, though. He wouldn't be so eager to have his Scarlett Letter wearing daughter mingling with his picture-perfect new family, that's for sure.

"I don't know. My schedule is really packed. I'm meeting

friends and we've got things planned for every night." She justified her horrendous lie by telling herself she was saving them both from embarrassment. "Maybe some other time?"

An uncomfortable silence filled the room while her dad studied her over steepled fingers, his stare inscrutable. She had the distinct feeling he knew she wasn't telling the truth. *Damn, he was good.* He probably had criminals confessing in the first five minutes of an interrogation. She resisted the urge to squirm in her chair.

Deputy Lovell bailed her out when he poked his head into the room. "Sorry to interrupt, sir." He looked over at Paige. "Miss, do you own a Ford Edge with Illinois tags?"

What the heck?

"Um, yes. I do."

"I just thought you'd like to know it's being towed."

"Towed?" She jumped up and dashed toward the exit. "Why? I was parked legally." She called over her shoulder at her father. "I was!"

Paige sprinted across the town square. Sure enough, the hood of her car was open, and a pair of jean-clad legs was hanging out of it. A tow truck idled in the street.

"Oh, there you are."

The now familiar voice of Bernice Reed stopped Paige in her tracks.

"Wouldn't you know it," the woman said. "Chet was at the diner when I went in. I told him about your car troubles. Lucky for you he wasn't busy today. He brought the wrecker over to take a look."

The woman had some gall. "I told you I would call Triple A if I needed help."

Bernice shrugged. "I saved you a phone call. Besides, they would have sent Chet. You wouldn't want anyone else anyway. He's the best mechanic around. And a straight shooter." She winked at Paige. "He wouldn't dare rip off a pretty young woman."

"Afternoon, Chet." *Great.* Her father must have followed her. He stepped around Paige and leaned an elbow on the car. "What are we looking at?"

The rest of Chet emerged from beneath the hood. His beard was gray against his black skin. He tugged his T-shirt over his round belly. Chipmunk cheeks and the deep crinkles fanning out from his maple syrup eyes made him look a lot like Santa Claus.

Chet wrinkled his nose. "Well, that smell usually only means one thing. Catalytic converter."

Her dad made a tsking noise. One that didn't sound the least bit encouraging. Beads of sweat began to form on the back of her neck.

"The catalytic convertor?" She tried and failed to tone down the hint of panic lacing her voice. She had no idea what a catalytic convertor was. Only that it sounded expensive. "What does that do?"

Chet's eyes were sympathetic. "It filters out the harmful emissions and makes your car run more efficiently."

"Okay." Paige nodded. "But can my car run without it?"

"Sure."

She let out a breath of relief.

Her relief was short-lived, however.

"But it's not a long-term solution." Chet gestured to the hood of her car. "And by the looks of it, your car has already been running without one that works properly for some time. She ain't gonna go nowhere now without a new one."

She braced for impact. "How much is a new one?"

Chet pulled a rag out of his pocket and wiped his hands. "Won't know until I get inside her. But my best guess? The parts alone could be a couple thousand."

"I'm sorry? Did you say a couple *thousand*?" she choked out before staggering over to one of the park benches and plopping down.

Unless this town had its own currency she didn't know about, this was a disaster. She was already going to have to dip into her emergency savings to pay her rent and student loans next month. Repairing her car would be a significant hit to what was left of her bank account. Not to mention the pesky fact she'd been blackballed from teaching or nannying and wouldn't be bringing in any income for the foreseeable future.

"How long to fix it?" she heard her father asking.

Chet said something about calling around for parts and getting them sent in. His 'best guess' was the day after tomorrow.

And just like that, Paige was trapped in her very own Hallmark small town nightmare.

"I PASSED a Hampton Inn on my way into town," Paige said. "I can stay there." At least she'd earn some points for a vacation she might not ever be able to afford to take.

Her father kept his eyes on the road and his hands at ten and two on the steering wheel of the Bronco presumably belonging to the sheriff's office given the lights on top. Sitting in the passenger seat, she could sense the disappointment rolling off him. Now he knew the only reason she'd stopped in Chances Inlet was because her car broke down.

"Nonsense," he said curtly. "Tricia owns a B & B. She always keeps a room open for family."

Paige nearly laughed. Just as Summer suspected. Except, as she kept having to remind everyone, she wasn't family. And the last time she'd checked the B & B's website, the price tag for even the smallest room was close to four hundred a night. If she ever made it to Myrtle Beach, she'd be dining on Ramen noodles and juice boxes.

At this point, though, arguing with her dad seemed pointless. Not to mention, churlish.

"Don't most of her kids live in town now?"

The sounds of the ocean grew louder when he steered the Bronco down a long gravel drive. A canopy of Spanish moss hanging from the live oak trees on either side of the road created a shaded tunnel.

"All but Elle," he said. "She works for a publisher in New York City. Miles and his wife live in DC during the week. But they're home most weekends."

He pulled around a circular drive and brought the Bronco to a stop in front of a gorgeous Victorian mansion. Three stories high, the B & B had twin spires that likely offered a fabulous view of the ocean. A porch wrapped around much of the building with rockers and Adirondack chairs strategically placed to form conversation areas for guests. Hanging baskets of flowers gave the entire area a pop of color. Off in the distance, Paige made out a gazebo surrounded by azaleas and lush green grass.

Patricia McAlister came out the screen door before her father had even killed the ignition. Paige recognized her from New Year's Eve. She wasn't as elegantly dressed as she had been that night, but even in worn jeans topped with a long, peach sweater, she looked chic. Her shoulder length champagne-blonde hair was pulled back into a messy ponytail making her appear youthful and vibrant. Out of the corner of her eye, Paige looked on as her father's face softened watching his wife hurry down the steps.

"Welcome to the Tide Me Over Inn," Patricia said when Paige got out of the SUV. "It's so good to finally meet you."

She leaned in for a hug. Paige awkwardly hugged her back.

"You must be exhausted after your drive." Her hazel eyes

took in Paige's disheveled outfit. "Not to mention all the other unplanned events of the day. Come in and we'll get you settled."

Her father was already unloading her suitcase from the back of the Bronco. Paige grabbed her computer bag and her duffel and followed Patricia inside. The interior of the B & B was as stunning as the outside. Tigerwood floors gleamed throughout the entry hallway. Tall ceilings gave the place an open, airy feel. An eclectic mix of antique and rustic farmhouse furniture was interspersed about each room. The scent of fresh flowers and baked bread added to the inn's welcoming ambiance.

"We have tea every afternoon at three in the main salon, just over here." Patricia indicated a room with floor-to-ceiling windows offering a stunning view of the beach and ocean beyond. "Nothing fancy. Just light refreshments of scones, cookies, and finger sandwiches."

Paige's stomach rumbled loudly as they climbed up the elaborate staircase leading to the second floor. Patricia shot her a concerned look.

"Have you eaten anything at all today? I'm happy to fix you a sandwich or something."

"I'm fine, really. You're already being too gracious. Thank you, though. I'm sure I'll survive until teatime."

Patricia led them to the end of the hall where she opened the door to a lavish space. "This is the Glasgow suite. It's my daughter Elle's favorite. Gavin's wife Ginger also stayed here when they were filming the 'Historic Restorations' show."

Paige stepped into the sitting room at the center of the suite. A love seat and two stuffed armchairs filled up the space. Beyond them was a massive four poster bed that looked so comfortable, Paige was tempted to face plant in the middle of the mattress and sleep for two days.

"This is—this is amazing." She spun around trying to take

the space in. No wonder they could charge such a high rate for the rooms. The suite was exquisite, yet homey at the same time.

Patricia's smile was all pride. "There's a claw foot soaking tub in the bathroom and a robe in the closet. Help yourself to any of the toiletries."

A warm bubble bath sounded heavenly after the shitshow of a day she'd been having. But there was no way she could afford this. Not now.

"Really, this is too much," Paige said around the boulder of embarrassment clogging her throat. "I'm sure you've got a waiting list of guests wanting to rent this room."

"There are seven other guest rooms in the inn. All of them turning a profit. But I always hold one back for when a surprise guest drops in." Patricia seemed to sense her unease. She reached over and gave Paige's arm a gentle pat. "And the room is always comped for family."

"But I'm not—"

The pat on the arm was a little firmer this time. "Nonsense. Like it or not, you are as much family as my own two daughters. Settle in," Patricia ordered. "When you're ready, take the backstairs down to the kitchen. That's where the family hangs out. They are all so excited to get to know you."

Paige's voice didn't seem to want to cooperate, so she nodded like a simpleton. Her wallet would be relieved, but she still felt like she was taking advantage of the woman's generosity by staying. Especially when Patricia didn't know the truth about her.

Patricia turned to her husband and began ushering him out of the suite. "Come on, you. I'll fix you a sandwich to take back to the office."

Paige shook her head in amazement at the formidable woman her father had married. No wonder her children were standouts in their professions. She doubted anyone stood a chance when Patricia got something into her head.

Seeing how her plan to meet her dad's family on her own terms was now out the window, Paige decided a nice soak in the tub and a short power nap would go a long way toward refortifying her armor for the "get to know you" session looming.

CHAPTER FOUR

ALMEDA'S FRIEND didn't know CPR. Not only that but she seemed a little flummoxed when Tanner inquired about it. The roly-poly grandmother took offense, announcing she'd cared for "countless babies," all of whom were now productive members of society. Tanner backed off immediately, telling himself he was overreacting. The woman at the sheriff's office —*Paige*—had gotten into his head, that's all. Whitney would be fine staying with his housekeeper's friend.

His golf game, on the other hand, was *not* fine. Not even close. Tanner shot seven over par on a nine-hole course he knew like the back of his hand. He chalked it up to the distraction of the past few days. Not that he was sharing any of that info with his swing coach. The man's lips tended to get loose in the bar after a few shots of Glenlivet. Tanner didn't need him blabbing all about his personal life to one of the other guys on the tour. Or worse, a reporter.

"Are you sure your back is fit enough for this tournament?" His coach leaned on a golf club. "We can always sit this one out before we head to Augusta in two weeks."

No way was Tanner sitting anything out. He was number one in the rankings and poised to show everyone who doubted him that he wasn't just a playboy, flash-in-the-pan who didn't take the game of golf seriously. Tanner took it seriously. He took everything seriously.

Too bad no one took *him* seriously.

Tanner had a reputation of being cold and aloof with a killer instinct on the course. That part was true. He played to win. Was there any other way? He let his work speak for itself. His reputation off the links was that of a spoiled wild child. He'd earned it the hard way, and he had the emotional scars to prove it. Despite the fact he'd cleaned up his act a few years ago, the rumors persisted. Tanner didn't see the need to bother refuting them. The only person he was responsible for was himself. And he liked it that way.

"My back is fine," he told his coach. "Everybody has an off day. Be happy I'm having mine today and not next weekend."

The coach eyed Tanner shrewdly but wisely kept any further opinions to himself.

Two hours later, Tanner was in his home office, nursing a beer and watching Whitney play with her stuffed bunny. Unaware that he was spying on her, she danced around the screened porch to a silent tune only she could hear. She seemed none the worse for wear after this morning's episode.

The child was a beautiful, even-tempered, well-mannered little girl. Not for the first time, he wondered how a mother could just abandon her kid. On a stranger's doorstep, no less.

He fingered the vague note Whitney had arrived with for what felt like the hundredth time.

Please take care of my precious little girl. She is my world. Whitney is a good girl, and she won't give you any trouble. I wouldn't impose on you for her care if it wasn't important. As soon as I get my life together, I'll be back for her.

IT WAS SIGNED SIMPLY "DONELLA." Not much to go on. Donella —or whomever left Whitney here—blacked out the mother's name on the Nevada birth certificate. Tanner's name was left intact, though. Ironic, since he wasn't the girl's father. A few simple calculations and he was certain. He'd been in Europe the year in which she was conceived, in a monogamous relationship with his fiancée, Shelby.

Too bad Shelby hadn't been monogamous.

Not going there.

He took another pull from his beer. Sheriff Hollister had friends working in both local and federal law enforcement in Clark County, Nevada, the home of Las Vegas. Hopefully, one of them would turn up something on the birth certificate soon.

Ironically, Nevada was one of the few states where the birth records are closed. Only the principals named on the birth certificate can access the actual birth record containing the parents' names. Tanner's attorney was in the process of filing a motion with the court to unseal the file, but since the case wasn't life or death, the court was taking its sweet time hearing his case.

Tanner swore violently.

Sonny entered the room and glanced in the direction of Tanner's gaze. "Do you think Almeda's friend is gonna work out?" he asked quietly.

Not you, too.

"She'll be fine," he replied, hoping like hell he could make himself believe it.

The caddy took a seat in the leather recliner. Both men fell silent as they contemplated the little girl. Tanner couldn't tell for sure, but he thought she might be humming to her bunny.

"Do you think my parents cared if the nannies they hired to watch over Tristan and me were trained in CPR?" he asked.

Sonny paused with his can of Cheerwine halfway to his mouth. "I think your parents care about you very much."

Tanner saluted his friend's judicious answer with his beer. "That was never in doubt."

Marcus and Blythe Gillette were doting parents—when they were around. His mother was the number-one-ranked female golfer in their native Australia, as well as Asia, while Tanner and his brother were growing up. When she wasn't golfing, she was traveling around the world with their father, a wealthy developer who designed prestigious golf course communities, including the one in Chances Inlet where Tanner currently lived.

During school holidays, the two brothers were able to accompany their parents to wherever in the world they were working. Tanner gravitated to the links at a very young age. Tristan wasn't as hardy as a child, often suffering debilitating asthma attacks. So it went that Tanner became his mother's shadow, while Tristan, the older of the two boys, was quickly taken under their father's wing as the heir apparent to Gillette enterprises. Each boy accepted his path in life as a given. There was never any animosity between them. They were roommates at boarding school and each other's best friend.

"I think parents today spend too much time on the Internet. They worry about everything that could harm their kiddos. And that makes them hover more," Sonny said, interrupting Tanner's thoughts. "That's why they call them 'chopper parents.'"

"I think the term is 'helicopter parent,'" Tanner replied with a grin. "My parents weren't like that at all. They knew that when they were gone, Tristan and I had each other. We'd always take care of one another."

If Tanner ever needed proof of how much their parents loved them, it was evident in the devastation they suffered—and were still suffering—at the loss of their oldest son. Their thirty-five-year marriage nearly collapsed under the strain. The constant media scrutiny didn't help. Thankfully, they'd found solace in one another again and were enjoying a three-month cruise.

"Well, whatever the saying is," Sonny continued. "It's none of that nosey parker's business, anyway."

Tanner chuckled at Sonny's description of Whitney's defender from the sheriff's office. *Paige.* They hadn't exchanged names on New Year's Eve, but he'd bet his best irons that her last name is Hollister. Anyone looking at them closely could connect the dots. Tanner had never seen anyone with the same faded-blue eyes as the sheriff—until Paige showed up in town.

Damn, she was stunning in her ire. A man didn't forget a woman with her moxie, and it had taken Tanner the drive home from town to recall where they'd met. In the few moments they spent together outside the wedding, he'd been intrigued by her. Not to mention her decadent-looking mouth. The memory of her beguiling smile kept him up for hours that night, his body frustrated by not following-up on the spark that simmered between them.

She'd felt it, too. He'd seen the heat in her eyes. But she'd been running from something. Tanner joked about her running from the law. Some of the pieces fell into place today. Paige was running from the law that night, so to speak. For some unknown reason, she was hellbent on getting away from her father, the sheriff.

The question was why?

His mobile phone buzzed with a text.

DR. ALDEN BRYANT

Hey, mate, I should have the paternity test
results any time now. In the meantime, I'll be at
the inn this afternoon. Why don't you bring
Whitney over to play with Emily. Kids often let
down their guard when they are at play. Not to
mention, my daughter is a force of nature.
Perhaps Em can get Whitney to open up.

Tanner wasn't too concerned with the DNA results. But the idea that the pediatrician's daughter could get Whitney to open up was as good as any of the others they'd tried. He chalked-up the uptick in his heart rate to the hope Whitney might shed some light about her mum. It had nothing to do with the fact that, if Paige Hollister was still in town, she'd most likely be staying at the Tide Me Over Inn.

IT TURNED OUT, Paige didn't need to brace herself for meeting the McAlisters at all. The only two who showed up for tea were both pint-sized, with sticky faces and hands after inhaling a plateful of cookies and scones between them. So much for Patricia's family being eager to meet her. Not that she wasn't relieved to be among a familiar demographic.

"He's not really family," Emily, the daughter of Patricia's oldest, Kate, announced around a mouthful of snickerdoodle.

"Am, too," Henry, the tow-headed boy seated at the table with them, argued. "My mom is dating Ryan."

Emily rolled her big, blue eyes. "My Gigi watches him after school every day because his mom works."

"And because Ryan is dating my mom!" the little boy insisted loudly.

Paige got the sense this was a familiar debate between the

two and it wasn't going to get resolved today. The other guests in the salon began to cast leery looks their way.

"Who do the two dogs belong to?" she asked, hoping to change the subject to one less animated.

"The little scruffy one is mine." Henry puffed his chest out proudly. "His name is Kringle."

"His real name is Sparky, and he used to belong to Santa Claus," Emily added.

"Really?" Paige expected Henry to counter Emily's point.

Instead, both kids nodded earnestly.

"The big dog is Midas. He's Uncle Gavin's," Emily continued. "Aunt Ginger had to go to the doctor to get the baby in her tummy measured. Gigi is watching him today because Midas was a bad dog and tore up some of the new baby's things."

"It's not his fault." Henry defended the dog. "He probably thought the baby toys were for him."

The little girl sighed dramatically. "Babies are so annoying."

"I hope you're not referring to your new brother when you say that, my little one," a very British voice said from behind Paige.

Emily's eyes went wide before she jumped from her chair. "Daddy!"

Paige turned in her chair just in time to see a light-haired man wearing wire-rimmed glasses lift Emily high into the air. "Good gosh, Em." He set the girl back on her feet and immediately reached for his lower back. "How many of granny's cookies did you eat today?"

Henry snickered while Emily flounced back to her chair. The girl's father winked at Paige. He didn't look like he missed much time at the gym judging by the way his scrubs clung to the hard planes of his body.

'Good gosh' was right. What was in the water here that the men all looked so dang hot?

"You must be Paige. I guess that makes me your brother-in-law." He extended his hand. "Alden Bryant, husband of Kate and father of this little sprite and her newly arrived brother, Maximus. Kate sends her regrets. Max had a particularly restless night last evening and they are both catching up on some needed sleep. She promises to pop by to say hello tomorrow."

The words 'brother-in-law' had Paige too stunned to respond. She pumped her hand up and down and nodded, hoping like hell she was at least smiling. Were Patricia's kids as eager as their mother to accept her as one of their own? They might be now, but surely not when her newly tarnished reputation caught up with her. Her stomach tightened up at the thought.

With any luck, Chet would fix her car quickly and she'd be out of town before then. Not that luck was exactly on her side lately. Still, a girl could hope.

"If you two are done with your snack," Alden said. "I've brought a young friend over. She's new to town and could use a few playmates."

Emily scrambled out of her chair. "A girl? Yes! All Henry wants to do anymore is play baseball. Where is she?"

"She's out on the veranda getting to know the dogs."

Both kids made a beeline for the front porch.

"Be gentle, Emily," Alden called after them. "Whitney is shy."

"Maybe she could be our catcher," Henry suggested.

Not that Paige heard him. She was too surprised by the name Alden mentioned. "Did you say 'Whitney?'"

He seemed to hesitate, using the pause to scrutinize her from behind his glasses. "You know her?"

"We met this morning. She got lost in town." She narrowed her eyes at the doctor. "Don't tell me he pawned her off on you so he could go play golf?"

"Pardon?"

She didn't bother waiting for a reply, instead following the children outside. Whitney was sitting in one of the child-sized Adirondack chairs. Emily and Henry stood on either side of her, bombarding her with questions.

As soon as she saw her, Whitney sprung from the chair and wrapped her arms around Paige's thighs.

"Hello again, Miss Whitney." Paige brushed her palm against the top of the little girl's head, gently smoothing the hair back from her face. "I'm glad to see you, too."

"Do you know her?" Emily demanded. "Is she one of your students?"

"Students?"

Paige flinched at the sound of Tanner Gillette's voice. She whirled around to see him standing at the bottom of the steps, smartly dressed in freshly pressed chinos and a green golf shirt with an unfamiliar logo on his sculpted chest. The Oakley sunglasses he wore prevented her from seeing if the green in his shirt brought out the green in his eyes.

We. Don't. Care, she chastised herself.

Both dogs stared at him just as intently, drool dripping from the Golden Retriever's mouth. Paige had no trouble picturing the many women who did the same thing at the sight of the sexy Australian.

Tanner flicked a mangy tennis ball between his fingers. "You're a teacher?"

"Aunt Paige teaches kindergarten," Emily said, making Paige flinch a second time.

Since when had she become "Aunt Paige?"

"You don't say?"

Happy barks filled the air when he launched the tennis ball across the lawn. Both dogs bounded down the steps in pursuit.

"My turn," Henry yelled as he chased after them.

"Come on, Whitney. I'll show you and your bunny the fairy garden Gigi and I made." Emily tugged on Whitney's shirt.

The little girl loosened her grip on Paige's leg ever-so-slightly and tilted her chin up. The expression on her face was conflicted.

"Go see it," Paige encouraged her. "I'll be here when you get back. You can tell me all about it."

Whitney hesitated for half a second before following Emily down the steps. The two girls linked arms and skipped across the lawn toward the gazebo.

Tanner stared after them. "Do you think she'll do it?"

"Do what?"

He shoved his sunglasses up to the top of his head, pivoting his gaze back to her. Something flickered deep in her chest at the look of helplessness in his eyes. He charged up the steps. "Do you think she'll tell you about the fairy garden? Do you think she'll talk to you?"

He was so close she could smell the tangy scent of his after-shave. The wintergreen of a breath mint. She could see the burnt gold and green flecks winking in his eyes. The small cut where he'd nicked himself shaving. The sensory overload made her nerve-endings dance.

"I need her to talk." His voice was hoarse with emotion. "I need her to tell me who her mother is. *Where* her mother is. I need to for the woman to come and take Whitney back so I can get back to my life. The one without kids."

Wait, what?

"You...you don't know who her mother is?" That was a piece of the puzzle Paige wasn't expecting.

He edged in closer. "No."

The porch felt like it was spinning. Her temples began to throb trying to process what he was saying. He didn't know Whitney's mother? Or he didn't remember her? Was he one of those scummy guys who slept with so many women, he couldn't remember who he might have fathered a child with? Dear God, was he just like Jon?

And damn it, why was this the type of man her body was continually attracted to?

"Why are all men such assholes?" she snapped.

"What the hell is that supposed to mean?"

The sound of footsteps crunching on the gravel had Paige jumping back. Tanner's heated stare effectively pinned her to the wall.

"Ah, there you are." Her father's gaze landed on Tanner before shifting to Paige. There was no way the intuitive man could mistake the tension crackling between the two of them. He hesitated for a brief moment before climbing the steps.

"I just spoke with Chet. As he suspected, the catalytic convertor in your car is totally shot. Because Ryan is co-owner of the garage, you get the family discount. I'm afraid even at cost, though, the parts are going to run you over a thousand dollars. He needs to know if he's got the green light to go ahead."

She closed her eyes and let the back of her head rest against the Hardy board. *For the love of God, universe, why must you continue to pile on?* She huffed out a sigh.

"It's not like I have any choice."

"Paige?" The concern in her father's voice had her opening her eyes. "If you need help with anything, all you have to do is ask."

Her dad was a good man. There was no doubting that. That didn't mean she wanted to be in debt to him, though.

She'd been turning down his money since he offered to pay for college. Looking back, that probably wasn't the wisest decision now that she was unemployable, and her student loan payment was half her monthly debt. But teenage Paige was full of pride. She wasn't taking money from a man who hadn't been a part of her life since she was three. And even then, he'd been deployed for most of those three years.

Adult Paige just wanted Lamar Hollister to know she'd turned out to be a strong, self-sufficient woman without his help. That she didn't need a father in her life to turn out well-rounded. Of course, once he found out about her latest poor choices, he'd know that for the bullshit it was.

She shook her head. "Thank you. I'm good."

The look in his eyes suggested he didn't believe her once again. Thankfully, he dropped the subject. "I'll let Chet know." He slipped past her into the inn.

Paige blew out another slow breath before stepping away from the wall. She moved to follow her father inside where she could make a phone call in private. Her dad was one thing, but she wasn't above asking her mother for a loan.

"Do you know CPR?"

Tanner's sharply uttered question had her whirling around. "Wh-what?"

"It's a simple question. Do you know how to perform CPR on a child?"

"Of course I do. I have to in order to teach at my school." She didn't bother mentioning it wasn't her school any longer.

"Good. You're hired."

The throbbing in her head grew more intense. "I'm sorry, what?"

"I need someone to watch Whitney while I'm away at this week's tournament. You're a teacher. You know CPR and she seems to like you. Clearly, you're stuck in town for a few days. Stay the week."

Of all the...

"I don't know what kind of ego trip you're on, but I don't recall applying for the job." She jammed her fists into her hips. "And as soon as my car is fixed, I'm out of here. Not that it's any of your business, but I have plans for the week."

Sort of.

He took a step closer. "How are you going to pay for your car, Paige?"

She swallowed a gasp.

Tanner grinned malevolently. "You're easier to read than the back of a cereal box. You don't have the money to fix your car. Stay and watch Whitney this week and I'll pay for it. Hell, the purse for the tournament includes a car for the champion. If I win—and I rarely lose—the car is yours."

Her cheeks burned with embarrassment. And frustration. *How dare he?* She didn't have to kowtow to his demands. The I-told-you-so's that would no doubt follow groveling to her mother would be painful, that's for sure. But Paige could survive them. It was preferable to sticking around Chances Inlet until her father and his new family figured out her shame.

She opened her mouth to tell him no, but he beat her to the punch.

"I was surprised when Patricia said today was the first time she met you."

Her stomach dropped to her knees.

"I would have thought you two would have met on New Year's Eve. When you and I met." He must have sensed the blood in the water because he took a step closer. "Imagine how hurt she will be—how hurt your dad will be—when they find out you came all this way and never bothered to say hello."

It was a hell of a threat. Judging by his smug grin, he knew it, too. Paige's beef—if that's what one would call it—was with her father. She would never want Patricia to be collateral damage. The woman had not done anything to warrant Paige hurting her feelings.

"You're a dick, you know that?"

Tanner shrugged. "Most of the players on the tour feel the same way. That's because I play to win. Every. Time." He settled his Oakley's back onto the bridge of his nose. "I need to be on the road by nine a.m. tomorrow. If you want to wait to start until morning, Sonny will be here at eight sharp to pick you up."

———

PATRICIA SLIPPED OUT onto the porch of the little carriage house tucked behind the inn. Darkness had settled around Chances Inlet, bringing with it a sea breeze, thankfully warm for late March. Lamar sat on the steps of the porch, quietly staring off into the distance.

She knew he had nights like this occasionally, where work, or worse, memories of his days in combat, threatened to overwhelm him. Most times, she left him alone in contemplative silence. Tonight was different, however. He wasn't staring at nothing. His gaze was firmly focused on the window of the Glasgow room where his daughter had been holed up since teatime.

The tree frogs chorused as she wrapped her arms around his shoulders from behind and sat down on the top step. He sighed as he leaned his head back against her chest.

"I don't know how you survived parenting five kids," he said. "This not knowing what the hell is wrong with her is killing me."

Patricia chuckled. "Waiting them out is hard, but it's the only thing you can do when they are adults."

"I honestly thought she came to see me. To meet you."

She hated the heartache she heard in his voice. "Don't be so quick to rule it out. Chances Inlet isn't exactly on the way to Myrtle Beach. At least not when you're driving from Chicago."

"Mmm. My gut tells me she only meant to pass through. She didn't count on her car breaking down."

"Your gut, huh?" She kneaded his shoulders with her fingers.

"That and the fact Hayden recognized her. She's been her before."

Patricia's hands stilled. "Is he sure? When?"

"The boy has an eidetic memory. He never forgets a face." He tilted his back to look at her. "Paige was in Chances Inlet New Year's Eve. She was at the weddings, Tricia."

The rawness in his expression made her chest squeeze. "She came all this way just to watch from afar and then leave?" That didn't seem right.

"Something or someone spooked her." He fixed his eyes back on the inn. The lights in Paige's suite clicked off. "And today, I got the distinct impression she's lost somehow. Maybe even a little frightened."

She kissed the top of his head. "Then she definitely came to Chances Inlet to see you."

He harrumphed. "How do you figure that?"

"Because you're her father. You may not have had a hand in raising her, but deep down, she knows you care. That you'll fix whatever is bothering her."

"How can you be so sure?" he whispered.

"Mother's intuition." She gently guided his head back against her thigh so she could see his eyes. "Trust me, Lamar. You're the reason she's here. I know how hard it is for a protector like you to be patient, but you're going to have to wait for her to let you in."

"What if she doesn't?"

The desperation in his softly uttered words nearly broke her. All of her senses screamed Paige would come clean to her father. But they were just feelings. She wouldn't ever lie to her husband as much as she wanted to ease his pain.

"You'll still have me." She pressed her lips to his. "Come to bed, Lamar," she murmured against his mouth. "I'm sure we can find something to do that will take your mind off Paige for the time being."

She was relieved when, after a slight hesitation, he stood and reached down a hand to help her to her feet. He pulled her against his broad chest.

"Have I told you today how much I love you?" he asked as his lips hovered above hers.

"I'd rather you come inside and show me."

With a low chuckle and a passionate kiss, he did just that.

CHAPTER FIVE

Tanner swirled the dregs of his scotch around the bottom of his crystal glass. A single lamp illuminated his desk, pitching the rest of his study in darkness. It suited his mood.

He deserved every name Paige called him earlier today, and a whole lot more. His mother would tan his hide if she knew how he'd manipulated the woman to bend to his will. Still, he wouldn't regret it. His anxiety of the past few days had lessened exponentially knowing Paige would be here caring for Whitney while he was away. His mind was free once again to focus on his game.

Best of all, the little girl seemed delighted her protector would be staying with her. He'd announced the plan to Whitney when he was putting her to bed. It was the first time he'd seen even a glimmer of a smile since she arrived.

It was also the first time he'd tucked her in. Almeda was responsible for handling Whitney's primary care since she arrived. He only hoped he'd done everything the correct way. He had no idea what kids liked and didn't like. The queen-size bed in the guest room practically swallowed up the tiny girl.

Did she have a bed more suitable to a child at home? Tanner

pictured her in a princess bed with netting and fairy lights above it. One of the players on the tour had a similar setup for his little girl and the guy couldn't stop showing off pictures to anyone and everyone.

He wondered if Whitney had trouble sleeping in the big bed here. Should he get her a smaller one? He could, except she wasn't staying. As soon as they found Donella, Whitney was going back home. If she didn't have a princess bed there, he'd simply send one home with her as a parting gift.

Finding the girl's mother was proving difficult, however. It was as if Donella had vanished without a trace. Sheriff Hollister followed up on all the local leads, scouring home surveillance cameras, interviewing local gig drivers and rental car staff. Nothing turned up. The sheriff's buddies out west were still investigating leads, but, so far, not even a whisker, as his granddad would say. It was almost as if someone was punking him.

Not for the first time in the last year and a half, Tanner wished he could call Tristan. His brother always claimed to have the higher functioning brain. Tanner could use a different perspective right now. Of course, his brother would always find the funny, lighter side to any situation. And somehow, he'd find a way to place the blame for everything squarely on Tanner's shoulders. If it meant Tristan would still be alive, he wouldn't mind being the butt of the joke this time.

He could always call Tristan's widow, Melinda. She possessed the same keen sense of humor as her husband. It's what had made their relationship work. It was no secret that Tristan was far from perfect.

It was two hours earlier in Arizona, though. Melinda likely had her hands full getting sixteen-month-old twins fed and ready for bed.

Twins Tristan never got to meet.

With a growl, he tossed back what remained of his scotch.

His mobile chimed with a call from the guard house at the neighborhood's front gate.

"Sorry to bother you, Mr. Gillette, but there's a Dr. Alden Bryant here. He said you are expecting him?"

Tanner glanced at his watch. Alden said he'd call as soon as he got the paternity results. He didn't expect the doctor to deliver them in person, however.

"Sure," he said, his curiosity piqued. "Send him along."

He turned on another lamp in the room before wandering down the hall to check on Whitney. She was lying on her side, her bunny tucked in close to her body. He took some solace that her sleep seemed less restless than in previous nights.

Tanner reached the front door just as Alden was parking his car.

"Sorry to stop by at this time of night," the doctor said as he entered. "I thought I should go over this with you in person."

"No problem." Tanner ignored the uneasy feeling that threatened. This case was cut and dry. There was no way Tanner could be Whitney's father. He led Alden back to his study. "Things are pretty self-explanatory, though, aren't they? I mean either someone's the father or they aren't."

"In most cases, yes."

Tanner felt a big 'but' coming. He reached for the bottle of scotch and refilled his glass. "Drink?"

Alden shook his head. "I promised Kate I'd deal with Max tonight." He pulled a sheet of paper from his messenger bag and handed it to Tanner.

Tanner took a fortifying swallow from his glass before glancing down at the results. He immediately wished he'd downed the entire bottle. "What the fuck is this? This can't be right. The test is flawed." He snapped his gaze up to meet Alden's sympathetic one. "How can this be?"

"We can do another sample," Alden said. "But these things aren't usually off by very much." He paused for a long moment, seeming to choose his next words carefully. "Tanner, if you look at each metric carefully, you're a very *close* match. But not an *exact* match."

An icy wave washed over Tanner. The glass in his hand felt heavy. It slipped from his fingers, but Alden grabbed it before it hit the floor. The doctor sighed before chugging the rest of the scotch. He carefully placed the glass on the desk.

"It goes without saying that this remains between us," he said quietly. "Whatever you need, I'm here for you."

Tanner wasn't sure how long he stood there, frozen in disbelief. But when the thaw came, it was followed by a searing hot rage. Breathing unsteadily, he marched over to the credenza, picked up a photo of his twin and hurled it at the wall.

"Have you lost your mind?!"

Paige held her cellphone at arm's length to prevent Summer's explosive rant from damaging her eardrum.

"More like my dignity," she muttered while unpacking her toiletry bag in the Jack and Jill bathroom she was sharing with Whitney. She pushed aside the shower curtain and set the open bottles of shampoo, conditioner and body wash she'd pilfered from the inn on the rim of the tub. It's not like Patricia could reuse them, she reasoned. Too bad she'd used up all the body lotion after her bath yesterday. The stuff was decadent, with an amazing scent and texture.

"This is serious, Paige. You can't just move in with a stranger," Summer protested.

"I'm not 'moving in' with anyone. I'm simply taking a nannying gig for a week. One where the only person home is the child."

Tanner didn't stay one minute longer than necessary once

Paige arrived earlier that morning. The man practically snarled as he slapped down a credit card, the keys to his car, and an emergency contact list on the kitchen counter. The whole ride over, she steeled herself for another one of his cocky triumphant smiles. Instead, she was greeted with a series of grunt-like instructions and nothing resembling a "thank-you" before he took off. For some reason, part of her was disappointed not to have the opportunity to spar with him. The rest of her, though, was taken aback by his unpleasant demeanor, not to mention the dark circles under his bloodshot eyes.

"So now you're home alone in a strange man's house?" Summer went on. "Wow. You're right. That sounds *sooo* much safer."

Paige ignored her friend's sarcasm.

"It's a gated community. The house has a state-of-the-art alarm system that practically scans my eyeballs when I want to enter. And if all that weren't enough, you're forgetting that my dad is the sheriff in this town. I imagine he'll have his deputies patrolling by here on the hour."

Her father, of course, was delighted to have Paige sticking around for the week. So much so that he'd put up far less objection to her living in a stranger's house than Summer was presently giving her.

"Why couldn't you and Whitney stay at the inn?" Summer asked.

Because it was only a matter of time before Paige's story reached her father's ears. And those of the rest of the McAlister family. She'd rather have a buffer of at least a couple of miles when that embarrassment came raining down, thank you very much.

Paige glanced into the opposite bedroom where the little girl was quietly coloring. She lowered her voice. "Whitney has had too much upheaval already. This is a better plan."

Summer grumbled something unintelligible. "Do you think

Tanner is telling the truth? That he doesn't know the mother? Because clearly, *she* knows *him*. You don't just pick a random celebrity out of a hat and drop off your kid at the country club where he's playing golf."

"Yeah." Paige sighed. "No doubt he's leaving a lot of the story out. I'd like to say I'm surprised, but nothing about the male species surprises me anymore. I've found it's best not to believe a word they say."

"Not all men are that way," Summer said.

"Not all, no. You've found one of the few who isn't a lying, cheating SOB. But the good guys seem to be few and far between these days."

Something feeling a lot like despondency settled in Paige's chest. She wanted what Summer had. What Patricia McAlister had with her father. Heck, what the woman's children likely had with their mates and significant others. But she doubted she'd ever be able to trust a man again. And she certainly didn't trust Tanner Gillette to tell the truth.

"More than likely, Mr. Gillette hasn't paid his child support and momma wanted a little vacay. So, she dropped her kid off with her baby daddy the kid has never met." She slammed her hairbrush onto the counter in disgust. "But let's not forget, Whitney is an innocent in all of this. Her well-being takes priority over everything else. And caring for little ones is what I do best."

"You do," Summer said. "And she's lucky to have you. I feel a little better now, knowing there won't be a sexy golfer coming on to you at every turn. From what I read about him online, he's quite the playboy. Do you know what they call him on the tour? Mr. Swipe Right or Tanner Tinder. Rumor has it he has a woman in every city. He seems to be as proficient at charming the panties off women as he is with his putter."

Paige snorted. "You're forgetting who you're talking to, Sum. I'm immune to charming liars, remember? Don't you worry. I'm never giving another guy like that access to my heart again."

AFTER SETTLING into one of the guest rooms, Paige inspected the rest of the house. Whitney and her bunny silently shadowed her. The rooms were large and elegantly decorated.

"I'll bet this was a model home for the community at one time and Tanner just left everything as is," she said to Whitney.

A screened porch stretched along one side of the back of the house. The yard looked to be the fairway from a golf course.

"No going out back without a helmet on," she warned Whitney. "I don't want you taking a golf ball to the noggin."

The little girl's eyes went wide as she nodded.

The great room was a bit stuffy for Paige's taste, with its white sofas, perfectly placed pillows, and sterile artwork. It had a fabulous view of the golf course, however, thanks to an entire wall of windows.

"I wonder how many times one of those have been cracked with an errant golf ball."

Whitney moved in close to inspect the windowpanes.

There was a study off the great room. Paige took a peek inside. It was the only part of the house with any personal articles. Photos of Tanner holding various trophies hung on the walls. The trophies themselves were displayed on the built-in bookshelves.

A hallway leading to the opposite end of the house likely contained Tanner's bedroom. Paige was proud of herself for resisting the urge to snoop. Instead, she steered Whitney toward the huge kitchen at the back of the house.

"Well, we won't starve," she announced to the little girl after cataloging the contents of the fridge and the pantry. "Tanner's housekeeper keeps this place well-stocked. What I don't see, though, is any ice cream."

Whitney's face lit up.

"We can't have a week-long slumber party without some, can we?"

A slow grin formed on the little girl's lips as she shook her head.

"You look like a cookies and cream kind of girl to me."

Whitney nodded and Paige held out her fist for a fist bump. "Atta girl. Me, too. But I'll never say no to Ben and Jerry's Fudge Brownie. How about we go to the store and grab some ice cream and a few things to keep us entertained this week?"

There was one of those big box discount stores on the way into town. She could pick up ice cream and some puzzles and games to occupy Whitney with one stop. The little girl didn't have a bathing suit or swim floaties, either. Paige may not be going to Myrtle Beach, but she was determined to return to Chicago with a tan. And Tanner's ritzy neighborhood had four pools to choose from. They'd just go to a different one every day.

She grabbed the keys to the car, along with the credit card, from the counter and headed for the garage, only to stop short.

"Seriously? He left me a Porsche to drive?"

The only car sitting in the three-car garage was a two-door 718 Boxster coupe in candy-apple red. Paige's pulse danced with excitement. She'd been driving since the age of thirteen. Her stepbrothers were both dirt-track junkies and saw no reason why their little sister shouldn't be able to enjoy the sport, too. As a result, Paige could drive just about any vehicle, under any type of conditions.

Too bad she hadn't paid much attention to the mechanics and upkeep of the cars. She might not be stuck in Chances Inlet if she had. But maybe things were looking up. Driving a

Porsche was on her bucket list. Given the car's ridiculous price, she never thought her dream would come true.

She practically skipped over to the driver's side and carefully opened the door. "It even smells luxurious. This is going to be so much fun." She ran her hand over the leather seat reverently before lowering herself into it.

The sound of rubber soles squeaking on the Epoxy floor brought Paige back to reality. Whitney shuffled up next to the open door, her bunny clutched to her chest. Paige eyed the only other seat in the car—the passenger seat. Even if Tanner Gillette did own a child's booster—the very idea was laughable —there was no way she was going to allow the little girl to ride upfront. It was way too dangerous. Not to mention against the law.

Sighing, she propped her forehead against the leather-trimmed steering wheel. "Just when I think I've found some luck, fate keeps snatching it away."

Her father informed her this morning that her car would be ready the following afternoon. Too bad that didn't help her today. Walking five miles to the big box store was out of the question. It was only two miles to the center of historic Chances Inlet, however.

Yesterday, she'd spied an ice cream stand and a bookstore. There was also a little park by the water. They could make an afternoon out of it. Tonight, Paige could order anything else they needed online. Including a booster seat. It would cost a fortune for a rush delivery, but she had no remorse sticking the rich professional athlete with the bill.

"How about the three of us take a walk to get some ice cream?" Paige would likely be carrying the child on her back half the way, but it beat sitting around the house.

Whitney squared her shoulders and gave Paige an enthusiastic nod. Paige pulled her sunscreen from her backpack and dabbed some on both their faces. The little girl grinned softly when Paige pretended to rub some on her bunny's ears.

"Now, all we need are some hats."

Fortunately, Tanner's sponsors kept him well-stocked in that area. Paige grabbed two from a box of new ones sitting on a shelf by the mudroom door. The brim covered Whitney's eyes, so Paige flipped it around.

"No red neck for you!" Grabbing two bottles of water from the fridge, she took the little girl by the hand and headed for the garage's side door. Whitney suddenly began dragging her feet. She tugged on Paige's hand and pointed to a flat cart stacked with bags of mulch.

"Oh my gosh, you are a genius!"

Paige unloaded the four bags and went back into the house to grab a beach towel. She spread the towel on top of the metal cart and bowed down to Whitney.

"Your chariot awaits, Princess."

Whitney climbed aboard, her bright smile her biggest one yet. Paige felt a little wave of disappointment she wasn't able to coax a giggle from the little girl. For some reason, it was important that she be the one to unlock Whitney's voice. And she wanted to do it by the time Tanner returned. He may have blackmailed her to stay with Whitney, but Paige was always a "make lemonade out of lemons" type of girl. Her professional pride was on the line. Not to mention getting the little girl to open up and tell her where to find her mother would give her the upper hand with Tanner Gillette.

Less than an hour later, they were both sitting cross-legged on the cart, enjoying ice cream cones and the shade of the century old live oak tree in the Chances Inlet square.

"Do you have a favorite bedtime story?" Paige asked as she wiped Whitney's hands with a wet wipe.

Whitney's face dimmed slightly, but she nodded.

Paige felt crappy because now the girl was probably thinking of her mother.

"How about we go into the bookstore to see if they have a copy. Then we can read it together tonight."

They entered the Whale of a Tale Bookstore to the happy tinkling of bells. Dust motes danced in the sunlight streaming through the big picture window. A woman of Asian descent was crouched in the window case organizing a display of spring and Easter books.

"Hello there," she greeted them. "Welcome in."

Another woman, this one wearing a dress circa the 1950-s with a full shirt and matching scarf came out from behind the counter. She bent over to meet Whitney eyes. "You must be the little girl that handsome fella was looking for yesterday. He said you had a distinguished looking bunny. Your daddy was very worried about you, sweetheart."

Whitney slipped behind Paige's leg.

"Oh my gosh, Lou, you're scaring the poor thing." The Asian woman crawled out from the display, dusted off her jeans and held out a hand to Paige. "Apologies. I'm Denise. And this is my wife, Lou. We were actually very worried about your daughter yesterday until Deputy Lovell came by to tell us she'd been found."

Paige was stunned by the two ladies' assumption. "Oh, no, she's not my daughter. I'm her . . . um . . .nanny." She didn't dare give out any additional details. It wasn't that she wanted to protect Tanner's reputation as much as it was that she wanted to keep Whitney's situation private.

"Ah," Denise said as if it all made perfect sense.

Both pairs of eyes didn't seem as convinced.

"I see a copy of *The Velveteen Rabbit* in the window," Paige said, trying to steer the conversation back to safer ground. "Do you have a copy I can buy?"

"Do we ever," Lou replied and cocked her hip. "They're right back here in our children's section."

She led them to the rear of the store where the shelves were lower—easier for little bodies to reach. A child-size table took up the middle of the section, the surrounding floor covered in brightly covered cushions. There was an actual fainting couch to one side with small pillows shaped like books littering one end.

"Wow, this is amazing," Paige said.

Lou pressed her hands together. "Isn't it? I copied several elements from a shop I visited in Sweden. Its children's section was four times this size and aways teeming with kids." She tsked softly. "We haven't quite gotten to that level of patronage yet."

"There, there." Denise patted Lou's shoulder. "I have to keep reminding her this is a beach town. The kids who come here are more interested in sand toys and boogie boards."

"That's why it's important we promote the puzzles," Lou said. "Did you put the Easter egg puzzle in the window?"

She hurried off to the display window, presumably to check. Denise shrugged. "It's always been her dream to open a bookstore. I promised her we would have our own when I retired from my job as a set designer. We couldn't afford a space back home in Manhattan." She spread her arms wide. "So here we are."

"How long have you been open?"

"A little over a year. Not everything in life turns out as picture-perfect as we dream it should be," Denise said, cryptically.

Paige huffed. "Don't I know it."

Whitney pulled several books from the shelves and piled them on the fainting couch.

Denise chuckled. "Well, at least she's enjoying the selection.

Stay as long as you like. I'd better go check to see that Lou hasn't undone all my handiwork."

The woman walked away just as Whitney crawled up on the couch and patted the place beside her. She held out a book to Paige.

"Ahh, you've found one you want me to read, I see." She settled onto the chaise. "*A Bad Case of Stripes*! Excellent choice. My students love this one."

A lump formed in her throat as she thought of someone else reading it to her kindergartners. Whitney nestled in against her, as if sensing Paige's sadness.

"We're both gonna be okay," Paige whispered. She drew in a deep breath, transitioned to her teacher voice and began to read about Camilla Cream and her love of lima beans.

CHAPTER SIX

TANNER CROUCHED DOWN on the green in order to get a better look at the tin cup three feet in front of him. His body was so tense he was surprised he could even bend his knees. Of the first nine holes during the afternoon's practice round, this was by far the shortest putt he needed to make. He should be able to do it with his eyes closed. Of course, after missing his previous eight putts, maybe he should just close his eyes and take the damn shot.

"The green slopes to the right about six inches in front of the hole," Sonny advised from where he was bent over Tanner's back, studying the same line.

The caddy could read the greens better than anyone in professional golf. Both men knew his advice wouldn't matter for shit today, though. Tanner couldn't seem to sink a putt from six inches away much less thirty-six. That's because every time he gripped his putter, his wrists began to twitch.

He got to his feet and stepped up to address the ball. Sure enough, there was the damn twitch again. He could feel the eyes of the other golfers and caddies in his foursome looking on sympathetically. None of them looked his way when the ball rolled past the hole, however.

A few years ago, a much less mature Tanner would have angrily tossed his putter into the pond to his right. The tantrum would have fueled headlines for weeks. Fortunately for his family—and the prototype putter his sponsor let him experiment with—the anger management techniques he'd spent a fortune to master were helping him keep his frustrations from becoming social media fodder.

But just barely.

"I think that's it for me today, gentlemen," he announced to no one's surprise. "Obviously, I'd be better off spending my time on the practice green."

The other men all murmured their agreement, trying, and failing, to hide their relief. Golfers were a superstitious lot. They all knew it just as easily could be one of them self-destructing during a practice round days before a tournament. None of them wanted any part of what Tanner was experiencing to rub off on them. And they certainly weren't going to acknowledge Tanner's condition for what it likely was: a bad case of the yips.

"There's already a crowd over at the practice green," Sonny said quietly. "You sure you want to go over there?"

"It's only a matter of time before everyone in the clubhouse is talking about it," Tanner replied. "But you're right. No amount of practice is going to fix this. Let's head back to the condo."

He needed a stiff drink and some privacy to make the phone call he'd been dreading since learning the truth about Whitney last night. The shock of the paternity results was messing with Tanner's head. Not to mention his game. The sooner he resolved the situation, the sooner he'd leave the yips in the rearview mirror of his golfcart.

An hour later, his wrist was twitching for another reason as he dialed his phone. He needed to get this conversation over with, but a big part of him wished he could just remain oblivious. To go back to playing the game he loved at a level he'd worked hard to attain.

Except there was a living, breathing child he couldn't ignore. A child that had his twin brother's DNA but Tanner's name on her birth certificate.

Tanner needed answers. Unfortunately, the one person with all the answers was no longer among the living. That meant he had to go to the next closest source.

Melinda answered on the fourth ring.

"Tanner," she said. "What's up?"

His brother's widow always sounded breathless and harried on the phone, like she was doing the caller a favor just by answering. Tanner got along well enough with her when Tristan was alive. She adored her husband and likely deserved some sort of monument for putting up with Tristan's idiosyncrasies and superiority complex. Not only that, but she was a good mother who doted on her twin boys.

Now that Tristan was no longer around to act as a buffer, Melinda's frosty indifference toward Tanner held a bit more bite. No doubt her view of him was tainted by whatever tales Tristan told her about their childhood. His reputation as a hothead on the links and a playboy off the course likely didn't help their relationship either. Still, she never denied him access to his nephews.

"I wanted to check in on the boys," he said. Not entirely a lie. With Tristan gone, Tanner was determined to be the devoted uncle/father figure to his brother's sons. "And you, of course. It's been a few weeks since we last spoke."

"Has it?" Her tone implied she hadn't been waiting by the phone for his call. "Time seems to run together when you have little ones."

Melinda was far from a frazzled mother. She was born with

a silver spoon in her mouth just as shiny as the ones Tanner and Tristan were born with. The Arizona home she shared with her sons was by no means a shoebox, either. Not to mention the staff of three that came with it.

"How are the boys doing?" He thumbed through the photos on his phone to find the weekly snapshot of the twins she religiously sent to Tanner and his parents. At nearly seventeen months, the boys already had the same twinkle in their eye as their father and uncle.

"Both are getting their two-year-molars right now. Liam continues to walk with his arms above his head as though he's got a gun pointed to his back."

Tanner chuckled at the image.

"And Luca still does all the talking for both of them," she continued.

Shit.

The twitch in his wrist suddenly became more pronounced. He dropped onto the sofa, unsure how to proceed from here.

"Listen, Mel, I'm trying to locate someone from the Silver Canyon project." Tristan spent three years developing the six-thousand-acre community just north of Las Vegas. The timeframe coincided with Whitney's conception. On the day of her birth, however, his brother was on his honeymoon in Fiji. "Do you happen to know if Tristan kept a staff directory?"

The line was quiet for several long heartbeats before Melinda answered. "I have no idea. Your dad would have all of that, anyway. You should check with him."

Except Tanner couldn't ask his dad. Not without the man becoming suspicious. Tanner never cared about the company or its property development before. Sure, he showed up to promote the golf courses and surrounding homes when asked. He benefited from the company's success after all. The day-to-day operations were well beyond his sphere of interest, however. His father would immediately know something was up if Tanner started asking for an item as innocuous as a staff directory.

And he wasn't sure how to broach the discovery of Whitney yet. His parents were both so fragile right now. They would relish having another living part of Tristan, though.

But would the woman on the other end of the line?

What the fuck was he doing?

He dragged his fingers through his hair. As much as he wanted to hand this problem off to someone else, he couldn't very well ask Melinda if Tristan ever mentioned a woman named Donella. He certainly couldn't tell his brother's widow her twin sons had a half-sister.

The mum accidentally left her with me before she disappeared. Tag. You're it.

Nope. He couldn't pull the trigger. Not now anyway. Maybe not ever.

The answer to his problems was out there somewhere. Just not with Melinda. So far, none of Sheriff Hollister's contacts had turned up anything. Tanner would hire a private detective to track Whitney's mother down, that's all. Hell, he'd hire five it that was what it would take.

"Is that all you needed, Tanner?"

"Um, yeah. Some guy who says he used to work out there claims Tristan promised him a round of golf with me. I'm happy to honor it if the guy's legit." Tristan had promised countless people a round of golf with his famous brother. Melinda would never suspect the lie. "I'm sure Dad can verify it for me."

"Your parents will be in the States later this spring," Melinda said. "Hopefully, you can fit us all into your busy tournament schedule. It will be good for the boys to see you."

He hung up saying a fervent prayer that the situation with Whitney was cleared up long before then. If not, he wouldn't have to worry about a busy tournament schedule. His days would be wide open.

PAIGE CLOSED the book then nearly jumped off the chaise at the smattering of applause filling the bookstore. Aside from Lou and Denise, two other women were clapping a little bit too enthusiastically. The taller woman had a mischievous grin to go with her wavy shoulder-length dark hair. The blue eyes behind her glasses seemed vaguely familiar. An infant carrier was strapped to her chest, the only evidence of the sleeping baby inside was a tiny foot sticking out from one of the leg holes.

The other woman wore her long blonde hair in a messy braid to the side of her head. Her almond-shaped eyes practically twinkled within her delicate face. The rest of her was just as slight, except for the large baby-bump protruding from her middle.

"That's Emily's favorite book right now. Alden and I pride ourselves on being good bedtime story readers," the dark-haired one said. "But your rendition puts us to shame."

Lou charged forward. "She's right. That was amazing." She clapped her hands. "I've been wanting to start a story-time hour here in the store for months, but I couldn't find the right person. You would be perfect. Oh, please say you'll do it."

The four women stared at Paige expectantly. As though it was a perfectly reasonable request.

"Um—"

"Whoa there, Louella." Denise gently pulled her wife back toward the front of the store. "You're scaring the poor woman."

The blonde woman laughed. "Stand down, Lou. Paige is only visiting for the week." She turned to Paige. "Acclimating to life in a small town can be a little overwhelming. Trust me, I should know." She extended her hand. "I'm Ginger, Gavin's wife. And this is Kate."

Paige already surmised the taller woman was Patricia's eldest daughter based on her earlier comments. What she couldn't figure out was why they were here. She shook hands with both of them.

"How did you know where to find me?"

"It's hard to fly under the radar in Chances Inlet," Ginger replied. "We ran into Deputy Lovell outside Knotical. He mentioned seeing you come in here."

Kate elbowed her sister-in-law. "Knotical is the yarn shop next door. His mom owns it. It's not like he was tailing you or anything like that."

Of course not.

Paige's expression must have telegraphed her thoughts because both women laughed.

"I didn't say your father isn't keeping tabs on you," Kate teased. "But then, that's a father's prerogative. Especially with their daughters."

There was no point in explaining that "keeping tabs" on her didn't make Lamar Hollister a father. Whatever issues she had with her dad had nothing to do with these women. Or anyone else in Chances Inlet. She didn't come here to tear down the good reputation he had within this town or the McAlister family. Their lost relationship was water under the bridge.

At least that's what she kept telling herself.

Kate bent down to shake Whitney's hand.

"And you must be Whitney." She reached for the rabbit's paw and shook it. "And that makes you Gladys. So nice to meet you both."

Gladys?

Kate winked at Paige. "Emily noticed it written on the tag," she murmured. "She confirmed it with Whitney. What can I say? My daughter comes from a long line of formidable women. She scares me sometimes with her superpowers."

Paige glanced down at Whitney. "Gladys?"

The little girl nodded.

"That's a perfect name for a bunny." Paige glided her palm over Whitney's head. "Why don't you pick out three books to take home with us and put the rest away."

While Whitney quietly sorted through the books, Paige turned to Kate and whispered, "Did she say anything to Emily?"

Kate shook her head in defeat. "I'm afraid not." She laid a hand on Paige's arm. "But she will. I've seen these kinds of cases before and all it takes is for the child to trust someone. It's obvious she's comfortable with you. We are just going to have to wait it out. Be patient with her."

Patience was not exactly one of Paige's virtues. She only had a week to unlock Whitney's secrets.

"Those books are wonderful choices," Ginger was saying to Whitney. She patted her growing belly. "I may need your advice for some books for my baby. Do you think you can help me pick some when the time comes?"

Whitney gave Ginger a shy grin as she nodded.

"It's a date," Ginger said.

The kindness everyone kept showering Whitney with was touching. However, the assumption neither of them was ever leaving Chances Inlet was starting to freak Paige out a little bit.

The little girl proudly carried the books she'd chosen to the counter. Lou shot Paige a pleading look. Something fluttered in her chest. It had been nearly three months since she'd read aloud to a child. Truth be told, she'd forgotten how much she missed it.

Damn you, Jon, for taking that away.

"I'll be in town through Sunday," she heard herself saying. "I'm happy to come back later this week."

Lou raced around the counter and pulled her into a tight hug. "Thank you! Thank you!"

"Any day but Saturday," Kate chimed in. "She's busy that day."

Paige eyeballed the other woman.

Kate pointed at Ginger's belly. "Saturday is Ginger's baby shower," she said as if that explained everything.

Ginger nodded. "It'll be a great opportunity for you to meet everyone."

It wasn't until they were on the sidewalk outside the bookstore that the full force of what just transpired hit Paige. Her father would certainly have unearthed Paige's embarrassing secret by the weekend. She would likely be too paralyzed with humiliation to read aloud in front of a crowded bookstore. The realization had her feeling gloomy. For some unknown reason, it meant something to her to have these people respect her.

Whitney climbed aboard the gardener's cart.

"Don't tell me you pulled her on that all the way from Tanner's place?" Kate asked.

Paige shrugged. "It's not that far. And I like the exercise."

Kate narrowed her eyes. "Let me guess. 'Number One in the World' didn't think to pick up a booster seat?"

"Bingo. And the car he left me is only a two-seater. My car should be ready tomorrow afternoon. I'll use Tanner's credit card to order a booster online. Hopefully it will be here by then."

"You'll do better than that." Kate pulled a key fob from the baby carrier and pointed it at a giant SUV parked three doors down. "I'm on my way to grab some diapers for this little poop machine. My car is equipped with built-in booster seats. I'll give you two a lift to the super-store. You can use his credit card to buy one there. And whatever else we think you'll need."

Whitney looked at Paige expectantly.

Paige grinned back at her. "Only if they sell ice cream."

"Well, it looks like that problem is solved." Ginger had to maneuver around her belly to give Paige a hug. "I'm so glad to meet you, finally, Paige. Your father always talks about you with such pride."

An uneasy tremor shot through Paige.

Ginger gave Whitney a squeeze. "We will definitely see you Saturday, if not before. Now, I'm off to the studio to get ready for my afternoon dance classes."

A strangled sound escaped Whitney's throat. All three women stilled.

Kate cocked her head to the side. "Do you like to dance, Whitney?"

The girl's chin bobbed up and down swiftly.

"Oh my gosh, we are going to be great friends, then." Ginger sat down on the cart next to her. "I'm thrilled to share my love of dance with little girls like you. Emily has dance class tomorrow. You're welcome to come with her." She quickly glanced up at Paige. "If that's okay?"

One look at Whitney's eager face and Paige realized this could be an opportunity to unlock the little girl's voice.

"It's not like we have any other solid plans." She cupped Whitney's cheek. "And we'll need a way to work off all that ice cream, won't we?"

TANNER ACKNOWLEDGED the man inside the guardhouse with a quick wave. He didn't have time to stop and make small talk with him. Especially since the guy's first question would likely be to ask why Tanner was returning home before this week's tournament even began.

"We need to stop at the club," Sonny reminded him.

The caddy was a bit obsessive-compulsive about storing Tanner's clubs in a temperature-controlled environment. He preferred they be kept under lock and key in the clubhouse. It always annoyed Tanner that he couldn't step out onto the golf course behind his house in the late evenings and drive a few balls just for the fun of it.

Since it was highly unlikely Tanner would be using them anytime soon, he didn't bother protesting. Instead, he steered the Cadillac SUV in the direction of the golf course, two miles deep into the community.

"We should at least hit the range tomorrow," Sonny said. "It won't do you any good to let the rest of your game slip."

Tanner leveled a glare at the man in the passenger seat. "You should have gone on the bag for someone else this week. At least you would have earned some prize money."

Sonny earned a salary for being Tanner's caddy, but the opportunity for the big bucks came from tournament play. Most golfers on the tour shared a percentage of their prize money with their caddy. Tanner was no exception. If he finished the year number one in the rankings and won the year-end championship as he planned, Sonny would earn seven figures this season.

This was the trickle-down effect to Tanner's yips. He squeezed his fingers around the steering wheel trying to alleviate the frustration and guilt swallowing him up. Both men stood to lose a lot if the Whitney situation wasn't resolved quickly.

"As my momma used to say, 'I'll dance wit the guy that brung me,'" Sonny mumbled.

Tanner thought his caddy was being a fool, even though he was grateful for the loyalty. A few years ago, he'd taken a chance on Sonny when the rest of the golf world had written the guy off. Alcoholism had ruined two of his marriages and lost him the bag with three top ten professionals.

At the time, both men were looking for someone to believe in them. Tanner helped Sonny find his way to sobriety while the caddy taught him to trust his innate golf skills. Their relationship was mutually beneficial ever since.

Until now.

"I've got video chats with two private detectives Sheriff Hollister lined up," he told Sonny. "My lawyer should have the birth record any day now. We'll get this mess cleared up by the end of the week."

Sonny made a noncommittal sound before leaning forward in his seat. "Um, Tan Man, is that who I think it is?"

Tanner did a double take in the direction Sonny was pointing.

"What the hell?"

Paige Hollister was strutting along the golf cart path dressed in an outfit that left little to the imagination. The white blouse she wore over a lavender two-piece bathing suit might as well have been made from tissue paper, it was so sheer. He'd long suspected her figure would be enticing, but he wasn't prepared for just how mind-blowing it actually was.

A pair of golfers in a cart slowly passed by her, both men nearly getting whiplash trying to sneak another peek at what was a very fine ass. A wolf whistle filled the air just as a pickup truck nearly collided with Tanner, the driver presumably getting an eyeful of Paige.

"Is that Whitney?" Sonny asked.

Sure enough, the little girl was huddled beneath a big beach towel on top of the flat cart Tanner's lawn service stored at his house. Paige kept her gaze forward and her chin up as she pulled Whitney along the cart path. Her ponytail was swinging angrily as she marched along.

"For the love of Pete." Tanner made a sharp U-turn so he could pull up alongside the pair. He jerked the car into park and jumped out. The icy look she greeted him with when he stormed around the hood of the car nearly had him moving his hands to cover the family jewels. Recognition quickly dawned and her expression relaxed into a scowl that wasn't any more welcoming.

"You're supposed to be in Charleston," she practically hissed.

"What and miss whatever this—" He waved his hands at the cart and then at Paige's outfit. "—is."

Paige narrowed her eyes to slits. "For your information, 'this' is a bathing suit that is perfectly respectable for the beach —where I'm supposed to be this week, I might add. It is also acceptable for wearing to a swimming pool. Unless said pool is surrounded by horny, middle-aged men who prefer to act like middle school boys."

She pulled her coverup more firmly against her body. Not that it did any good. The fabric clung to her, accentuating her lush curves even more. Paige let out an angry growl.

"None of the reviews mentioned this thing practically disintegrated when it got wet," she mumbled. "No wonder it was so inexpensive."

This close he could make out her nipples. They were hard beneath the wet cloth. The breath stilled in his lungs as all the blood rushed to his crotch.

For fuck's sake.

He was no better than the jerks who had just been ogling her. He forced his gaze up her body. Hell, was that one of his limited-edition golf hats she was wearing? The ones he was saving for Augusta?

Anger is good. Lust is bad.

"I was referring to the cart and the horse business going on here. I seem to recall leaving you the keys to my car." He moved to block her from view of the on-coming traffic. "You'd get a lot less attention in the Porsche. Why the hell are you pulling Whitney on a cart like a circus animal instead of simply driving to the pool?"

She threw her shoulders back and stepped forward. He could practically feel the anger radiating off her.

"I would have loved to drive your fancy Porsche had it been properly equipped with a back seat and suitable child protection," she snapped.

The heat was scorching off Tanner now, although for a very different reason. The scent of coconut and sunshine had him glancing down at the exposed skin on her chest. A tiny bead of perspiration was meandering down into the valley between her breasts. He licked his lips.

"Oh my God, you're as bad as the rest of your infantile

golfer buddies." With a huff and a stomp of her foot, she yanked on the cart and pulled it forward, narrowly missing his toes. "Come on, Whitney. We need to get home and get ready."

Tanner shook his head to regroup.

"You're not pulling her on that thing all the way home," he argued. "It's more than a mile."

She swung around, walking backward as she continued to pull Whitney. "Ooo. A whole mile, is it? I'm sure that distance is probably daunting for most of the paper-doll women you surround yourself with. Newsflash, though, Down Under Dude. You should probably find yourself a woman with more stamina."

With a flick of her ponytail, she spun back around and continued walking. Tanner meant to follow, but he was trying to convince his body that she had not just issued a blatant sexual challenge.

A woman with more stamina?

For the love of fuck.

"Um, Tanner," Sonny was saying from somewhere behind him. "Cell phones are rolling."

Shit.

At least that got his feet moving in the right direction.

"Get in the car," he demanded once he caught up with her.

Paige stopped short, this time nearly taking off his shin with the side of the cart.

"Do you have a child's car seat in that car?" she asked, a touch too sweetly.

Tanner looked down at Whitney. "She's not a baby anymore. She doesn't need a car seat."

"Children forty pounds and under are required by law to ride in a booster seat." Her smile was smug. "Seeing as that car does not have booster seats, Whitney will not be riding in it. Now, if you'll excuse us, we need to hurry home and get changed. Whitney has a ballet class this afternoon."

Booster seats? Ballet? The woman was certifiable. What had he been thinking leaving her in charge of Whitney?

He watched her walk away from him, her sweet ass sashaying from side to side. Yeah, he'd been thinking with the wrong head.

"Take the car," he growled at Sonny. "I'll meet you back at the house."

"You sure?"

No! He needed to get as far away from her lush lips and provocative body as he could. Except he couldn't let her walk home like that alone. His mother—and a few nannies—raised him better than that.

He waved Sonny off and trudged after Paige. Whitney looked back over her shoulder at him, her eyes wide. Tanner relaxed his face and tried to smile at her. At the very least, he attempted not to scare her.

"I'll pull it," he said once he caught up to them. He reached for the handle before Paige let it go. Heat raced to his junk when their fingers tangled. She pulled her hand away as if he'd scalded her. She cleared her throat while he did everything he could to catch his breath. They walked along in a tense silence for several yards.

Tanner looked back at Whitney. "You okay back there, Whit?"

The little girl moved her chin up and down slightly.

"You tell me if I go too fast, okay kiddo?"

Whitney's shoulders relaxed and the nod she gave him this time was slightly more pronounced.

He focused his gaze back to the front, only to find Paige studying him quizzically.

"Why are you looking at me like that?"

A ghost of a smile flitted over her lips. She shook her head.

Tanner sighed. "I may not know all the ins and outs of

keeping a four-year-old safe, but that doesn't mean I want any harm coming to her."

Paige acknowledged him with an arched eyebrow and nothing else. They continued in silence for another quarter mile.

"I thought you were going to be gone through Sunday," she finally said.

"Yeah. So did I. Something came up."

She jerked her gaze over to him. "Something about—" She motioned behind them with her head.

"Yeah." It wasn't a lie. He wouldn't have the yips if Whitney hadn't shown up.

Paige moved in a little closer and lowered her voice. "Have you found her?"

He didn't have to ask who the "her" she was referring to was. "Not yet. But we've got a new lead."

Mainly that his brother was the little girl's dad. Not that he was sharing that with Paige. Or anyone else right now

"I take it I'm not getting a new car, then?"

He looked over to find her lips twitching at the corners. It made him want to take her by the damn ponytail and kiss those luscious lips of hers senseless.

"No, but your car is ready. And paid for. I told Almeda she could have the entire week to spend with her daughter and new grandson, though."

She was quiet for a long moment. "I'll hold up my end of the bargain."

The intensity of the relief that washed over him was unexpected. He told himself it was because Paige was just what Whitney needed, a protector, an educator, a friend. And caring for Whitney was his main priority.

He glanced back over his shoulder. The beautiful little girl sitting on the cart was his niece. His brother's child just as much as Liam and Luca. Everything suddenly looked different.

Yes, he needed to find Donella. But that didn't mean he would let this part of Tristan slip back out of his life.

Now all he had to do was figure out how he was going to share a house with the temptress beside him for the next six days without combusting into a cloud of lust.

PAIGE WAS GOING to spend the next six days sharing a house with Tanner.

Her heart was still on lockdown. And her brain knew enough not to trust a man who up until now, ignored responsibility for his own daughter. But her body . . . that was an entirely different can of worms. Just the brush of his fingers against hers moments ago had her nearly losing her balance. The sizzle she'd felt New Year's Eve was definitely not a fluke.

"Still doing okay back there, Whit?" he called over his shoulder.

His attentiveness to the little girl warmed her. He did seem to have her best interests at heart. Of course, it all could be a smokescreen. Jon had pretended to be an entirely different person with Paige—one who didn't have a wife and three young kids at home in Champagne. And Paige bought it quicker than a Lululemon markdown.

Not this time.

Sure, there were likely extenuating circumstances surrounding Whitney's parentage, as her father insisted. Two sides to the story and all that. But that didn't mean Paige was going to trust a man again. Particularly not a sexy golfer with an Australian accent and heart-stopping dimples.

"So, Whitney is already enrolled in ballet," Tanner said. "How much is that going to cost me?"

Paige snickered. "Lucky for you, I seem to be related to the instructor. Ginger invited Whitney to sit in on Emily's class this afternoon. But I did buy her a leotard and some tights to wear."

"Mmhmm. My credit card alert pinged me frequently yesterday."

"Again, lucky for you I'm a thrifty shopper."

"That's not what the account balance said."

Fortunately, his words didn't hold any bite.

"You told me to do whatever it took to keep her happily entertained this week," she said. "I don't have a carpet bag like Mary Poppins. And from the looks of it you can afford it."

He laughed, the sound of it so relaxed it made her grin.

Tanner stopped suddenly. "There it is."

Paige sobered up. "There what is?"

"That smile you beguiled me with New Year's Eve." His gaze was filled with wonder. "I was beginning to think it might have been a mirage."

Oh. My.

She was light-headed again. Fortunately, the sound of someone clearing their throat snapped Paige back from doing something stupid. Like melt at Tanner's feet.

They turned in unison to discover her father leaning against his Bronco parked in Tanner's driveway.

"Afternoon." His tone was relaxed, but Paige had no doubt his eyes were spearing both of them with a pointed look behind his Aviator's.

Great. Had he discovered her ugly truth? She could only imagine what he thought of her. Not to mention that her current outfit backed up whatever assumptions her dad had.

Beside her, Tanner stiffened slightly. "Afternoon, Sheriff. What brings you around?"

Her dad stepped away from the Bronco, his mouth softening into an easy smile he aimed in Whitney's direction. "I'm here to escort one little girl and her nanny to ballet."

Paige's body relaxed with relief. Her reputation was safe for another day. "I thought Kate was coming to pick us up?"

"Max took a while settling down for his nap, making Kate late to pick up Emily," he explained. "The logistics were starting to get complicated, so I offered to come by and get you two."

It sounded innocent enough. "That's . . . nice of you."

"We all do our part in this family."

Paige ignored the reference to her being a part of the McAlister family. It was easier that way. "We'd better get changed then, Whitney."

The little girl tried to scramble off the cart, but her foot got stuck in the towel she was wrapped in. Tanner quickly scooped her up before she hurt herself.

"You're all wrapped up like a little burrito there, Whit." His indulgent smile brought out those knee-weakening dimples. "How 'bout I just carry you inside."

Tanner whistled as he carried Whitney into the house. Paige bit back a sigh at the sweet image.

"I'm surprised to see Tanner back in Chances Inlet," her father said.

Paige risked a glance at him. As usual, his face was inscrutable.

"That makes two of us. He just arrived a few minutes ago. He said there has been a new development in the search for Whitney's mother."

"Did he?" Her father nodded. "That's good news."

A painful silence stretched between them until he finally spoke again.

"And you? Will you be staying now?"

Wasn't that the twenty-thousand-dollar question?

"Tanner's housekeeper won't be back until Sunday. It's a big enough house that Whitney and I can keep out of his way," she assured him.

If her father didn't think it was a good idea for her to stay alone in a house with Tanner Gillette, he kept his thoughts to himself. He followed her through the garage and into the kitchen. Tanner was standing in the center of the room with his hands on his hips staring at the countertops. They were littered with water-colorings Whitney painted earlier in the day.

Tanner cocked an eyebrow at Paige. "Are we opening an art gallery?"

Paige bit back a smile. "It's good for her to express herself through art. It helps with emotional healing." She hastily stacked all the paintings into a pile.

"But do any of them give us a clue as to where her mother disappeared to?" Tanner asked.

She met his frustrated gaze. "No," she replied softly.

Tanner turned and walked into the great room. He stood silently staring toward the golf course.

Paige sighed. "I'll hurry and get changed so we can go. I'm sure you've got someplace more important to be."

"Nothing is more important than you, Paige," her father said.

She wanted to call him on his blatant lie, but she was emotionally drained from all the competing feelings swirling inside her. It was simply easier to head down the hall and distance herself from both men.

CHAPTER EIGHT

"W HITNEY HAS DEFINITELY BEEN to a dance class before," Ginger remarked. "Given how graceful and flexible she is, my guess is she's been dancing since before she could walk."

"Seriously?" Paige asked. "You can tell that by just observing her playing 'Ring Around the Rosie?'"

Ginger, Paige, and Kate looked on as seven little girls were skipping and twirling around the wood floor of the Tiny Dancers ballet studio. There was nothing tiny about the space, however. Twenty-foot ceilings gave the room a cavernous feel. It didn't help that two of the room's walls were mirrored, making the studio appear never ending. Soft sunlight streamed in through the high transom windows leaving shadows on polished floors. A row of folding chairs lined the back wall.

Yet, Whitney didn't seem intimidated at all. She moved about the room with graceful confidence, her chin held high. Her supple body seemed to be primed for the lesson.

"Because Ginger was born into the ballet world," Kate said. "Like recognizes like."

Paige turned to the petite blonde. "Really? How did you go from being a ballerina to a soap opera actress?" The soap opera

'Saints and Sinners' was her guilty pleasure after school. Ginger starred on the show for several months a while back.

"Now there's a story," a male voice announced from the doorway.

The little girls all squealed when the golden retriever, Midas, raced into their circle.

"Uncle Gavin!" Emily skipped across the room and into the man's arms.

The studio was housed inside an old torpedo factory along the banks of the Cape Fear River. The offices of McAlister Construction and Engineering took up the other side of the building's first floor. From what Paige could tell, it doubled as the district office for Congressman Miles McAlister.

Upstairs, Gavin McAlister converted the top floor to a swanky loft apartment similar to ones he designed for his New York City clients. Second to the Tide Me Over Inn, this building seemed to be ground-zero for the McAlister clan. Although Paige was beginning to think she couldn't swing a cat in this town without hitting one of the McAlisters. Or someone related to them.

Gavin had his mother's hazel eyes and the same laugh lines fanning out from them. His hair was brown and wavy like his sister Kate's. He also had a wicked dimple when he smiled. That smile was presently directed at his niece.

"You do realize I just saw you yesterday?" he teased.

"I know," Emily said. "But I just wanted you to know you are my favorite uncle."

Kate sighed.

Gavin loosened his grip on his niece. He let her nearly drop to the floor, before catching her and setting her on her feet. "Spit it out. What do you want from me?"

Emily pressed her little fists to her hips. "Henry says I won't like anchovies on my pizza. I told him you always get them on your pizza and he dared me that I couldn't eat a whole slice tonight. Please, can I have a slice of your pizza at dinner?"

Ginger made a gagging sound at the mention of anchovies. "Oh please, no," she whispered before hightailing it to the bathroom. Gavin raced after her.

"What did I tell you about trying to one-up boys?" Kate admonished her daughter. "You don't have to do everything Henry says."

"Yeah. What your mom said. And who says you have to eat the anchovies?" Paige added. "How do we even know Henry is telling the truth about liking them himself? Or if he's even had one."

Emily narrowed her eyes. "Yeah. How do I know he's not trying to trick me?"

"It's hard to tell with boys," Paige said. "They're sneaky that way. They'll do and say anything to get what they want. If I was you, I'd stay away from them for as long as I could."

The girl threw up her hands. "Ugh. Boys," she said before stomping back toward the other girls.

Kate cocked her head to the side. "Sworn off men, have we?"

"Something like that." *Especially ones who publicly humiliate you and rob you of your career.*

"Huh. That should make it easy to resist a particular golfer with a smoking hot bod and a sexy accent, then."

Paige slammed her eyes closed. "When you've been burned as badly as I have, it's easy to resist any man. Even the sex-on-a-stick ones."

Kate was quiet beside her. Paige slowly lifted her eyelids to find the other woman wearing a fierce expression.

"Whoever he was, he doesn't deserve someone as special as you, Paige."

The unexpected kindness of her words made the breath catch at the back of Paige's throat rendering any kind of response impossible.

"And I hope his penis shrivels up and falls off," Kate continued.

Paige choked out a laugh that had Kate pounding her on the back.

"I know we barely know each other," Kate said. "But your dad has been so good to our mom when she needed it the most. Just know that I'd be happy to return the favor if you ever want to talk."

The back of Paige's eyes burned. "Thanks," she croaked. It would be nice to unburden herself to Kate. Paige suspected she'd be a sturdy shoulder to cry on. But in doing so, the other woman would know just how gullible Paige had been. How downright stupid. It was a relief to be free of that embarrassment these past couple of days. To be treated with respect once again. She didn't dare risk it.

Ginger returned, looking a little less green. Gavin hovered beside her. When he spotted Paige, he stuck out his hand. "You must be Paige. I've got the keys to your car. I parked it out front. The sheriff installed the booster seat to the manufacturer's specifications." He wrapped an arm around Ginger. "No need to go to the fire station to check to see if our baby seat is secured properly now that we've got our own law enforcement in the family."

Gavin whistled for Midas. "Come on, you. Let's go for a run. If I tire you out, maybe you won't go snooping in all the baby's things."

The girls chorused their goodbyes to the dog.

"I'm looking forward to chatting more, Paige. I'll see you tonight for pizza," he said.

"Pizza?" Paige asked.

"Once a week, we all try to get together for a family dinner," Kate explained. "As much as mom loves to entertain, we'd rather she take a night off to enjoy herself. So, we meet at the pizza place most weeks during the winter. I have to warn you, though, it's not Chicago deep-dish, but it's pretty darn good, anyway."

Paige sank her teeth into her bottom lip.

"Face it, girl." Kate slipped her arm through Paige's. "You're a part of this family whether you want to be or not."

And there it was again. The mention of the word "family." As hard as Paige tried to resist the McAlisters, the more they kept sucking her in. They were part of her father's life, though. Paige wasn't. She didn't want to like them.

Except it might be too late for that.

"Come on," Kate pleaded. "We only have a week to get to know you. Did I mention they serve the best wines?"

"Sure, torture the pregnant chick why don't ya?" Ginger groaned.

Paige smiled at both women. Any day now, they'd find out the whole sordid story about her bad choices and they would feel differently about her. Why not enjoy an evening out with them before then?

"You had me at wine."

<hr>

TANNER LEANED against the bar of the Slice and Sip nursing a beer. The pizzeria was a favorite from the first week he had relocated from Europe back to the States. The restaurant's space was long and narrow with brick ovens lining the back wall, the bar running lengthwise along the side, and a cluster of long tables that forced diners to eat family style. During the summer months, Tony put out bistro tables under the red and white awning outside for added seating.

Tanner wasn't sure what the hell he was doing crashing a McAlister family dinner except that the sheriff invited him. That and Whitney was here. And she was only here because Paige was here.

Paige.

Whitney's nanny. Who was right now accepting a glass of wine from Deputy Dog, Hayden Lovell. The deputy said something to Paige making her laugh. Tanner's teeth clicked in the back of his mouth. Women were constantly fawning over the deputy with his square jaw and rippling muscles. Tanner suspected the guy's prosthetic leg was some sort of chick magnet, as well. Women were natural care givers. And who better to care for than a good-looking guy with a Purple Heart for losing his leg to an IED in Afghanistan.

Congratulations, Tanner. You win the 'asshole of the night' prize for being jealous of a disabled veteran. Shame on you.

Try as he might, he couldn't keep his eyes from trailing Paige as she wandered over to where Whitney sat beside Emily. Both little girls were coloring on their kid's menus. Paige seemed more comfortable around the children. She was a kindergarten teacher, so it made sense.

Except the McAlisters were a warm welcoming bunch who never met a stranger. Yet Paige wandered around the restaurant as though she was trying to keep her father and his new family at arm's length. Her guarded demeanor piqued his interest. What kept her from announcing herself at the wedding New Year's Eve? Why did she still have her guard up?

"You're moving too well for it to be your back that had you backing out of this week's tournament."

Tanner turned to see Dr. Jane Sheffield standing beside him.

Christ, how long had she been there?

The physical therapist worked at one of the more prestigious sports rehab centers in the South. Luckily for Tanner, it was located right here in Chances Inlet. She'd been treating him for on-and-off-again bouts of back spasms over the past two years. She was also a de facto member of the McAlister clan, being Kate's best friend and now Ryan McAlister's girlfriend.

"The back's fine, Janey."

She studied him while she sipped her wine. "The only other explanation for you cutting out early is what's being reported on social media. They're saying it's the yips."

Tanner tilted his head back. "Jesus, even the word sounds ridiculous."

Jane pressed her back against the bar. "But the condition isn't. It's very real. And it's curable."

"Sure it is. Just alleviate all the stress from my life."

"Now *that* is ridiculous. Not to mention impossible." Jane swirled her wine around in her glass. "But we do have some visualization techniques we can try, if you're interested."

"I'm hoping it won't get to that point." Tanner took a pull from his beer while his gaze involuntarily continued to follow Paige. She made her way back to where Deputy Dog waited for his to-go order. Tanner willed the brick ovens to cook the pies a little faster so Lovell would scram.

"She's cute," Jane said.

"Yeah," he replied, absently.

Jane chuckled beside him. "You do realize I was talking about Whitney?"

Tanner whipped his head back to where Whitney, Emily, and Jane's son, Henry, were crowded around the restaurant's two arcade games. He slowly shifted his gaze to the woman beside him.

The physical therapist had the nerve to grin. "Sex is another great stress reliever. Although, you might not want to mess with the sheriff's daughter. Just sayin'."

A skirmish between Emily and Henry saved Tanner from responding.

"Ugh." Jane drained her wine glass. "Here we go again with

those two. Excuse me while I go attempt détente over anchovies."

Sheriff Hollister took Jane's spot at the bar.

"I heard you were throwing my name around in Las Vegas," he said with a teasing glint in his eyes. "I'm glad you interviewed both the private investigators I mentioned. Let me know if you choose either of them. My friends in law enforcement are happy to share whatever they've got."

Tanner liked both investigators the sheriff recommended. He'd already decided to go with the female P.I. He wasn't sure why, but he figured it would be easier for a woman to locate another woman.

"Appreciate it," he replied. He braced himself for the keep-your-hands-off-my-daughter speech, but it didn't come. Instead, the man surprised the hell out of him with what he said next.

"This is quid pro quo, Tanner. I'm happy to help you out, but I need your help in return." The sheriff's gaze landed on his daughter who was helping Whitney navigate the claw machine. "She's been hurt. Badly by the looks of it. If she tells you anything at all, I want to know."

"You're not planning on putting a horse's head in the guy's bed, are you?" Tanner joked.

The sheriff's steely gaze sent a shiver up Tanner's spine.

"I don't like it when someone hurts one of my own."

Shots fired.

Tanner acknowledged the sheriff's words for what they were: a warning. The man had a unique way of delivering it, that's for sure.

"Understood."

"Nice talk," the sheriff said before moving toward Deputy Lovell. Hopefully to give the man the same damn speech.

"It just takes some good, old-fashioned hand-to-eye coordination," Sonny was saying to Whitney. "We'll get you a prize."

Tanner wandered over to where his caddy stood with Paige and Whitney. "The claw giving you trouble, Whit?"

"Ah ha." Sonny handed Tanner some game tokens. "Here's the guy with the best hand-to-eye coordination in the room."

Any other day, Tanner wouldn't have disputed that claim. Tonight, however, was a different matter. He gave his caddy the stink eye. Sonny hiked up a bushy eyebrow in challenge. Whitney gazed up at Tanner with a hopeful look on her face. Sighing, Tanner sank down into the game's seat.

"Won't your bunny get jealous if you get another stuffed toy?" he asked.

Whitney shook her head and pointed at Paige.

"You want me to win one for Paige?"

The girl nodded.

Tanner looked up at Paige. Was it his imagination or were her eyes a little misty?

"What'll it be, Miss Hollister?"

She gnawed on her bottom lip as she sized up the options. "I've always loved panda bears."

He studied the stuffed animals in the case before swearing beneath his breath. "You do realize the panda is at the bottom of the pile?" He shouldn't have bothered asking. Of course, she did.

Paige aimed a serene smile at him. "Then it's a good thing you are the best."

Whitney clapped her hands together and bounced up and down on her toes. It was the first time he'd seen her so animated. So delighted. She wanted to make Paige happy. Truth be told, Tanner wanted to make them both happy.

"I'm gonna need a co-pilot, Whit." He tapped his thigh. "Climb aboard and I'll teach you how it's done."

Her hesitation was barely noticeable. She crawled up into his lap. Tanner took her little hands in his and wrapped her fingers around the joystick controlling the claw. Whitney's tiny body shook with excitement. Tanner smiled at the back of the child's head. The joy she felt in giving a gift to a woman she barely knew made him proud to be her uncle. Her mother raised her right. He just hoped he found her soon so he could tell her that.

"Okay, Whit. Time to go bear hunting."

CHAPTER NINE

PAIGE SETTLED against the pillows she'd stacked behind her in bed. She couldn't help the ridiculous grin that formed whenever she peeked over at the stuffed panda sitting in the place of honor on the nightstand. Watching Tanner and Whitney bond over an arcade game did all kinds of things to Paige's insides. Father and daughter were both beginning to relax in each other's company.

Whitney was sweet, well-mannered and smart. There wasn't anything for Tanner not to love about her. Even if he didn't find Whitney's mom by Sunday, the pair would be okay together.

Paige, on the other hand, might not be. She was growing ridiculously attached to the little girl. And maybe just a little attached to the girl's father. Which would be an epic mistake, she reminded herself. Tanner Gillette was not the type of guy women should fall for. Sure, he was doing right by his illegitimate daughter, but she was likely the only female a guy like him could commit to. It was a good thing Paige was no longer interested in having a man in her life, then.

Still, she'd felt the weight of his stare all through dinner at the pizza place. And there was definitely heat in his gaze when he confronted them outside the pool earlier today. Her nerve endings began to dance just recalling the way he gave her body the once over.

"A fling with Tanner Gillette is out of the question, too," she reminded those body parts that tended to have a mind of their own.

She snatched up one of the beach-reads she'd brought from home. The well-worn paperback was one of her "comfort" books. Part of a Victorian era romance series featuring a group of wallflowers trying to find love. The familiar words kept swimming on the page, however, before Paige finally slammed it closed.

"There's more to life than finding a man, sister," Paige mumbled. Sighing heavily, she smacked her head against the pillows. "Yet another thing Jon ruined for me. Romance novels."

She was about to reach for the TV remote when a sound from Whitney's room caught her attention. Flipping back the covers, she listened intently for it to come again.

"It was probably something outside," she told herself.

Except it wasn't. Whitney was crying out in her sleep. And it sounded like she was calling for her mother. Paige raced through the bathroom and into the adjoining bedroom. Whitney was tossing and turning as sobs wracked her small body. As sweet as it was to finally hear the girl's voice, Paige was devastated by her cries.

"Shh." Paige crawled into the bed, gathering Whitney up beside her. "Shh," she repeated. "Everything is going to be okay. You're safe. I'm here."

Whitney's gulping sobs eventually subsided. She curled against Paige, remarkably, still fast asleep. Paige rubbed the girl's back, softly whispering reassurances. She wiped Whitney's tear-stained cheeks with the sheet. Within minutes, the child was sleeping peacefully.

A noise in the doorway alerted Paige they were not alone. She looked up to see a shadow of a man illuminated by the hallway lights. After resettling Gladys in Whitney's arms, Paige replaced her own body with a pillow. She waited a moment to make sure Whitney was settled before slipping out into the hallway where Tanner waited.

A shirtless Tanner.

"She okay?" he whispered.

Paige picked a spot beyond his muscled shoulder where she could fix her gaze to avoid openly drooling at the man.

"Mmhmm," she answered with a nod.

He took a step closer. "Are *you* okay?"

She wanted to be blasé and mature, but she wasn't that skilled at playing it cool. The man's chest was a freaking work of art. And who knew golfers had six-pack abs? Weren't they supposed to be pot-bellied or some damn thing? It was the trail of dark hair disappearing beneath his flannel joggers that sent her over the edge.

"Could you—" She wiggled her fingers in the direction of his chest. "Could you cover that up, please?"

He looked at her as though she'd just asked him to shoot a hole-in-one on the moon. Then he chuckled sadistically before turning on his heel and padding down the long hallway leading to his bedroom.

"Water." Paige fanned herself. "I need some water."

Hurrying to the kitchen, she filled a glass using the dispenser on the refrigerator door. She was gulping down its contents when Tanner reappeared. Thankfully, he was wearing a T-shirt with what looked like German writing on it. A pair of sheepskin moccasins covered his feet.

"I've got something stronger in my study," he said when he walked past, presumably on his way there.

A smarter woman would have returned to her bed and listened for signs Whitney might be having another nightmare.

"She usually settles down after the first episode," he called back to her, seemingly reading her mind.

"You mean this isn't the first time?" Paige followed him into the study.

A small lamp illuminated his desk. Tanner clicked a switch and the museum lights inside the built-ins bathed the room in a soft glow. The landscape lights from outside cast cozy shadows on the walls.

"Nearly every night since she's been here," he said as he poured liquor from a bottle into two glasses.

"Really? You knew she could talk, and you didn't tell me?"

He rolled his eyes at her when he handed her a glass. "You're too smart not to have figured out Whitney's mutism was caused by trauma."

Paige tried not to preen at the knowledge Tanner thought she was smart. But damn, his praise was good for her flagging ego. She tucked her legs beneath her as she settled into the corner of the suede sofa.

"It was just a shock hearing her voice, I guess. It's pretty. Like the rest of her." She took a sip from the glass.

"Mmm." Tanner leaned his hips against the desk.

A comfortable silence settled in the room as they both sipped their drinks.

And then Tanner ruined it.

"What's the story with you and your dad?"

Paige bristled. "There *is* no story between me and my dad."

"I gathered as much. Why?"

Paige studied the shadow of a tree branch dancing on the wall. That area of her life wasn't a secret. There was no harm in answering his question. She drew in a breath.

"He's never been a part of my life." She shrugged. "Even

when my parents were married, he was deployed most of the time."

"How long were they married?"

"Long enough to know they weren't suited." She took another fortifying sip. "My mom grew up on a farm in the middle of Iowa. The same place I grew up, actually. She couldn't wait to get out of there. When my aunt told her about a job opening at a military base in Cedar Rapids, she jumped at the chance."

"Cedar Rapids being a busy metropolis and all that," he teased.

"It's all relative when you grow up in a small town. Anyway, within the first year, she'd met my dad and gotten pregnant. By all accounts there was a shotgun wedding and voilà, here I am. My dad deployed shortly after I was born. My grandmother passed away suddenly, so my mom returned to the farm to help my grandfather. I don't think my parents lived together for more than a couple of months."

"I can't picture Lamar not playing a role in your life, though."

Paige pulled at a string of a blanket draped over the back of the sofa. "He always made an effort, but it's hard when you only see someone two weeks every year. Most of the time he was deployed in areas that weren't safe for dependents. And when he wasn't, well, my mom is kind of nutty about my safety."

He arched an eyebrow. "You don't say?"

She snorted. "You can't be too careful with kids."

"So I'm learning."

"I always felt like I was holding my mom back." The words slipped past her lips before she could stop them. She'd never admitted that to anyone else before.

"How?" Tanner asked quietly, almost as if he knew they were wandering into uncharted territory.

Paige rested her head back against the cushion. "All she ever wanted was to be free of our little farm. To have some big, glamorous life. And then I came along and messed everything up. Don't get me wrong, she's never come out and said the words. But I've always sensed them." She stared at the amber liquid in her glass as if it held all the answers. "I'm sure my father regrets my existence, too."

"Your dad is an honorable man. He doesn't seem like the type of guy who has regrets. And the way his face lights up when he sees you doesn't look like regret to anyone looking on."

Something squeezed in the vicinity of Paige's chest. The booze, the mood-lighting and Tanner's kind words were all casting a spell on her. She needed to get back to her room before she did something *she* would regret.

Paige downed the rest of her whiskey in one gulp, letting it punish the back of her throat before getting to her feet. "It's a little late for psychoanalysis this deep. I'm going to get some sleep. Whitney is an early riser."

She was walking over to the bar behind the desk to return the glass when she stepped on something sharp.

"Ow!"

Tanner swore violently. "Don't take another step. There's glass on the floor over there."

Paige froze while he turned on all the lights in the room. He wheeled his desk chair up next to the back of her legs, its wheels crunching over the shards of glass on the tile floor as it moved.

"Sit," he ordered.

She didn't argue, immediately lifting her foot to check for blood.

"Give me that." Tanner wrapped his fingers around her ankle and suddenly it wasn't the pain of the cut making her breathing unsteady.

He was crouched down before her tenderly examining her

heel with the pads of his fingers. How was it that this man's touch on her foot could be so sensual? A breathy moan escaped her lips before she could stop it.

His chin shot up. "Does that hurt?"

She shook her head. "No. It's fine really. I'll just go rinse it out and put a bandage on it."

His grip tightened. He bent the arm of the desk lamp so it was shining on her foot.

"I don't see any glass stuck in there." He grabbed a tissue from a nearby box. "Press this firmly to the cut until I get back."

"I can take care of it my—"

"Do. Not. Move."

"Oh, for heaven's sake. I'm not going to sue you over a cut," she said to his back.

Tanner murmured something unintelligible before leaving the room.

Paige slumped back in the chair. With all the lights on, she could study the photos behind his desk. She picked up a frame containing a picture of two adorable twin boys giggling together on a baby blanket. After setting it back in its place, she spied a photo of what had to be Tanner's parents. He had his father's build and his mother's eyes.

There was an empty spot on the credenza where it looked like a frame should have been. Was that why there was glass on the floor? Had a photo fallen and broke? She leaned under the desk to check. Sure enough, a silver frame lay face down. Paige picked it up to find another photo of twin boys. In this one, the boys were older—maybe tweens? And they looked exactly how she pictured Tanner looking as a boy.

He hustled back into the room, stopping abruptly when he saw what she had in her hands. Then he was slamming the box of bandages onto the desk. He dropped to his knees again and grabbed for her foot. Something about his demeanor told her not to go there, but Paige was never one for ignoring her curiosity.

A trait that often left a mark.

"You're a twin?" It was more statement of fact than question because she held the answer in her hands.

He dabbed antiseptic on the cut a bit too aggressively. "Was."

"Was?"

His eyes locked with hers. "Yes, Paige. I *was* a twin."

The heavy silence that descended wasn't as comfortable as it was moments ago. Why, oh why, didn't she listen when her brain told her to shut up?

"I'm sorry," she whispered.

Tanner ripped open a bandage. "Why do people always say that? It's not like you had anything to do with his death."

"I'm sorry that his death hurt you."

Her words seemed to catch him off guard. His fingers stilled for a long heartbeat before resuming their first-aid. His touch was much gentler as he smoothed the bandage tenderly over her foot. "It's been a year and a half. It hurts a little less every day."

"The twins in the other picture? They look a little like you."

Tanner rocked back on his heels. "They're Tristan's. They were born six weeks after his death."

The enormity of what he revealed made her stomach clench. Paige's brothers were only her stepbrothers, but she could only imagine the pain of losing one of them. Losing a twin would probably feel like losing a body part. She covered Tanner's hand where it rested next to her on the arm of the desk chair.

"That had to be awful for you."

His eyes softened. He nodded.

"How? How did you lose him?"

Tanner sighed heavily. "Helicopter crash. We were both in

San Francisco—me for a tournament and him for work. We were supposed to meet for dinner, but I got delayed on the Pebble Beach course due to weather." He dragged a hand through his hair. "Fog rolled in grounding flights throughout the region. Tristan was anxious to get home to his wife, Melinda, who was seven months pregnant with the boys. She had just been put on bed rest. I had a chopper lined up to take me to San Diego after our dinner, but I wasn't making the pilot fly until the fog lifted." He turned his head to stare out into the shadows on the screen porch. "Somehow, Tristan found out I had a copter reserved. He pretended to be me and demanded they make the flight. From San Diego, he could get a flight back to Phoenix easily. The pilot was flying blind, but he couldn't clear the Berkeley Hills. None of them made it."

He got to his feet and pushed her in the chair toward the door.

"That's . . . tragic. For everyone." Paige felt bad for leading him down such an emotional path. "I always wondered if twins really did switch identities," she said, trying to lighten the mood. "Did you two do that often?"

"I never did," he said. "And Tristan stopped doing it when we left boarding school."

Paige snorted. "Obviously not."

Tanner stopped the chair so suddenly that he almost dumped her on the floor.

"I hope you're better at driving a golf cart," she teased.

But Tanner wasn't laughing. Instead, he unleashed a tirade of violent obscenities before storming back toward his bedroom.

What had she done? What had she said?

"Tanner?"

But he didn't answer. The only sound she heard was the slamming of his door.

Paige remained where she was, perched in his chair in the

doorway of his study, for several minutes. She should apologize. As usual, she'd gone too far. It didn't matter that she had no idea what she'd said to set him off. Grief came with many triggers.

Forcing herself out of the chair, she hurried back to her room to slip on a pair of flip-flops. She only made it as far as the kitchen, however, before she realized Tanner Gillette's happiness wasn't her concern. She was Whitney's nanny.

For only six more days.

After that, she'd be back in Chicago with her own ridiculous problems to deal with. Comforting a sexy jock wasn't in her "single forever" rehabilitation plan. She was sure Tanner had an entire contact list of women he could turn to for that.

Trudging to the laundry room, she retrieved the vacuum. She'd just clean up the mess in Tanner's study before someone else got hurt. Not that vacuuming was in her job description, but it was a whole lot safer than being around Tanner Gillette.

CHAPTER TEN

TANNER DROVE the ball off the tee with a resounding whack.

"He was pretending to be me," he told Sonny through gritted teeth.

"That was a hell of a shot. So whoever you're mad at, maybe stay that way until the end of the season."

"I'm likely to be mad at my brother for the rest of my life," Tanner said as he handed Sonny his driver. "The jerk was pretending to be me when he was with Whitney's mother. That's the only possible explanation for my name being on the birth certificate. All this time, this Donella person thought *I* was Whitney's father."

Sonny whistled through his teeth. "Holy shit."

Tanner ripped off his golf glove and shoved it into his back pocket. "At least their relationship took place before he and Melinda were married."

Tristan was a lot of things, but he was devoted to his wife. He always claimed he'd fallen in love with Melinda the moment they met. They were married six months later.

The burning question that kept Tanner up the previous night, though, was whether Tristan knew. Did he know he had a daughter? Tanner liked to think his brother didn't know. That Tristan would have been a part of Whitney's life had he been aware she existed.

But then, there were lots of things about his twin brother he thought he knew but didn't.

"Tristan pretended to be you all the time," Sonny remarked.

Like that.

"What?" Tanner's voice carried down the fairway. A golfer from the group in front of them aborted his putt mid-swing. Tanner waved his hand in apology and lowered his voice. "How do you know that?"

"I wasn't drunk all the time," Sonny grumbled. "There was always chatter in the clubhouse."

Tanner's pulse throbbed painfully at the back of his skull. He pulled an ibuprofen from the pocket of his shorts and swallowed it dry in an effort to ward off a migraine.

Sonny searched for Tanner's ball in the rough at the side of the fairway. "If it makes a difference, I don't think he was doing it for money or fame. Or out of spite. I got the sense he was just pretending to be you for shits and giggles." He pulled back the grass around the ball with his foot. "It was more like he was bored with his life and wanted to walk in someone else's shoes for a while. And since you and he were practically the same person, it was easy for him to be you. If I had to guess, it was simply an escape for him."

What the hell would his brother need to escape from? Tristan was the favorite son, working with their dad running a multi-billion-dollar company that would become his legacy. He had a beautiful wife. Multiple homes and a family who loved him.

Unlike Tanner, Tristan didn't have to justify every one of his life choices to their father. Marcus Gillette thought his "spare" lacked ambition, not to mention the drive to make a success of himself. Ironic, since the man was married to a professional athlete. A woman whose career thrived because of the support of her husband—even though that same husband considered it his wife's hobby. Her golf game was a unique way for him to meet prospective wealthy clients.

While Tristan had been the over-achiever in school, Tanner did what he had to do to pass. He spent the rest of his time learning the science and the math behind the game of golf. His father's perception of the sport was men spending time in the sunshine striking a ball all day and carousing in the clubhouse all night. It was beneath the Gillette name to play a game. He didn't understand that it took the same mental toughness to excel in sports as it did to close a deal in the boardroom.

Part of that was Tanner's fault. He hadn't done a damn thing to refute his reputation as the spoiled little rich kid riding on mama's coattails when he first turned pro. On the contrary, he'd lived up to every bit of that reputation and then some. It wasn't until he was politely asked to leave the tour at the ripe old age of twenty-five that he realized he needed to do an abrupt about-face.

He headed over to tour in Europe, where he could lick his wounds and grow-up. There, he met a misfit caddy who not only taught him how to sharpen his God-given talent, but who stood beside him as they both went through the painful, but necessary self-improvement process. The transformation wasn't easy. Yet, both men survived.

Now, Tanner was on the precipice of proving his father wrong. To show him that he was as smart as Tristan. As mentally tough. That he wasn't wasting his life having a good time. That he was a winner, too.

Once he got rid of the yips, that is.

He forced himself to relax his grip on the club. To regulate his breathing so all that negative energy left his body. The club whooshed by his ear as he drove the ball directly at the pin. A surprised cheer went up from the golfers leaving the green.

Tanner looked back at Sonny. "Did I hole it?"

The caddy shot him a thumbs up. "That's one way to avoid having to putt. Keep it up."

Three hours later, Tanner returned home still in a foul mood. The eagle was the high point of his round. His hands continued to shake each time he gripped his putter, while the rest of his game was firing on all cylinders. None of it made sense.

Sonny suggested that Tanner might want to consider Jane's offer of alternative treatments. Except Tanner knew the only solution to this mess was finding Donella, reuniting her with Whitney. Then, he could get the answers he needed to move on.

The sound of giggling coming from the direction of the great room had him headed that way. He wasn't prepared for the scene that greeted him. The once pristine room had been transformed into a giant blanket fort. Several of the throws usually adorning the sofas were pinned together using what looked like chip-clips to create a warren of sorts. Beneath one of the blankets, he could just make out string-lights twinkling.

Paige's muffled voice was followed by another round of belly laughs that could only belong to Whitney. The sound of it stole Tanner's breath.

His anger bubbled up from the surface again just thinking about how desperate Donella must be to have left her daughter with him. Which made him even more pissed at Tristan. Why hadn't he provided for them?

Closing his eyes, he ran through another cycle of breathing exercises to calm his pulse and his temper. None of this was Whitney's fault. The most important thing was keeping her healthy and happy. Fortunately, he had Paige for that. Almeda was good with the child, but he couldn't picture his pleasingly plump housekeeper crawling into a blanket fort on her bad knees with Whitney.

Tanner was relieved to find Paige still here this afternoon. After the way he'd stormed off last night without giving her any explanation, he was glad to see she hadn't packed up Whitney and decamped to the Tide Me Over Inn. Not that he would have blamed her. He needed to apologize. Except he had no idea what he'd say to her. It was better off to let her keep believing he was Whitney's father. He wouldn't throw Tristan under the bus until he had all the facts.

And maybe not even then.

Besides, it was safer having Paige think the worst of him. There was already too strong of a pull between them. As much as he wanted to act on it, he didn't need another complication in his life. A brief fling with his temporary nanny would be something old Tanner might have done, but not new Tanner.

It took everything he had to remind the rest of his body of that.

If he was going to finally prove to his father that he was worthy, he needed to remain laser-focused. The immediate goal was to resolve Whitney's situation, so that he could get rid of the yips. Only then could he get back on tour and finish what he started this season.

Paige murmured something else causing Whitney to giggle again. Tanner bent down and peeked beneath one of the blankets. "Is there a password for this fort or can anyone come in?"

He heard Paige's sharp intake of breath from deep within the warren. "Can't you read? There's a big sign that explicitly says no boys allowed."

Sure enough, there was a piece of paper bearing those exact words taped to one of the blankets. Tanner chuckled to himself. Leave it to Paige. He should walk away and let her keep doing her job. From the sound of it, Whitney was having fun.

The joy he heard in the little girl's laugh was like a drug, though. He didn't get to see Tristan's sons often. But right now, he had a little piece of his brother that was all his. And she was slowly coming out of her shell. More than anything, he wanted Whitney to feel loved rather than abandoned.

He lifted up one of the blankets. Paige shot him a death glare. Whitney jerked up before backpedaling beneath the blanket until she was hidden within the depths of the fort. It was the look of dread on her face that had him dropping the blanket.

She still didn't want anything to do with him.

Maybe it's for the best.

Once he found Whitney's mother, Tanner's role in her life would likely be limited to that of her financial guardian. Just as he had no business seeking out a fling with Paige, he had no business trying to forge a relationship with Whitney.

The thought twisted painfully in his chest. He turned on his heel and headed for the study. Paige whispered something to the child before crawling out from beneath the blanket.

"Wait," she called.

He looked back over his shoulder at her. She swiped at the hair falling into her face as she got to her feet. He let his eyes drink her in. The khaki shorts she wore offered a pleasant view of her toned legs, pale pink from her time at the pool the day before. The white V-neck she had on stretched nicely over her ample curves.

"I'm sorry," she said quietly. "This is your house. I should be more thoughtful. I got a little carried away. It won't happen again. From now on, I'll confine our mess to our two rooms."

Christ, did she think he was that much of an asshole?

He waved her words away. "You're welcome to use this room whenever you want. I just wanted to speak with you, that's all."

Her eyes widened. "About?"

"Uh, about last night." He dragged his fingers through his hair. "I was rude to storm off like that. It's just—"

She closed the gap between, placing her palm on his arm. "I'm the one who should apologize. I asked questions about memories that are painful for you. I'm sorry."

He was a bit dumbfounded at the fierce pleasure her touch brought and all he could do was nod.

Paige lowered her voice. "And don't take Whitney's reactions to heart. She's skittish with everyone right now." Her fingers stroked his forearm gently. "You're doing great with her, though. It's just going to take some time."

Up close, he could see that the rims of her irises were a deeper blue than the rest of her eyes. Again, today she smelled like sunshine and—cinnamon. Several pieces of pink glitter were stuck to her cheek. He lifted his hand to wipe them away, but thought better of it. Touching her would not be wise.

"You—" He pointed at her cheek. "You have some glitter stuck to your face."

He regretted his words immediately when she lifted her hand from his arm. She swiped at her cheek, missing the glitter altogether.

"No," he said. "Higher."

She brushed her fingers along her cheekbone in frustration, nowhere near the glitter.

"Not there."

"Where?" She was starting to sound a little pissy.

He reached for her hand to guide her fingers to the correct spot. They both froze at his touch. One of them groaned. He was pretty sure it was him. Her blue eyes were suddenly dark as flames.

Ah, fuck it.

Tanner was past caring at this point. He leaned in, inhaling the light scent of soap on her skin, and pressed his lips to the glitter. Her surprised exhale of breath brushed against his neck, practically urging him on. He gently pinned her body against the wall with his own. Her pulse raced in the wrist he still held.

He traced the curve of her cheek with his lips until he found the corner of her mouth. Her free hand landed on his biceps nearly scalding him with its heat.

Dammit, he wanted to feel that heat all over his body. Skin on skin. Releasing her hand, he delved his fingers beneath her T-shirt to lightly skim along her waist, then further up to her full breasts. Something primal roared within him when he came in contact with her pebbled nipples.

She feels it, too.

Paige moaned softly when he toyed with the hard nub. The sound of it had him straining against his zipper painfully. He couldn't remember ever wanting a woman as much as he wanted Paige Hollister. His head was practically ringing with desire.

"Tanner," she breathed.

"Mmm." He traced the line of her lips with the tip of his tongue.

"Tanner," she said more forcefully, her fingernails digging into his arm. "There's someone at the door."

THE DOORBELL RANG AGAIN. Tanner froze with his lips hovering near her neck. It took everything she had to slip from his arms. He banged his forehead against the wall.

Paige was feeling the same frustration. Another minute and she likely would have embarrassed herself by climbing the man like a tree. And that would have been monumentally stupid.

Good thing Paige was done being stupid with men.

"Um, it's probably Kate," she explained, swiping aimlessly at the glitter.

With a single nod, Tanner shoved himself away from the wall and disappeared into the study.

Paige took a deep breath and counted to ten before she felt calm enough to answer the door.

"Oh my gosh, this is so fun," Kate exclaimed a few minutes later. Emily and Henry were already tunneling through the blanket fort chasing one another. "But I may have to re-examine our friendship because now Emily is going to be scheming about a way to recreate this in our family room."

"Okay, children." Paige turned on her teacher voice. "We need to clean this up before we can go."

A chorus of groans came from beneath the blankets before all three kids crawled out. Emily unclipped the blankets while Henry attempted to fold them up. Whitney stacked the books they'd been reading carefully. Paige turned off the fairy lights and rolled them into a ball.

"Well done, team," Kate praised them. "Now, who's ready for some golf?"

Emily and Henry cheered while Whitney clapped her hands.

"What's this about golf?" Tanner asked from the doorway to his study.

"We are going to play putt-putt." Henry pretended to swing a golf club, knocking over a lamp in the process.

Tanner caught the lamp before it hit the floor. "First of all, we need to work on your swing. Secondly, putt-putt isn't golf. It's a carnival game."

All three kids went so still it was as if he'd announced there was no Santa Claus.

Paige glared at Tanner. How dare he ruin the kids' enthusiasm. "Of course it's golf. You play with a golf ball and a putter," she reassured the children. "Don't listen to him."

Tanner scoffed. "Golf isn't about avoiding windmills or pirate ships with a brightly colored ball. It's about reading the greens, adjusting the torque of your swing to fit the wind speed. It's calculating distance and topography."

She crossed her arms in front of her. "So, what you're saying is putt-putt is too easy for a talented professional like you?"

His eyes darted to her chest for a brief moment, making her panties damp just thinking about his fingers there moments before. He met her eyes, looking as if he knew exactly what she was imagining.

"That's exactly what I'm saying," he replied, silkily.

Paige lifted a hand so she could study her fingernails. "Too bad we can't put your ridiculous theory to the test."

What was she doing? She'd just barely escaped the dragon's lair with her panties intact and now she was baiting him to join them? She should be running in the opposite direction.

"Um, Paige," Kate whispered from beside her.

It was Tanner's turn to throw his arms across his chest. "What's that supposed to mean?"

She shrugged. "Just that if putt-putt is so easy, you'll have no problem taking us on." She gestured to the three children who were watching the exchange with rapt attention. "But I do have to warn you, I hold the course record at both the Lake Geneva and Mackinac Island putt-putt courses. That said, I'm sure I'll be no match for the likes of you."

His fingers twitched briefly before shoving them in his pockets. She wasn't sure, but she thought his forehead looked a little damp. Still, his gaze never wavered. Almost as if he'd gone to the Lamar Hollister school of interrogation.

"Game on," he surprised her by saying.

Henry did a little whoop. Emily handed Whitney her shoes. Kate shook her head in warning.

"I hope you know what you're doing," she murmured as she led them toward her car.

CHAPTER ELEVEN

PAIGE MAY BE DONE BEING stupid with men, but she wasn't done *being* stupid, period. Case in point? Baiting Tanner into joining them for miniature golf. After their near-kiss in the hallway, she would have been smart to avoid the man altogether. Instead, they'd somehow formed a fivesome with Tanner instructing Emily, Henry, and Whitney while Paige trailed behind them. Kate, the traitor, was enjoying a glass of wine at the "clubhouse" aka the restaurant adjacent to the ocean-front course.

"They're reasonably well behaved," she told Paige. "No need for man-to-man coverage. I've got the rest of the week to enjoy maternity leave and I intend to make the most of it."

"Nice putt, Whit," Tanner said.

Whitney smiled up at him.

See, this wasn't about being stupid, she told herself. *It's about giving him more time with Whitney.*

The pain on Tanner's face when Whitney shied away from him earlier nearly tore Paige in two. Clearly, he cared for the little girl. He was determined to put her first in his life, even skipping a golf tournament this week. It was important to

Paige that Whitney become comfortable with Tanner. Who knew how long it would be until her mother returned.

"Make a vee with your thumb and forefinger, Emily," he instructed.

"A vee goes the other way," Emily mumbled, but she did as she was told and sank the putt.

"Woohoo!" She and Henry danced around the fake log meant to obstruct the hole.

Paige grabbed Henry's club before he accidentally beaned Whitney with it.

"Whoa," Tanner said sternly. "A player never raises his club above his shoulders unless he's driving the ball. That would be considered bad etiquette, not to mention bad sportsmanship."

Henry sobered immediately.

"You're up, kiddo." Tanner gave the boy's shoulder an encouraging squeeze. "Remember what I said about keeping your toes pointed forward and your hips still."

The boy chewed on his lower lip in concentration. After an agonizing minute, he finally tapped the ball with his club. It rolled straight into the cup.

"Atta boy!" Tanner fist-bumped Henry. "You've got it now."

The three kids hurried on to the next hole. Paige waited for Tanner to follow. He didn't. Instead, he tucked his hands in his pockets and arched an eyebrow at her.

Like that was going to hurry her up. She shooed him away with her hand. "Stick with the kids. I'll be right there."

He leaned a hip against the wood railing. "There's a backlog up ahead. They won't need me for a few minutes."

"Well, I can't concentrate on my shot with you hovering." Truth be told, she couldn't concentrate on much of anything just knowing the man was on planet Earth.

"A true professional learns to tune out the world around them." He smirked at her. "Besides, someone has got to keep you honest. How do I know you're not padding your scorecard back here?"

She pointed her club at him. "Did you just accuse me of cheating?"

He grabbed the head of the club and lightly tugged it from her hands. "I doubt you've cheated a single moment of your life," he said, softly.

If you only knew.

Her shoulders slumped. She was living on borrowed time here in Chances Inlet. The news that Paige did cheat—whether she knew it or not—was only a phone call away for her father. In fact, she was surprised she'd made it this long without her dad discovering the reason she'd run from Chicago.

"Hey." Tanner was suddenly beside her. "Where did you just go?"

To hell and back.

"I just don't like being accused of something I'm not," she said stiffly.

He studied her intently for several heartbeats as if he was trying to unearth all of her secrets. She wouldn't let him have them, though. She wasn't letting any man have them ever again.

"You almost done, lady?" a teenage boy called from the front of the hole.

"One sec." She took her club back from Tanner and lined up for her putt.

"Not that way," Tanner said. "You'll drive it too far left."

He stepped up behind her, sliding his arms around her torso. Her breath hitched when he wrapped his fingers around hers.

"Shift your feet ten degrees toward the hole," he instructed, his warm breath fanning her now tingling neck.

She did as he asked and suddenly her hips were pressed against his. They both froze. She could feel his heart pounding against her back. Of course, her body would line up perfectly against his. Fate was a bitch that way. His fingertips slid along her wrists, his touch a barely-there caress. She stifled a groan.

"Tilt your wrist this way," he whispered, his lips skimming the surface of her jaw. "We're going to take this real slow." He dragged out the last two words.

And just like that, her panties were wet. Again.

Why, of why, was it always the bad boys she was attracted to? Tanner Gillette was charming, sexy, athletic, famous—and so not for her. The man apparently had so many notches on his bedpost, he couldn't remember the women he slept with. He was a prime example of why Paige had sworn off men.

For. Ever, she silently screamed at her traitorous body.

She jerked her hands free, smacking the ball so hard it soared over to the next hole. Untangling his arms from around her waist, she stomped off to where Whitney, Emily and Henry were waiting to tee off.

"Maybe you should get Botox," Sonny suggested.

Tanner turned from the mirror in the club's locker room where he was getting dressed after his shower. He'd just finished another disastrous eighteen holes when his hands could barely grip the putter. "What the hell are you talking about?"

The caddy looked up from his phone. "It says right here that Botox can help relieve the tension in your hand muscles." He glanced around the locker room which was empty apart for the two of them. Sonny lowered his voice anyway. "It's a recommended treatment for, you know, the yips."

Tanner turned back to the mirror to finish shaving. "Jane has some sort of visualization mumbo-jumbo she wants me to try first." He doubted it would work, but the physical therapist had done wonders for his back and his migraines. He could at least give it a try. Besides, he'd been holding a migraine at bay since last night. If the visualization was a bust, at the very least she could help ward off his headache.

Too bad he couldn't get any relief for the other part of his anatomy that ached.

Paige Hollister and her sultry body were torturing him. Remembering the feel of her torso pressed up against his made other parts of his body twitch uncontrollably.

He'd never taken advantage of a woman before. Yet, twice yesterday he'd tried to do exactly that with Paige. The woman was so far from his type, it was laughable. She was too outspoken. Too stubborn. Too bold. The fact that she had lush lips that invaded his dreams nightly and a body built for all kinds of sin shouldn't have him this fired up. There were plenty of golf groupies on the tour with the same characteristics.

It's simply her close proximity that had his libido racing, that's all. That and her devotion to Whitney. He didn't know another woman who would unselfishly shower a little girl she'd just met with such adoration and care. Sure, he'd practically blackmailed her into it, but she'd never taken it out on Whitney. He wasn't sure some of the other women he'd been involved with would be that unselfish. Hell, he wasn't sure any of the other women he'd been involved with possessed the backbone Paige did.

Not to mention that no other woman dared to challenge him the way Paige did. The way she'd hustled him into playing putt-putt with them yesterday was amusing. And downright cute. He knew she'd done it to get him to spend more time with Whitney. Part of him, though, wished she'd done it to spend more time with him.

Then there was the mystery surrounding her sudden appearance in Chances Inlet. Sheriff Hollister's instincts were likely correct, and that intrigued Tanner. His daughter was hiding something. He got the sense someone had hurt her. And that didn't sit well with him. Not at all.

"What time are you seeing Janey for physio?" Sonny asked, interrupting Tanner's thoughts.

"Not until this afternoon."

The rest of the day stretched out before him. As much as he wanted to return home and hang out in a blanket fort with Whitney and her alluring nanny, he didn't dare. Not when all he wanted to do was strip Paige naked, lay her out on one of those damn blankets and have his wicked way with her.

Jesus. He needed to get a grip.

"I think I'll kill some time reading by the pool," he said. The day was unusually warm and sunny for the end of March. If Tanner had to slog through a prospectus from Gillette Industries, he'd just as soon relax while doing so.

Since Tristan's death, he'd made it a point to become more involved in the family business. Not that he ever planned to take his brother's seat at the table. He just wanted to be up to date in case his nephews ever needed guidance.

And now, there was Whitney to consider.

A few minutes later, Tanner headed from the clubhouse to the pool area, stopping along the way to order a club sandwich and fries. Unfortunately, he forgot to factor in that it was spring break. The pool deck was crowded with kids of all ages, presumably visiting grandparents. A group of coeds in brightly colored bikinis eyed him over their sunglasses. He felt the stares of some of the mums, too. It was no secret that he lived in the community. It was also no secret that women parked themselves by the pool in hopes of getting some face-time with him.

Swearing beneath his breath, he scanned the pool deck to find the waiter who'd just taken his order so he could redirect it back to the bar area. A familiar purple bathing suit caught his attention, however. The woman wearing it was lounging in a chaise, her skin glistening beneath the mid-day sun, her nose buried in a paperback book. Even better, the chaise next to her was empty.

Tanner was already halfway to her when his brain kicked in, reminding him that this was unwise. He was supposed to be avoiding Paige. He couldn't be trusted around her. But he couldn't retreat now. Not when he could feel the eyes of every woman at the pool tracking him.

Make that every woman except Paige Hollister. She was too engrossed in her book to notice.

"Where's Whitney?" he practically barked when he tossed down his towel onto the chaise next to her.

Paige jolted at the sound of his voice before pulling her sunglasses down and eyeballing him. "She and Emily went joyriding in your golf cart."

"Not funny." Her snark had him relaxing. He needn't be worried about Whitney. Paige took her role very seriously. Likely, she was off with Kate and Emily somewhere. He stepped out of his slides before lowering himself down to the chair.

"What are you doing?" she asked.

"That should be obvious." He let out a satisfying sigh, crossed his bare feet at the ankles and closed his eyes.

Paige huffed beside him. "Fine. Kate is taking the kids for lunch after visiting the sea turtle rescue hospital." She shoved her book into a canvas bag. "I'll just finish my book on the porch at home."

Let her go, his brain screamed. The rest of him wasn't listening, however. Without opening his eyes, his fingers reached between them, finding her wrist, gently encircling it.

"Stay," he heard himself saying. Opening his eyes, he turned toward her. "Please," he whispered, not liking the pleading tone of his voice one bit.

Paige's eyes leapt from his hand on her wrist, up to his face, only to drop back down to where her skin was scorching his. Judging by the wary expression on her face, she thought it was a bad idea, also. Still, she sank her teeth into her bottom lip before nodding.

Relief raced through him. He brushed the pad of his thumb against the pulse throbbing at her wrist. Time seemed to stand still.

"I've got your lunch, Mr. Gillette," a voice from above announced.

Paige yanked her hand away. The server was holding a folding table, but he seemed unsure where to put it until Paige gestured wildly to place it between them. She grabbed a fry from the plate and popped it into her mouth before he'd even set it down.

"Mmm. Do you have any ketchup?"

The server produced several packets from his pocket. "Anything else, sir?"

Paige picked up half the club sandwich and unabashedly took a bite.

Tanner sighed. "Apparently I'm going to need another one of those."

"And an Arnold Palmer," Paige mumbled around the food in her mouth.

Tanner held up two fingers. The befuddled server nodded and disappeared.

"Enjoying yourself?"

"Mmm," she replied. "You might have mentioned lunch was part of the deal. I wouldn't have been in such a rush to leave."

He shook his head to avoid laughing at her cheekiness. "Thank you."

She paused mid-bite. "Does that mean lunch is on me?"

This time he did laugh. "No. Thank you for staying."

Her eyes darted away. Despite her outward bravado, she

was skittish around him today. Not that he blamed her. He turned into a fool whenever he was near her.

The server brought their drinks. Paige swallowed half of hers in one gulp.

"I doubt you would have been lonely too long," she said.

"Precisely what I'm trying to avoid."

She lowered her sunglasses again. "Are you telling me I'm the . . . what? Some sort of *decoy*?"

"It's been my experience that women won't approach me if I've got a beautiful woman by my side."

Paige choked on a fry. Tanner leaned over to slap her on the back. She glared at him when he let his hand linger too long.

"Puh-lease. I'm no competition for those women." She waved a hand in the direction of the co-eds shimmying to an R&B song blasting from one of their mobile phones.

Was she kidding?

How could this woman not know she was a stunner? He let his eyes wander down her torso, lush and full in all the right places. Her legs were sturdy and toned right down to the purple nail polish on her toes. But it was the challenge in those pale blue eyes of hers that always seemed to draw him in. That and her saucy, sinful mouth.

"Why do women always do that?"

"Do what?"

"Put themselves down. Find fault with their appearance no matter how gorgeous they are."

Her mouth opened and closed twice. "Well—"

"No," he argued. "Don't you dare shame your body, Paige Hollister. It's magnificent just the way it is. *You* are beautiful just the way you are. Any man who doesn't see that is a damn fool."

Tanner was breathing unevenly. He was surprised at the ferocity of his words. But he needed her to know she was perfectly desirable. Hell, after yesterday, she had to know he was attracted to her. Had some jerk made her feel less than enough? If he ever discovered the guy's name, he'd wrap his driver around the dude's neck. Paige was worthy of any man. And Tanner was determined that she know it.

She tore her gaze away. The waiter with the impeccable timing arrived with Tanner's sandwich. Paige swiped another fry, then picked up her book and focused intently on whatever was between its covers. After inhaling his sandwich, Tanner tugged his golf shirt over his head, balled it up, and put it behind his head as a pillow.

"You should probably warn a girl before you do that. I need to get my stick ready to beat the women off," she teased.

"Have you considered a career in comedy?"

She mumbled something under her breath that he couldn't quite catch before she gestured to the five-hundred-page prospectus he was thumbing through.

"You could always beat them off with that," she suggested with a grin.

"Or just read it aloud. It's unbelievably boring."

"So why read it?"

He sighed. "Golf will be my legacy. But this—" He held up the report. "This will be my nephews' legacy. And Whitney's legacy."

When she didn't respond, he looked over at her. It was hard to tell what she was thinking with her sunglasses on, but the smile she wore looked amazed.

"What?"

Her lips twitched. "It's nice to know Whitney will be taken care of."

Her words shocked the hell out of him. "There was never any question of that."

They both went back to their reading.

"Do you think her mother will come back?" Paige asked after a few minutes.

Tanner leaned his head back and closed his eyes. "God, I hope so."

"At the very least so you can remember which of the many women you slept with is Whitney's mom."

It was a good thing he was sitting down because her accusation would have taken him out at the knees. *Jesus.* Did she really think that poorly of him? The idea that she did shouldn't surprise him. She was only judging him on the facts as she knew them. He should set her straight. He wanted to. And not just to see her have to backpedal from her ugly opinion of him. He wanted someone to share this immense burden with. Which was funny because he'd never needed to share anything with anyone before.

Except for Tristan.

But Tristan was gone. And he'd left a mess behind. A mess Tanner could better control if he kept the facts to himself. No matter how tempting it would be to lean on Paige Hollister's very attractive shoulders.

"Because no child should be abandoned by its mother," he replied tersely. He opened the prospectus and ignored her for the rest of the afternoon.

CHAPTER TWELVE

PAIGE WANDERED around her bedroom later that night, too out
of sorts to sleep. How could she when Tanner Gillette was
making her crazy with all of his "you're gorgeous" sweet talk
and a touch that left her skin zinging for hours afterwards. A
lesser woman would already be burning up the sheets
with him.

But Paige knew better.

At least she thought so.

She tried to ignore the tiny bit of her that melted every time
she watched him interact with Whitney. His declaration today
that the little girl would share in the birthright of Gillette
Industries rocked Paige. How does a man who denied his
daughter's existence do such an about-face? Her gut was telling
her Tanner must not have known about Whitney before she
was left in his care. The tender way he dealt with the little girl
certainly backed up her instincts.

He still seemed determined to locate Whitney's mom, but
she got the impression he did so in order to make things right
with the woman, whatever that looked like. Mostly, to make

Whitney happy, though. Paige couldn't help but admire him for that.

Except her ugly trust issues continued to haunt her. Her broken heart kept reminding her that she had no idea if Tanner was being genuine or not. Or if his actions were a ruse simply to get Paige to fall under his spell. Given her track record with men, the part of her that should detect that sort of thing was apparently never installed.

Like the pathetic bundle of hormones she was, she continued to be drawn to Tanner despite knowing the many ways he could hurt her. Something had to be done to quash her attraction to him before it was too late. So, she had lashed out at him with hurtful, inane accusations.

Hours later, she wasn't exactly proud of what she'd said. Her harsh comment about not knowing which woman he'd slept with was Whitney's mother still burned in her ears. Paige held a throw pillow up to her face wishing she could take back her words.

At the same time, she needed to keep the fact that Tanner could be another sleazy dude like Jon front and center in her mind. That knowledge was the best self-protection she had. No matter how much she wanted him to be different. The risk to her heart wasn't worth it.

Paige couldn't recall a single word she'd read while sitting next to him at the pool. When the silence between them became unbearable, she quietly slipped away. If Tanner noticed, he didn't acknowledge her. Later on, Sonny dropped by the house to say that Tanner was having dinner with some investors and wouldn't be home until late.

Relief and guilt ate at her the rest of the evening. After a dinner of tomato soup and grilled cheese, she and Whitney curled up in the blankets on the sofa and watched Frozen. Whitney fell asleep before Anna got a chance to rescue Elsa from Hans. Apparently, a day spent exploring the sea turtle sanctuary and its adjacent light house had exhausted the poor kid.

The sound of the garage door opening stopped her pacing. Tanner was home. If she had any hope of getting any sleep tonight, she needed to clear the air. Apologize. It wasn't like her to be so bitchy. Especially when Tanner seemed to be making up for his past sins with Whitney.

She ventured out into the hallway, hoping to catch him in his study. He often hung out there when he was at home. But the house was dark. He'd obviously gone right to bed.

An ugly thought formed. Was he alone in his bed? Had he really gone out with investors?

"None of your business," she muttered, slipping back into her bedroom. She was *not* jealous. Grabbing her book, she crawled beneath the covers and tried not to think about Tanner Gillette making another woman's skin tingle.

It took half an hour for Paige to finally become engrossed in her book. She was sighing at the hero's grand gesture when a barking noise shattered the quiet night. It came from Whitney's bedroom. The sound grew more panicked as Paige raced into the little girl's room.

"Whitney?" Paige clicked on the bedside lamp. "What's wrong, honey?"

The child was tossing and turning in her bed, her breathing raspy. She coughed again, sounding more like a sea lion than a tiny girl. Paige pressed her palm to Whitney's forehead. She was warm, but thankfully not too hot.

"Sit up, honey."

Paige piled up the pillows to help Whitney remain upright. Her breathing immediately became less labored. A wave of relief washed over Paige. She remembered seeing some children's acetaminophen in the bathroom. Another coughing spasm wracked the child.

"Try to relax," she said to Whitney. "I'm going to get you something to drink."

Before she could stand up, however, the door burst open and Tanner rushed in. Whitney barked again, her entire body shaking violently.

"Turn on the shower," Tanner ordered. "Nice and hot. Close both doors to the bathroom so the steam fills up the room."

Paige didn't bother contemplating how Tanner knew what to do. She dashed to the bathroom and did as he instructed. Then, she grabbed the acetaminophen and dosed it. When she returned to the bedroom, Tanner was pacing with Whitney in his arms.

"Here," Paige said. "Let's get some of this in her."

Tanner nodded and took the cup. "Sweetheart, I need you to drink this all up," he gently murmured. "That's a good girl." He brushed a kiss over her forehead when she did as he asked.

"Should I call Alden?"

He shook his head. "Not yet."

"Are you sure?" Because Paige was getting a little terrified by the rattling in Whitney's lungs.

"My brother used to get like this," he said. "A steam bath usually does the trick. Come on Whit, let's go sit in the sauna."

Whitney coughed violently in response. Tanner carried her into the now steamy bathroom, stepping into the tub and sitting on its edge. Whitney clung to him like a monkey.

"Can you fetch us some water?"

"Of course." Paige hurried to the kitchen. The light was on in Tanner's study. She was ashamed by the relief she felt spying only one glass with scotch in it.

A blast of steam hit Paige in the face when she returned to the bathroom. Thankfully, Whitney seemed more settled. Her head was resting on Tanner's shoulder, her eyes closed. Tanner was humming an unfamiliar tune as he lightly stroked her back.

It was then that she noticed Tanner was wearing nothing but boxer briefs. Her eyes drank him in, from the dusting of dark hair shadowing his well-defined thighs to the sleek planes of his back. His hair was damp from the spray. His boxers likely were, too, since he was using his own body to shield Whitney from the water.

Paige was unprepared for her visceral reaction to the gorgeous man in her bathroom. She bit the inside of her cheek to hold in the lusty sigh that threatened from escaping.

"Are you going to stand there and gawk at my body all night? Or can I get some of that water?"

Fortunately, her guilty blush could be attributed to the steam. She unscrewed the cap to the bottle and handed it to him. He guzzled half its contents. Not that she could blame him. The mist in the room nearly had Paige wilting.

"She seems more stable now." He grabbed a towel and wrapped it around Whitney. "Can you get her some dry pjs to change into?"

Paige went into the other room and began rummaging through the drawers. Tanner followed, gently laying Whitney on the bed. He went back into the bathroom. She heard the water turn off. He returned a moment later with a towel wrapped around his waist.

"Try to get her to drink some of this." He placed the bottle of water on the nightstand.

And then he was gone.

Paige hurriedly dried Whitney and helped her into new pajamas. She moved to put the wet clothes into the hamper when Whitney made a noise. The little girl's face looked stricken.

"Oh, honey," Paige reassured her. "I'm not going anywhere." She pulled the covers up to Whitney's chin and tucked Gladys in beside her. "Just let me get my phone and I'll come back to sleep in here with you."

She was surprised to find Tanner back in Whitney's bedroom when she returned. He'd changed into long flannel sleep pants and a dark T-shirt. His hair was still damp and unruly, though.

And he was crawling into the bed beside Whitney.

"What do you think you're doing?" Paige demanded.

"She'll rest better if her head is elevated."

He positioned himself against the pillows Paige had stacked earlier. Whitney crawled onto his chest without hesitation, resting her cheek against his pecs. She gripped Gladys by the ear. The bunny hung to the side. Tanner's lips turned up at the corners as he wrapped his hands around her back.

Paige tried very hard to not be jealous of the little girl. She should be glad that father and daughter were creating a bond. The strange tightness in her chest stemmed from the adorable picture the two of them made, that's all.

"I can sleep with her like that," Paige protested. If for no other reason than to get Tanner to go away. Far away. "You don't have to disturb your rest when you're paying me to take care of her."

He smirked at her. "If you're worried about earning your keep, be my guest." He patted the bed. "Keep us company."

"Don't be silly. There isn't enough room for all of us." She had more than enough will power to resist him.

Didn't she?

He arched an eyebrow at her as if to say now who is being silly?

Sighing, she grabbed a blanket from the end of the bed. No way was she getting under the covers with him.

"You'll need help if she needs a steam bath again," she said, trying to justify a decision she knew for a fact was a poor one.

Tanner wasn't buying it. He snickered softly as he slid over to make room for her. Within minutes, Whitney's breathing evened out. Paige peeked up at Tanner. His eyes were closed, but she could tell by the tense lines bracketing his mouth he wasn't asleep.

"Did your brother suffer from croup often?" she whispered.

His lashes fluttered, but he didn't raise his eyelids. "Mostly when we were Whitney's age. But sometimes when we were older, he'd have a bout when we traveled. His allergies were unpredictable."

She rolled on her side. "That must have been scary."

"Sometimes. When we were older, he didn't want anyone to know he still had them. He thought our parents wouldn't let us accompany them if they knew how often traveling upset his health. That's when I learned to take care of him."

"How old were you?"

"I don't know. Eight? Nine?"

Paige couldn't imagine any of the pampered second graders at Preston having the wherewithal to guide a sibling through something so traumatic.

"You must have loved him very much," she said.

He was quiet for so long, Paige thought he might have fallen asleep. Or he'd decided to ignore her inane comment. Of course he loved his brother. They were identical twins.

"Did you not have siblings growing up," he surprised her by asking.

"Two stepbrothers. The youngest is a decade older than me, so we were never that close. I know they care for me, but it's not the same kind of bond as they have for each other. They were a pretty tight unit before my mom married their dad."

"Lucky for you, then. Your McAlister step-siblings seem to be much better at welcoming newcomers into their fold."

Something that felt a lot like sorrow made her insides clench. *They wouldn't be so welcoming when they knew the truth.*

"I don't need any more step-siblings," she whispered with more force than was necessary.

"I don't think Patricia plans to have any more, so you're safe," he said with a chuckle.

She rolled her eyes. "That's not what I meant."

His eyelids cracked open as he tilted his head to the side. "Okay. Why don't you explain it to me."

She flipped over onto her back and stared at the stars the nightlight was casting on the ceiling. It was easier to avoid his scrutiny that way. He saw too much with those amber eyes of his. And no way was she going to tell him why she was keeping the McAlisters at arms-length.

"The McAlisters are my dad's family. After this week, I'll likely never see them again."

"You won't come to visit your father?" His tone was incredulous. "Ever?"

Paige swallowed roughly. As much as the thought of not seeing Kate or Ginger again stung, Paige knew it was for the best.

"What about Whitney? You're just going to leave at the end of the week and never look back?"

It was her turn to be incredulous. She snapped her gaze back to his. "You make it sound as if she is a permanent fixture in your life. Is she?"

She held her breath, suddenly desperate to know if what she hoped was true. The tense lines were back bracketing his mouth. Whitney coughed before squirming against his chest. He rubbed his palm against her back.

"Go to sleep," he whispered.

Given how harshly he uttered the command, Paige assumed it was directed at her. Once again, she'd wounded him with her prying. She couldn't help it, though. It was the best tool she had to keep from falling for the guy.

Except, she was beginning to think it might be too late to stop that from happening.

TANNER PEEKED IN ON WHITNEY. After a restless night, she was finally sleeping peacefully, cuddled up with her bunny beneath the covers of Paige's bed. He crept through the adjoining bathroom to check on the other woman he'd shared a bed with last night. Paige lay in the center of the mattress, arms and legs all akimbo, the blanket tangled around her luscious thighs. Her satiny pink shorts were bunched up high enough that he caught a glimpse of a silky-smooth butt cheek.

Damn. How was it that he wanted her so desperately? No matter how much he fought it, the force pulling them together grew more intense every day. She felt it, too. He could see it in the way her eyes darkened with passion whenever he got close. He could feel it in the way her pulse jumped whenever he touched her.

He had to hand it to her, though. She had more willpower than he did. The speed with which she'd slipped out of his embrace at miniature golf the other day was impressive. Not only that, it was obvious she didn't trust him.

Normally, Tanner didn't give a damn what people thought of him. He let his golf game do his talking. But it was beginning to eat at him that Paige thought the worst of him. He told himself to let it go. She wasn't going to be a part of his life after this week. What did it matter what she believed?

Yet, deep down it had begun to matter. It had begun to matter a hell of a lot. He wanted Paige to trust him as much as he wanted Whitney to trust him. He was desperate for both of them to believe in him. Not only that, but the need to protect them both burned fiercely in Tanner. Whitney would be easy to protect. Paige was an entirely different matter.

Tanner still had a nagging suspicion that she was deeply troubled by something. That someone had hurt her. The more he got to know her, the stronger his suspicions grew. She seemed committed to not letting anyone get too close. The forlorn tone in her voice when she declared the McAlisters were her father's family, not hers, nearly gutted him last night. And the painful ache that settled in his belly when she announced she had no intention of ever returning to Chances Inlet scared the shit out of him.

Which was kind of ridiculous since once Tanner located Donella and settled her and Whitney somewhere, he wouldn't be spending much time in Chances Inlet, either. He still had something to prove on the tour. And he wasn't going to let anything stand in his way until he'd succeeded.

How in the hell had his life gotten so fucked up?

Paige woke suddenly. She jerked up to a seated position, her eyes wide and several strands of hair glued to her jawline.

"What are you doing?" she croaked. "Standing there like some creeper watching me sleep?" She patted the mattress frantically. "And where is Whitney?"

He pressed a finger to his lips, motioning with his chin toward Paige's room. "She's still sleeping."

He nearly laughed at the befuddled expression on her face. She looked adorable all rumpled and sleepy. He'd had enough experience with women the morning after not to voice those thoughts, however.

"Why? What happened?"

"You've a bit of the Tasmanian devil in you when you sleep. I moved her to your bed when I got up. I didn't want to risk her ending up with a black eye as well as the croup."

Tanner was definitely understating the facts. Paige slept the way she seemed to live her life: full of gusto and passion. The thought of harnessing all her passion for a different activity among the sheets suddenly had his junk growing tight.

He raised his coffee cup toward his lips to cover up his groan, but Paige moved more swiftly. She managed to yank the mug from his fingers without spilling a drop. Oblivious to the coffee's temperature, she took a hearty swallow.

"Jesus, woman. What is it with you stealing my food?"

Her sigh was almost reverent. "Sorry. I'm not human until I've had coffee."

She reluctantly offered the mug back to him, but he waved her off. "Have at it. There's more where that came from."

He made no move to go to the kitchen and get another cup. He wanted to sit beside her on the bed and share the rest of his coffee with her. He wanted to share secrets with her. Hell, he wanted to kiss her until he'd broken down all her walls and she let him in.

"Paige—"

"I should check on Whitney." She scrambled off the bed and out of the room.

CHAPTER THIRTEEN

Waking up to find Tanner Gillette standing at the foot of the bed after she'd just enjoyed the most explicitly erotic dream about him had to be at the top of the list of Paige's most embarrassing moments. Which was saying something because that list was a long one. She gave herself a gold star for not stripping off her clothes and jumping him as soon as she opened her eyes.

She was finding it difficult to moderate her breathing recalling the way Sexy Dream Tanner had coaxed multiple orgasms from her using only his tongue. Watching him staring at her—as if he was undressing her and cataloging all her features—had her taut nerve endings vibrating so painfully, she had to clench her thighs together. She could barely meet his eyes. Making matters worse, Tanner looked downright yummy with his bedhead and a shadow of beard.

And wearing an expression like he knew *exactly* what she had been dreaming about.

"I should check on Whitney."

She vaulted off the bed and tried to edge past him. But he had the reflexes of a professional athlete. She didn't stand a chance. He wrapped an arm around her waist halting her progress.

"She's fine, Paige. I just checked on her. Come to the kitchen and finish your coffee." He chuckled softly. "Or my coffee."

The seductive rasp of his breath against her cheek nearly had her knees buckling. He maneuvered her back against his chest and her limbs suddenly went as limp as a ragdoll's.

"I might even know where Almeda hides the cinnamon rolls," he teased before lowering his lips to her neck.

Her laugh sounded perilously close to hysterical. "Don't make me like you."

She felt his smile against her skin. "Mmm. I think it might be too late for that."

Paige was afraid of that, too. She felt something give within her, though. Liking him didn't mean she had to hand over her heart for him to smash with his golf club. Maybe her *No Men Ever Again* plan could have a 2.0 version. One that permitted getting naked and sweaty with Tanner Gillette. After all, she was a modern woman. Sex didn't have to be about commitment.

"It's just lust," she murmured to herself as much as him.

"I can work with that." Tanner spun her around and cupped her face with his palms. "Tell me what you want, Paige. You have complete control over this."

She flattened her hands against his chest, surprised to discover he wasn't nearly as calm and collected as he appeared. His heart raced against her palm. His gaze was hungry. Feeling empowered, she slid her fingers slowly along the ridge of his pecs. He swore softly. Paige wiggled in closer to him.

"Damn it, Paige—"

Her lips found his before he could finish his thought. His surprise lasted less than a second before his hands left her face to thread through her hair, tilting her head to give him better access to her mouth. The kiss was raw and hot and like none she'd ever experienced.

And so much better in real life.

The sensuous slide of his tongue against hers was making her wild. She arced her hips into his, colliding with his very potent arousal. He nipped at her bottom lip in retaliation. She tugged at his T-shirt until her fingers burrowed under it to trace along his skin. He shivered beneath her touch.

Growling something unintelligible, he maneuvered them both back against the bed, tugging her down to straddle his hips when he sat. She threw her head back with a moan at the contact. Tanner immediately took advantage of their position, leaning forward to cover one of her nipples with his mouth. The scrape of the fabric and his teeth against the sensitive flesh had her squirming against him.

He wrenched his mouth away with an angry curse before capturing her lips in another searing kiss. His talented fingers found their way beneath her shorts and began kneading her glutes while his insistent tongue plundered her mouth. The tension ratcheted up to such a peak, her body began to tremble with overwhelming desire. She was ashamed of the small whimpering sounds of need coming from her as she ground against him.

"Let me help you, sweetheart," he murmured against her lips.

He slipped a finger between them and with three quick strokes she shattered.

When she came back to earth, she was slumped over Tanner's shoulder. Not that he seemed to mind. He was rubbing his palm in slow circles over her back.

"Still with me, sweetheart?"

Too embarrassed to face him, she answered by nodding against his shoulder. How had this happened? One minute his lips were on her neck and the next she'd jumped straight into ecstasy. Her cheeks burned. He must think she's the most sex-starved woman on the planet.

"I'm sorry," she whispered.

His hand stopped moving on her back. "For showing me you're even more beautiful in the throes of passion?"

She smacked him on the back. "Stop saying that."

His shoulders shook beneath her cheek. "Not until you realize it's true."

He shifted on the bed so that she had to face him. She childishly hid behind the curtain of her hair until Tanner brushed it off her face. The look of disappointment or disgust she expected to see on his face wasn't there. Instead, his eyes reverently searched her face.

"Don't hide from me, Paige," he whispered. "You're safe with me."

Oh, how she wanted to believe him. Unfortunately, her scars ran too deep. She was safe to slake her lust with the man. But everything else was off the table.

She moved to untangle herself from him, freezing when Tanner hissed.

"Oh, God. We didn't—You need to—Should we?"

Tanner grabbed her waist to hold her still. "Not with Whitney in the other room." He touched his nose to hers. "Because when we do—and the decision is always yours to make—it won't be quick. Or quiet."

Oh. My.

He leaned them both back so they were laying on the bed. Tanner rolled onto his side so he was facing her. He propped his head on his hand. With his other hand, he traced a finger along her jaw. "Your secrets are yours to keep." He pressed a soft, comforting kiss to her lips. "But when you don't want to keep them to yourself any longer, I'm here."

She felt like she had a golf ball stuck in her throat. Her gut was telling her he was sincere. It would be so easy to open her heart and spill everything out. But her gut had burned her before.

As thrilling and satisfying as the last several minutes were, she really wasn't the type to use a man. She'd given it a go, but it turned out she wanted it to mean more. And no matter what he told her, it never meant more to guys like Tanner.

"Hey." He pressed another kiss to her forehead. "Where did you go?"

She shook her head. "Nowhere. It's just that—"

"Okay," he interrupted her. "If you're not ready to spill, how about I do?"

"What?"

He dragged his lips along her jaw. "The only way to get you to trust me is to tell you something in strict confidence."

Something fluttered in her chest. Why was her trust so important to him?

"It's about my brother, Tristan."

Well, that piqued her interest.

He opened his mouth to say more when a woman's voice echoed throughout the quiet house.

"Tanner? Are you home?"

Tanner froze beside her, his face contorted with shock.

"Tell me that's not your housekeeper," Paige whispered harshly.

"It is *not* my housekeeper." Tanner slammed his eyes shut and swore violently. "It's my mother."

"ISN'T it so typically male to think sex is the perfect remedy for the yips," his mother mumbled into her coffee mug fifteen minutes after walking in on Tanner and Paige together on the bed.

Thank goodness they were both fully clothed.

Like Paige, she was already on her second cup of coffee. Tanner was trying to figure out how to make it to his study undetected so he could add some whiskey to his.

"Mum, what are you doing here?"

His mother arched an eyebrow at him as if it were obvious why she'd interrupted her cruise and traveled thousands of miles around the globe to pop in on her son at eight-fifteen in the damn morning.

"It's all over social media," she replied.

As if that cleared things up. "You posted on social media you were coming to Chances Inlet?"

She slapped her mug down with such force, it was a wonder the quartz countertop didn't chip.

"The. Yips." She practically spit out the word. "It's all over social media that the number one golfer in the world—" she pointed a well-manicured finger at him "—has the yips."

For fuck's sake. His mother couldn't be bothered to come home to play nursemaid when he broke his leg in fifth grade, but a case of the yips and she drops everything to give him some unsolicited advice face-to-face.

"It's nothing," he lied.

"I'm your mother. Don't lie to me."

Ah, the hell with it, he was a big boy. If he wanted whiskey in his coffee to help navigate this minefield, he was going to get it.

"I'm here to help you."

His mother's words stopped him in his tracks. "Help me how?"

She rolled her eyes. "You aren't the first golf professional to be afflicted with the condition."

He cocked his head to the side to study her more closely. "You had them?"

"I did, in fact. The year I won the Australian Open."

"Huh."

"The point is, you're having a good run. We can't let this situation get in the way." Her expression softened. "I've been so proud watching how far you've come with your game."

Tanner rocked back on his heels. She hadn't told him that since he was sixteen. "Thank you." He sighed. Unfortunately, he didn't think there was much his mother could help him with in this case. Not unless she knew where Whitney's mother was hiding. He sighed heavily. He really needed whiskey for the bombshell he was going to drop next. "Look, Mum, there is something I need to tell you."

"I think I've already guessed," she replied, motioning to a showered and dressed Paige who was wandering back into the kitchen for more coffee. "But shacking up with a golf hussy isn't going to cure the yips."

"Mum," Tanner groaned.

"The yips?" Paige looked between him and his mother. "What on earth are those?"

His mother made a tsking sound. "See? Does she even know anything about the game of golf? Besides the size of the purse at each tournament, that is?"

"That's enough, Mother," Tanner shouted.

"Hush," Paige shushed them. "You'll wake Whitney."

"Whitney?" His mother looked at him aghast. "Do you have another woman hiding back there? Don't tell me you're having another one of those throuple relationships."

Paige shot him a look of shock that quickly morphed into revulsion. Surely she didn't believe that?

"Jesus, Mum! I told you not to believe everything you read. That. Never. Happened." He aimed the words at Paige.

His mother swatted the counter with a dishtowel. "It's not like your father and I are prudes, but really, Tanner. Where there's smoke there's fire."

A movement at the end of the hallway caught his attention.

Both he and Paige headed toward the little girl at the same time.

"Whit. How you feeling, sweetheart," he asked as Paige gathered the girl up in her arms.

She kissed Whitney's forehead. "No fever," she mouthed.

At least something is going right this morning.

Whitney clutched her bunny while she eyed Tanner's mother warily.

"Who is this?" His mother's eyes narrowed as she tried to put together the pieces.

Time to rip off the band-aid.

"This is Whitney," Paige announced, beating him to the punch. "Whitney, *this* is your grandmother." She drew out the last word devilishly, probably to pay his mother back for all her snide remarks. Or maybe it was the throuple image. At this point, who the hell knew if either woman was sane.

The room started to spin around Tanner. He was too far away from the bar in his study, so he dropped down into one of the stools surrounding the kitchen island instead.

"I'm sorry? Did you just say I'm that child's grandmother?" His mother's voice cracked with emotion. Tanner felt it all the way to the soles of his feet.

"Mum." Tanner winced as he rubbed his throbbing temples. "I was just about to get to that."

"Just about to? Don't you think that might be something you mentioned before I arrived? Or perhaps before *she was born!*" His mother had her game face firmly in place, but the hurt in her voice betrayed her. "How could you keep this from your own mother?"

"Because I only found out about her last week." *In for a penny, in for a pound.*

His mother scoffed. "And that's supposed to make me feel better? Is she the only one? Never mind. I suppose I'll find out when they send me their Christmas list."

There was no point in defending himself. His reputation was already cast in stone with his parents.

A tense silence fell over the room until Whitney began to cough uncontrollably. Paige gave her some water, and the spasm subsided.

"That child is sick," his mother snapped.

"Yes, ma'am." Paige shifted Whitney in her arms. "I'm taking her to the pediatrician shortly."

"But you're not the child's mother?" The fact that Whitney was biracial apparently ruled out Paige in Blythe Gillette's mind.

"Her nanny."

His mother snatched up her keys off the counter. "I need to go back and speak with your father."

And just like that, his fresh hell had another chamber. "Dad's here?"

"Of course he is, Tanner. Melinda is coming with the boys this weekend. We thought it would be nice to all be together to support you." Her gaze dashed over to Whitney. Suddenly, his unflappable mother looked unbelievably vulnerable. "I didn't realize there would be so many of us."

Tanner blamed Tristan for the damage to their mother's once steely spine. His brother was their perfect son. And now he was gone. Leaving behind a huge hole in his parents' hearts and three precious children.

Dammit. He should rat his idiot brother out. Tell his mother who really fathered Whitney. Make the little girl someone else's responsibility. And salvage the shreds of his reputation with his parents.

He caught Whitney studying him, the beginnings of trust brimming in those gorgeous unique eyes. Speaking up wouldn't solve anything, he decided. It was better for everyone if he stuck to his plan. As soon as he found Donella, he'd buy her silence. Then everyone could go on living their lives none the wiser.

The door leading in from the garage opened. "Hey, whose golf cart is parked out front—whoa. Hello there, Blythe."

Sonny stopped at the threshold to the kitchen. To no one's surprise, Blythe Gillette wasn't a fan of her son's caddy. Whenever she was around, Sonny made it a point to make himself scarce. Given what the poor man was walking into, Tanner almost felt sorry for him.

"Good. You're here. I'll be carrying my son's bag for his practice round today," she announced. "It's time someone put an end to all this nonsense. We tee off at the Player's Club at noon, Tanner. Don't be late."

With that, she was gone. Tanner rested his forehead on the cool granite. Sonny whistled through his teeth.

"Holy shit—ake mushroom," the caddy said when he spied Whitney. "That was unexpected."

"Tell me about it," Tanner mumbled.

"Come on, Whitney. Let's get you dressed so Emily's daddy can check you out," Paige said.

Sonny gave Whitney a kiss on the head. "Is our girl sick today?"

"Hold up, Paige," Tanner said at the same time.

He signaled for Sonny to take Whitney.

"How about I slice you up a banana before you go," Sonny was saying. "I'll even let you put some cinnamon on it."

Tanner gestured for Paige to join him in his study, but, as usual, she ignored him. Instead, she stormed into her room and began throwing clothes into her suitcase.

"Where exactly are you going?" he demanded.

"Myrtle Beach. Where I'm supposed to be right now."

"You can't go yet. What about Whitney?"

"Your mother is here. I'm sure she'd love to take care of her."

The sound coming from Tanner's mouth fell somewhere between a maniacal and panic-stricken laugh. "You've got to be kidding? Did you not just meet the woman?"

He was shocked to see tears glistening in her eyes. "Yes." She tossed a pair of shorts into the bag. "And I was awful to her." She covered her eyes with her hands. "I can't believe I blurted out that she was Whitney's grandmother. But she made me so angry."

"Hey, hey." He took her hands in his and sat down on the bed, tugging Paige to stand between his legs. "She has that effect on most women." Sighing, he rested his head against her stomach. "My mum is intimidating. She had to be to compete in a sport that was dominated by males. And when the women had their own tour, well, it was just as catty."

He felt her exhale.

"Believe it or not, she respects a woman who speaks her mind. Give her time. She'll adore you."

She made a huffing sound. "It will do Whitney good to get to know her." She dragged her fingers back and forth through his hair. "And once she sees how good you are with Whitney, she'll be too proud of you to be angry any longer."

Her comment was a punch to his senses. Her steadfast belief in him was humbling. She may not fully trust him, but she was one of a handful of people who actually took him seriously. And that was good enough for him.

"My mother is a lot of things. A sensational golfer. A devoted wife. And a genuinely good person. But maternal, she's not. She wouldn't know the first thing to do with Whitney." He tilted his head back so he could see her face. "You're an amazing caregiver. Whitney has come so far these past few days. Please don't leave us now."

She drew in a deep breath while her fingers absently caressed his cheeks. "I don't know," she whispered. "Maybe it would be best if Whitney and I stayed at the inn."

He brushed his lips along her stomach. "I promise I'll behave."

"What if it's not you I'm worried about?"

Tanner was suddenly lightheaded as all the blood rushed from his brain to his crotch.

"Afraid you'll jump my bones?" he teased.

Paige maneuvered her legs so she was straddling his thighs. She touched her forehead to his. "Something like that."

He leaned in to tease the corner of her mouth with his lips. "I told you before, I'll give you whatever you want. All you have to do is ask."

She trembled slightly beneath his palms. His ego was relieved to know she wanted him as much as he did her. It was the trepidation lingering in her eyes that had his gut clenching, though.

A crash in the kitchen made them both jump.

"It's okay, Whitney," he heard Sonny say. "I'll clean it up."

Paige scrambled off Tanner's lap. He wrapped his fingers around her wrist before she could fully escape.

"Paige—"

Before he could get the words out, she bent down to lay a sweet, intoxicating kiss on him.

"I'll stay with Whitney," she whispered against his lips. "But I'm steering clear of your mother."

CHAPTER FOURTEEN

"Lookee, who's here. It's the star of our story time." Lou ran across the Queen of Hearts bakery and threw her arms around Paige's neck.

"Oh, um, hello." Paige just managed to hang on to Whitney's milk beneath the bookstore owner's enthusiastic embrace.

"Everything is all set for tomorrow afternoon." Lou pointed to a flyer in the bakery's window. "Bernice is helping us get the word out. We've already had lots of folks stop by the store to say they're coming." The woman bristled with excitement.

Truth be told, Paige was eager for the event as well. She agreed to do the reading in a fit of anger. Anger at all that Jon and a misogynistic bureaucracy had taken away from her. All week, she worried that her father would discover the real reason she was not in Chicago and she'd be too ashamed to get in front of a crowd of people. Except that had not happened.

Yet.

She hoped fervently that she'd have a reprieve until after tomorrow's reading. It would be a shame to disappoint Lou and Denise. Not to mention the kids. Everyone was looking forward to it. And Paige was enjoying living as her old self again.

"Have you thought about what you might read?" Lou asked.

Paige set the glass of milk down in front of Whitney. She was sitting quietly at a little bistro table, carefully dissecting an enormous chocolate chip muffin into little bite-sized pieces.

"Whitney has requested *Llama, Llama, Red Pajamas.*"

Lou clapped her hands together. The woman's enthusiasm rivaled most high school cheerleaders. "That will be perfect. I better skedaddle back to the store. Denise will be wondering about her apple fritter." She leaned in to whisper. "And I want to make sure we have several copies of the Llama, Llama series in stock. I just know everyone will want one after hearing your rendition." The woman bunched her shoulders and made a sound only dolphins would understand before skipping from the store.

"No pressure there."

Paige spun around to find Patricia sitting at the little table beside Whitney.

"How—where?"

Patricia laughed. "I was in the back meeting with Tatum, the owner. She's baking the cake for Ginger's shower." She beamed at Whitney. "I hope you like chocolate cake."

Whitney nodded profusely.

Paige slipped into her chair. "Is there a woman alive who doesn't love chocolate cake?"

"I'm glad to see she's feeling better." Patricia motioned to Whitney.

"Wow. I forgot what life is like living in a small town. Everyone knows everybody's business."

Patricia dipped her chin. "We're not all that bad. Alden mentioned it when he stopped by the inn this morning."

Great. In the span of two hours, Paige needlessly hurt two innocent women with her callous remarks. She took a sip off her lemonade trying to quash the ugly taste in her mouth at the role she played blindsiding Tanner's mother.

"Apologies," she said. "I didn't mean to offend you. It seems my filter is on the fritz today."

Patricia smiled graciously. "No offense taken. We're family, remember?"

"You don't have to keep pretending I'm family, either. You married my dad. But it's not like he and I are—"

The smile vanished from Patricia's face.

Paige slammed her eyes shut. "Oh, God. I did it again. I'm never this rude. I don't know what's gotten into me."

Except she did. She was feeling things for Tanner that she'd forbidden herself from ever feeling again. And that had her scared. Because she still wasn't willing to trust anyone with her heart. The prudent plan would be to pack up and leave town right away before it was too late. Before she was in too deep.

She looked over at Whitney, content with her muffin and wearing a milk mustache. Lou's flyer in the window caught her eye. The unbidden memory of Tanner's kiss made her belly quiver. Paige sighed wearily. She was already in too deep.

Patricia placed her hand on top of Paige's. "Something tells me you've been through a lot lately."

Crap. What did she know?

Her expression must have transmitted her thoughts because the other woman's face softened. She patted Paige's hand. "Mother's intuition."

It was only a matter of time, though, before Patricia did know. She would likely be as disappointed in Paige as her husband. And now, instead of hurting her dad with her reckless behavior, she would be hurting his kind wife, too.

"You don't have to like me," Paige whispered. "Just don't ever stop loving my dad."

"There's not a chance of that," Patricia reassured her with a sly smile. "And it would take something much more than a few regretful words to make me not like you."

Paige snorted. "Now I know you're just being nice because I don't even like me right now."

"Well, you know what always helps me when I have days like that?"

She couldn't imagine the capable woman sitting next to her ever having one of those days. Although Patricia did raise five children. And she'd lost her husband several years back, so anything was possible.

"The beach," Patricia surprised her by saying. "What do you say we grab a picnic and go plop our butts in the sand for a couple of hours? I have everything we'll need at the inn."

Whitney's eyes brightened. Alden did say fresh air would be good for her. And Paige had yet to put her toes in the sand this week. Patricia wasn't disappointed in her yet. Why not enjoy her company?

"I'd like that," Paige said.

"THIS IS like owning a slice of paradise," Paige said a few hours later.

She carried a drowsy Whitney up the wooden steps leading from the inn's private beach to the B & B. Patricia followed behind her with the picnic basket and a bucket of sand toys. The older woman was right. There was something about the surf and the sand that was rejuvenating. Paige's fears still lingered. They just didn't seem as overwhelming as they had earlier in the day.

"I fell in love with this place twenty-five years ago," Patricia explained when they'd reached the expanse of green grass leading back to the inn. "It's been a dream come true finally turning it into a B & B." A shadow passed over her face.

"Things didn't turn out exactly the way I envisioned them. But they worked out the way they were supposed to in the end. Life has a funny way of doing that. As long as you don't give up believing you're worth it."

Paige squinted over at her. "Being a mother of five certainly gave you some sage wisdom to pass along," she teased.

"Ha! All that gave me was wrinkles."

They were both giggling when they reached the porch.

"Well, isn't this a beautiful sight?" Her father slowly unfurled his rangy body from the porch swing. "My three favorite girls."

Patricia snickered. "Don't tell Emily that. She thinks she's everyone's favorite girl."

He hurried down the steps to relieve Patricia of the picnic basket and toys. She pressed a swift kiss to his lips.

"Well, I probably should get Whitney home so she can nap."

The corners of her father's lips twitched. "Looks like she beat you to it."

"There's a child's bed in the office off the kitchen. Emily used to nap there when she was Whitney's age. It's quiet there and I can keep an eye on her while I get ready for the tea," Patricia offered.

Her father was already reaching for Whitney, leaving Paige with no choice but to relinquish the child.

"Then I guess you should put me to work. How can I help you get ready for tea?"

One would have to be blind to miss the delighted look Patricia and her father exchanged. No doubt they considered her offer to help full assimilation into the McAlister family. For Paige, however, it was simply killing time. She didn't want to be at Tanner's house should his mother return. Or his father. Tanner had a lot of explaining to do. And one thing was for sure, they needed to clear the air without an audience.

"WHAT THE HELL do you mean you don't know where the child's mother is?" His father's voice boomed through the foyer of the Tide Me Over Inn. Marcus Gillette never did believe in subtlety. Tanner knew it was a bad idea to accompany his mother back to the B & B, but she was insistent. After the piss-poor round of golf he just shot, he was surprised she wanted to be seen with him.

"Good to see you, too, Dad." Tanner waved at the guests in the salon who weren't expecting a side-show with their after-noon tea. He lowered his voice. "Can we take this convo some-where a little more private?"

"I was just about to sit down to have something to eat," his father argued. "I've been on calls all day and I'm starving."

"I can bring you a plate if you want to sit in the library."

Tanner sagged with relief at the sight of Paige standing behind his father, carrying a tray of cookies.

Thankfully, his dad quickly acquiesced to her offer. "That would be lovely, dear, thank you. And if you can find some whiskey to go with those cookies, I've a big tip for you."

"This is the nanny, Marcus," his mother said. "I'm sorry. I didn't get your name earlier."

"It's Paige. Paige Hollister," she replied.

Tanner herded them into the library.

"Does that mean our granddaughter is here?" his father asked.

"She's napping back in the kitchen."

"What did the doctor say?" his mother demanded before Tanner could ask himself.

"Whitney is fine. Just a bout with the croup." Paige shot him a reassuring look.

"Nasty stuff that croup," his mother said. "It always used to scare me when Tristan came down with it."

"Her name is Whitney? I take it the mother named her?" Tanner's father arched an eyebrow at him.

"Since I wasn't involved in the child's life until last week, yes, Dad, her mother named her."

"Well, you were involved in the most important part of the girl's life. The conception."

His father's comment was meant to wound. Too bad this time Tanner wasn't guilty. His dad would be the one wounded if he found out the truth. Especially if his golden boy son knew about Whitney all along and never mentioned her.

Bile rose in the back of Tanner's throat. He wouldn't believe that of his twin. And he couldn't let his parents suffer any more anguish over Tristan. So, he took the punches for him.

"I'll just leave these here for you." Paige set the plate of cookies on the desk.

"Excuse me a minute," Tanner said to his parents, not caring whether they would or not. "Paige," he called softly after her.

Disappointment flashed in her eyes before she extinguished it. She still thought he was Whitney's father. He should have told her the truth this morning. He would have if his mother hadn't interrupted them.

Only he wasn't so sure now. Lying to his parents was making his head hurt. He'd feel worse guilt telling Tristan's secret to a stranger. Not that he wanted Paige to be a stranger. Hell, he wanted her with a fierceness that consumed him. He'd just have to find a way to circumvent the trust issues holding her back.

"She's really fine," Paige told him. "Alden said her lungs sound perfectly clear."

"Thank goodness."

One of the guests edged by them. Tanner took Paige's elbow and steered her into the music room.

"You've moved to the inn, then?" He had to work to hide the disappointment from his voice. He'd given his word that the decisions about where they went from here were all hers. He just hoped she would choose him.

"No," she replied softly.

Tanner bit back the ridiculous grin that threatened.

"I ran into Patricia after our appointment with Alden. She invited us on a picnic at the beach. The sun and the air wore Whitney out." She shrugged. "It was easier to let her nap here. I figured I'd help with the tea while I waited for her to wake up."

He gave his grin free-range. *She was letting them in.* That had to be a good sign, right?

"What are you smiling at?"

He edged her back against the gleaming grand piano that took up most of the room. "You." He planted his palms on either side of her. "Spending time with Patricia."

She swatted at his chest before letting her hands settle on his shoulders. "It's not like that."

"Oh, really?" he teased before grazing his lips along her cheek. "Admit it. You like her."

"Of course I like her," she whispered. "She's impossible not to like." Although her tone made it sound like that wasn't a good thing.

He lifted his eyes. The frustration in her eyes confused him. "Talk to me, Paige."

She kept quiet.

"Sweetheart," he sighed as he wrapped his arms around her waist and pulled her against him. He brushed a soft kiss to the tip of her nose before moving lower to toy with the corner of her mouth. She tasted like lemon and temptation. With a low groan, he swept his tongue along the seam of her mouth.

She made an angry keening sound before digging her nails into his shoulders and responding with a deep needy kiss. Not that he was complaining. Just like everything else she did, Paige kissed with an unbridled passion that had every nerve ending in his body aroused. He pressed his hips against hers to let her know just how aroused.

The sensuous slide of her tongue became a bit more frenzied. Tanner eased a hand between them to finger her breast. He sank his teeth into her bottom lip while he tortured her nipple. A lusty moan came from the back of her throat as she ground her hips against him. He was trying to figure out a way to lock the damn door without untangling their bodies when she suddenly yanked her mouth away.

"Stop," she breathed.

It took a moment for Tanner's muscles to catch up to her demand. He dragged his fingers through his hair as he took a step back. And then another.

"I'm sorry," she said. "I shouldn't keep starting something we can't finish."

"Well not here, anyway," he croaked.

"Not anywhere," she whispered.

He didn't like where this was going. Not one bit.

"This." She waved her hand between them. "I can't do this with you."

With a whispered "I'm sorry," she slipped past him and out the door.

Tanner sank down onto the piano bench.

I can't do this with you.

He told himself to be grateful for Paige's willpower. Of course she was right. A fling with the nanny would be the king of bad ideas. Not when he had bigger issues to deal with at the moment. Like his imploding golf game. And keeping his brother's secret. And finding Donella.

Too bad his body wasn't in agreement. It would be another minute before he could return to polite society.

"As soon as I find Whitney's mum, we can head back to the tour. They don't call it the 'Professional Groupies Association' for nothing. There will be plenty of women willing to take care of you."

Jesus. Now he was talking to his dick. He dropped his head into his hands. His body wasn't buying what he was selling. Tanner hadn't been with a woman since he crossed paths with Paige on New Year's Eve. No one else made his body hum like she did. And he was beginning to despair no one else would.

His father poked his head inside the room. "There you are. We are going to have to table this discussion about your illegitimate daughter until later tonight," he said. "I'm having dinner with the Myrtle Beach investors you met with last night. They still have questions. I'll need you to join me so I can show you how to properly close the deal. It's just as well your golf game is in the toilet. It's time for you to step up to fill your brother's shoes."

Tanner barked out a harsh laugh. If his father only knew.

"Text me the details," he said with a sigh. "I've got physio in fifteen minutes."

THE BOOKSTORE WAS PACKED the following afternoon. There must have been fifty people crowded into the shop. Half of them under the age of ten. Denise propped the door open allowing a slight breeze to flow through the packed space.

Emily patted the spot on the floor between her and Henry. "Whitney! We saved you a front-row seat."

Whitney didn't hesitate to yank her hand free and race to her new friends. Paige should have been happy with the little girl's newfound confidence. Especially since she would be out of Whitney's life—and Chances Inlet—in two days. Instead, she felt like that mom whose kid doesn't cry the first day of kindergarten.

"Will you look at this mob?" Kate jostled Max against her chest. "Denise and Lou have outdone themselves."

"I believe the credit goes to Bernice," Ginger added. "That woman is like a human bullhorn when it comes to getting the word out."

Two of Ginger's ballet students rushed over and wrapped themselves around her legs. Their excitement startled Max who dropped his pacifier. The baby immediately began to howl. Paige quickly grabbed it off the floor.

"Five second rule," Kate said reaching for the plug to calm her son.

"Oh my God!" Paige exclaimed. "You call yourself a doctor? Do you think germs count to five before they latch onto something?"

Max's cries grew louder, if that was even possible. The children covered their ears and began to mimic his wailing. Paige stormed toward the restroom, Kate and her little banshee on her heels. She rinsed the pacifier at the sink before handing it back to Kate. The silence was nearly deafening when she popped it back into her son's mouth.

Paige could feel Kate's eyes on her as she washed her hands. "What?"

"Are you nervous or something?"

"No!" She snapped a section of paper towel from the roll. "Maybe."

"Maybe no or maybe yes?"

Paige glared at Kate. "Aren't they both the same thing?"

Kate had the nerve to laugh. "I guess they are."

When Paige didn't join in with her laughter, Kate sobered up.

"What's really wrong?" she asked.

Everything.

Not that she was sharing that. "Just tired. I didn't get much sleep last night."

"Did Whitney have another bout of croup?"

"No, no," Paige responded quickly to alleviate Kate's concern.

"Ah." Kate donned a knowing smile. "Then that spark that's always there between you and Tanner is heating up?"

Oh my gosh! Was it that obvious? Were people talking?

"No! Definitely not that," Paige said a bit too harshly. "He's not my type."

Which was a lie. Thanks to a quirk of nature, guys like Tanner were very much her type. And *that* was the problem. Her brain was telling her *no,* but her body was screaming *yes, pretty please with sugar on top.* And her heart, well, that particular organ was useless because Paige was pretty sure she was already falling for the guy.

It was a good thing she was leaving in two days.

"I'm just feeling down about heading back to Chicago." Paige was surprised to have blurted that out.

Of course, she didn't mention the reason she didn't want to return home. Her ugly truth about being ostracized from a job she loved. Summer called last night to tell Paige what she'd known all along. The contract she'd signed with Preston had an iron-clad morals clause. The board wasn't backing down despite threats of legal action by Summer's brother.

The proverbial nail was finally in the coffin of her career.

Kate draped an arm over Paige's shoulders. "This week flew by. It's been great getting to know you." She gave Paige a squeeze. "But, hey, school will be out in a few months. You can come back and visit us this summer. I still haven't hired a nanny yet. You're welcome to the job."

Max nestled against his mother's chest with a sleepy sigh.

"Tell me you can't resist this adorable face?" Kate teased.

Paige drew her finger along the peach fuzz on Max's head. "He is pretty stinking cute. Loud. But cute."

"He gets that from the McAlisters," Kate said proudly. "Alden's family is very British and reserved."

It was a tempting offer. Especially since it was her *only* offer of employment. But she would be tempting fate being so near Tanner. From the snippets she overheard between his parents, it didn't sound like he'd be returning to the professional tour soon.

Last night, she googled the "yips" on her phone and discovered it was an actual neurological condition golfers suffered. Their wrists and hands shook uncontrollably when they went to putt the ball. The cause was unknown, but it was closely linked to stress.

And Tanner Gillette certainly had some serious stress in his life.

"Unless Tanner has already offered?" Kate said.

"Surely he will have located Whitney's mom by then?" For both Tanner and Whitney's sake, she hoped so.

Kate shrugged. "It's beginning to seem like she doesn't want to be located. The whole situation is a mess. I've got to hand it to Tanner, though. He's stepped up to the plate where Whitney is concerned. I'm not sure I'd be so tolerant of my brother's mistakes."

A trickle of unease ran down Paige's spine. "What do you mean by 'brother's mistakes?'"

Kate suddenly looked like she'd swallowed a bug. She hefted Max up and sniffed his bottom. "Oh wow, this little dude needs a change. I need to get the diaper bag." She made a face and squeezed by Paige before she could stop her.

Did she mean what Paige thought she meant?

Lou appeared in the hallway, blocking Paige from chasing after Kate and getting her to explain.

"It's showtime." Lou clapped her hands together. "Are you ready?"

Crap.

TANNER HUNG at the back of the store, propping his shoulder on a bookshelf. Pride swelled in his chest watching Paige entertain a swarm of kids and their parents with a story about a llama and his pjs. The kids all listened raptly as she pitched her voice this way and that for each character. Even his young nephews were captivated by the story.

"You were lucky to have found her," his mother whispered beside him.

"Whitney?"

His mother harrumphed. "As I understand it, Whitney found *you*. I meant Paige. She seems very responsible. I hope you're paying her with more than sex."

Tanner swore beneath his breath. "Really, Mum?"

"She seems too smart to let someone take advantage of her like that, though," his mother continued. "I like her."

I like her, too. "Paige is being paid with money, Mother. Not sex."

"Oh."

He tore his eyes away from Paige to look at his mum. "What does 'oh' mean?"

"I've known you all your life, Tanner. I've never seen you look at a woman like you look at Paige."

Don't ask. Don't ask.

"And how is that?"

"Like a man who's found someone he can't live without."

Damn.

Applause broke out in the room when Paige closed the book. With a pat to his shoulder, his mother snaked through the throng to where Melinda and the twins were waiting. The crowd spilled out onto the square where Tatum Fisk waited with a table filled with cookies from her bakery. Lou was frantically checking out customers while Paige made book recommendations to parents.

Tanner wandered outside only to come face-to-face with a beaming Sheriff Hollister.

"I always figured she was an amazing teacher," the sheriff said to his wife. "It's nice to get to see her in action."

Patricia slipped an arm through her husband's. "It's apparent she loves what she does."

"Whitney has been lucky to have her this week." Tanner ignored the guilt he felt for blackmailing Paige into it. She'd been paid handsomely. And she'd at least made baby steps toward getting to know her father and his new family.

Whether she wanted to or not.

One of the owners of the bookstore came by with a tray of punch. "My wife is taking up a petition to keep Paige in Chances Inlet," she announced. "Maybe you could fire your housekeeper so she'd have to stay?"

Tanner nearly choked on the syrupy drink. If he thought he stood a chance in hell with Paige, he might consider it. He could give Almeda a year's severance.

"She's got a pretty sweet teaching job," the sheriff said. "I doubt she'd give that up."

"As I understand it, teachers don't make much. Just offer her more," his mother advised as she joined their circle.

Tanner stared at her, slack-jawed.

"Your father is right," she said. "You need to learn to apply the same killer instinct you have on the golf course to your business life."

The sound of Paige's laughter drew his attention away from his mother. Deputy Lovell was chuckling at something with her. The breath hung up in Tanner's lungs.

"That look reinforces my theory," his mother whispered in his ear.

Tanner made a noise that sounded suspiciously like a growl. The damn woman had the nerve to laugh at him.

"Save it for the putting green." She threaded her arm through his and led him away. "We've got more work to do today if you want to get rid of those yips."

IT WAS dark by the time he returned home. His mother was relentless in her efforts to cure his ailment. Unfortunately, nothing she suggested helped. If anything, having his family in town made things worse.

Seeing Melinda and the boys only heightened his anxiety. He made excuses for Whitney at dinner, telling his family it would be easier for the little girl if her first meeting with his family wasn't all at once. The truth was, he didn't want to share her with them just yet. Not until he found Donella and hashed out how big of a role he'd be playing in Whitney's life.

And he would be playing a role, dammit. After getting to know her, he wasn't about to relinquish all contact with her. She was a part of Tristan. And Tristan was a part of him.

The house was quiet. Tanner was disappointed even though he knew it was for the best. Paige made her decision abundantly clear yesterday. Funny that she would have more willpower than him, but she did. He respected her for it. That didn't mean he had to like it.

He liked the idea of her leaving in two days even less. Almeda texted to say she would return on Sunday as promised. He was fairly certain that had Whitney not been here, his housekeeper would have asked to stay away longer.

Was his mother right? Could he convince Paige to stay? He knew she needed the money. And Paige sticking around would provide continuity for Whitney. Didn't the girl desperately need that right now? So what if he would be torturing his body having Paige so near, yet untouchable? Whitney's happiness was the only thing that mattered.

Except Paige's happiness matters just as much.

Being around her father and the McAlisters was painful for Paige for some unknown reason. Tanner had already blackmailed her into staying longer than she wanted to. He didn't think he could bring himself to do it again. Besides, she clearly loved her job in Chicago. And watching her in action all week with Whitney and again today at the bookstore, he knew she was damn good at it.

His neck grew tight. He wasn't going to solve this tonight. Tanner headed to his study to grab a drink. Lord knew he needed it after the day he'd had.

The sight that greeted him nearly had him tripping over the threshold. Paige was curled up on the sofa, her bare legs tucked beneath a Milwaukee Growlers T-shirt. Her hair was pulled back into one of those topknot thingies, making her look like a unicorn. As usual, her nose was buried in a book. He never knew reading could be so damn sexy.

Tanner propped a shoulder against the doorjamb, stuffing his hands into his pockets to hide their twitching. He wanted to touch her. Desperately. So much for being able to be around Paige and remain sane.

"Enjoying yourself?" he asked.

She casually marked her place in her book before looking up at him.

Jesus, she even made that look sexy.

"Just killing time waiting for you."

Every nerve ending in his body went on alert when she unfurled herself from the sofa and stood. Her T-shirt slid off one shoulder revealing a large expanse of smooth skin. Tanner bit the inside of his cheek.

Nope. Not dreaming.

A lick of panic ran up his spine. "Is something up with Whitney?"

Paige meandered over to the bar. "Whitney is fine. She's sleeping over at Kate and Alden's." She poured bourbon into two glasses. "With two doctors in the house, she'll be well cared for if anything comes up."

While that was a relief, Tanner felt anything but relaxed. Had she changed her mind? God, he hoped so. Was it possible to die from unresolved lust?

She moved closer, holding his glass out for him. He wasn't proud of how his hand shook when he took it from her. If she noticed, she didn't say anything, instead clinking her glass against his.

"To unresolved issues," she said softly.

The zipper in his pants was suddenly very uncomfortable. He took a large swallow of the whiskey, not really tasting it all. "And what would those be?"

Please, please, please, he silently begged her. *Let it involve the two of us naked on that sofa. On the floor. In the shower. Anywhere, for fuck's sake.*

"Let's start with this."

His mouth went dry when she slowly began lifting her T-shirt, revealing a skimpy pair of shorts beneath it. She pulled something from her pocket. It looked like a sheet of paper folded into a square. With a sly smile, she unfolded it before pressing it against his chest with a lot more aggression than one would expect of a seduction.

The room tilted as he stared at the results of Whitney's paternity test.

Son of a bitch.

"You're not Whitney's father," she said matter-of-factly.

"I never said I was."

"And you never said you weren't," she shot back.

Tanner downed what was left in his glass. He brushed by her to get a refill. "Snoop much?"

"Your housekeeper's been gone since Saturday. It was in the trash for anyone to find."

His laugh was humorless. "Anyone who was snooping, you mean."

"Why are you covering for your brother? Why are you letting your parents and everyone else think poorly of you?"

"What does it matter to you?" he snapped.

Her lips wobbled slightly. "It matters a lot to me," she whispered. "It means you're not the man I thought you were."

"Ha!" He dropped down onto the sofa. "I get that from a lot of people."

She charged across the room to stand over him. "Because you're letting them believe lies!"

"What choice do I have? Tristan is dead!" The words ricocheted around the room like a shot.

"Oh, Tanner." Paige climbed onto his lap, enveloping him in the scent of cocoa butter as she wrapped her arms around him. "I'm sorry your brother left you with such a mess."

He buried his face in her neck, reveling in her compassion. And the knowledge that she believed in him fully, at last.

"How did you figure it out?" he murmured against her skin.

"Just a hunch." She leaned back to study him. "The other night when I asked about switching places, that's when you figured it out, wasn't it?"

She was perceptive. "Yeah. The paternity test identified Tristan as Whitney's dad. But there were still so many missing pieces. The pieces fell into place that night you stepped on the glass." He reached for her foot and rubbed his thumb along the sole. "How is it by the way?"

"My foot is fine."

She went to tug it away, but he increased the pressure, massaging her insole until she went limp.

"Do you think he knew about Whitney?"

Tanner sighed resolutely. "I'd like to think he didn't, but I just don't know anymore."

"We have to find Whitney's mother."

We.

His heart felt like it was turning over inside his chest. He wasn't alone in this any longer. And damn, it felt good.

Tanner wrapped his fingers around her waist and maneuvered Paige's body until she was straddling him. Reaching up, he freed her hair from its ridiculous knot. He trailed his fingers through the soft strands as it cascaded down.

"I have a team of private detectives looking for her." He pressed a kiss to her collarbone while one of his hands worked its way beneath her T-shirt. She gasped when his finger came in contact with a pebbled nipple. "Something has to turn up soon. Good or bad. But until then, I'd really like to concentrate on something else."

She draped her arms around his neck. "What did you have in mind?"

"You. I want to concentrate on you until you're screaming my name in ecstasy. And then I want to do it all again."

She shivered at his words. "I'm all yours for the night."

Ignoring her last three words, he took her mouth with a kiss that he hoped conveyed a multitude of promises. Because he knew deep in his soul that one night with this woman was never going to be enough.

CHAPTER SIXTEEN

Somehow, she wasn't sure how, they made it to Tanner's bedroom. This after a pit stop in the great room where Tanner toed off his shoes and shucked his shirt, all while only breaking their kiss for a few seconds. Then it was a pass through the kitchen, long enough for him to grab two wine glasses. The man was a maestro at multi-tasking. By the time they made it to their destination, she was starting to feel a little ragged around the edges, she wanted him so badly.

"You have a mini bar in your bedroom?" she exclaimed.

Tanner released her to reach into the wine fridge and pull out a bottle of champagne. "Don't tell me you limited your snooping to my study?"

"I found what I was looking for right away. I didn't need to explore in here."

She was exploring now, though, taking in the inviting California king bed with its soft shearling duvet cover. The transom window above it provided a spectacular view of the night's full moon. There was a leather armchair, big enough for two people, positioned next to the French doors leading out to a private patio. A stack of magazines and books were piled high beside the chair. The matching ottoman had a chenille blanket draped over it.

Tanner came up behind her and wrapped his arms around her midsection, the bottle of champagne still in his hands.

"I guarantee you'll find *exactly* what you're looking for in this room, too," he murmured against her ear.

Paige shivered in anticipation. "That's some pretty big talk." She dropped her head back against his shoulder to give his wandering lips better access to her neck. "I hope you can back it up."

While artfully claiming her with his lips, he popped open the bottle of champagne. The spray dampened Paige's T-shirt.

"Oh, I'm sorry," he said, not sounding sorry at all. "Did I get you wet?"

In more ways than one.

He pressed the mouth of the champagne bottle to her lips, tipping it slowly so she could take a sip. It was delicious, but it did nothing to quench the desire threatening to make her knees give out. He took a healthy swallow of his own, before placing the bottle on the bar.

"Let's get you out of that wet shirt before you catch a cold."

Sliding his fingers beneath the hem, he took his time dragging the T-shirt up her body, his gaze growing more heated with every inch of her skin he exposed. He gently lifted it over her hair as if it was styled in an elaborate coif he didn't want to disturb and not a riotous mess from him running his fingers through it.

Standing in the center of his bedroom wearing nothing but a skimpy pair of running shorts, Paige tried not to flinch beneath the full force of his scrutiny. She knew she wasn't one of those stick-thin influencers on social media. She was taller than most women, with a full figure to match. But she treated her body well, exercising daily and eating right. *Mostly.*

"You're fucking gorgeous." His voice sounded almost awestruck. "Do you know that?"

Before when he'd told her that, she chalked it up as a line. Something he told every woman whose panties he wanted to invade and conquer. Now, though, seeing the hungry look in those amber eyes of his, hearing the reverent tone in which he uttered the words, Paige believed him.

Better yet, Paige trusted him.

"You should probably reserve your judgement until you've seen the entire package." She shimmied out of her shorts.

His nostrils flared, but there was a teasing glint in his eyes. He crossed his arms over his chest. "Twirl," he whispered.

"Seriously?" Paige's bravado was beginning to wane.

With a wolfish grin, he made a spinning motion with his fingers.

Sighing, she began to turn. "Just wait until it's your turn," she mumbled. "I'm going to—"

She never finished her thought. Growling, Tanner tumbled them both onto the bed. He rolled her over onto her back, hovering above her on outstretched arms. A sheen of sweat broke out on his forehead.

"Christ, Paige. It might kill me to hear all the things you want to do to me. I'm already having a hell of a time keeping it under control as it is." He was breathing heavily when he pressed his forehead to hers. "Ladies first, though."

His lips grazed her nipples just as his finger slipped inside of her. She was already so keyed up, she bucked off the mattress at his touch.

"I'm not always this easy," she admitted between gasps.

She felt him smile against the tender skin beneath her breast. "I'll take that as a compliment."

Then, he was backing off the bed, pulling her legs over the edge with him. Wearing a playful grin, he leaned down to swirl his tongue inside her belly button. Paige gripped the duvet with both hands when Tanner sank down on his heels. He gently pushed her knees farther apart. The breath from his ragged groan brushed against her inner thighs making her shudder. His lips were next, exploring the delicate flesh on one leg before moving to the next. He was torturing her with his slow pace.

"Tanner," she pleaded.

"Mmm," was the only response she got.

He chuckled when she swore softly. And then his tongue was right where she wanted it, delving inside of her. Slowly at first, as if he had all the time in the world to explore and indulge. She jerked her hips against his shoulders, and he kicked his tempo up a notch. Her breathing became fractured as the pleasure ratcheted up inside her. He made a sound of male satisfaction when she began to writhe beneath him.

His playfulness was beginning to annoy her when, suddenly, her climax blindsided her. The wave of ecstasy was so intense, it felt like all the bones in her body were disintegrating into dust. She didn't recall ever screaming during sex before. But she was fairly certain half the population of Chances Inlet knew what she and Tanner were up to right now.

He was shoving his pants down over his hips when she opened her eyes.

Oh. My.

Her nerve endings roared back to life. He wasn't done with her yet. In fact, they'd only just gotten started. She sank her teeth into her bottom lip to keep from cheering.

Tanner shot her a wicked smile as he prowled over her. "See something you like?"

It was her turn to tease. "Maybe."

Seconds later they were a sweaty tangled mess of limbs, both of them exploring and tasting each other's bodies.

"I have to be inside you," Tanner begged. "Now."

His eyes went wide with surprise when she shoved him over onto his back. He groaned with pleasure when she straddled him. She went to wrap her fingers around him, but he cinched his fingers around her wrists first.

"No. There's no way I'll last thirty seconds if you touch me."

He seemed uncertain what to do with her hands, so Paige snatched them back and began to trace her navel sensuously.

"Jesus."

He reached into the drawer of his nightstand and pulled out a sleeve of condoms. Using his teeth, he ripped one open, hissing as he rolled it over his straining shaft.

Moving as one, he hurriedly guided her over his erection. She sank down, letting out a satisfied sigh at the feel of him stretching and filling her. They both stilled once he was completely inside of her. Tanner was breathing roughly beneath her palms. Slowly, she leaned down to deliver a tender, deep kiss to his lips. They stayed that way for several moments, beneath the curtain of her hair, their tongues moving with a now familiar dance.

Without breaking the kiss, Tanner dug his fingers into her hips and began to move her up and down. Slowly at first, but it took only a few strokes before the fever enveloped them once more. Paige threw her head back with a cry, moving her hips to his now relentless rhythm. The pressure began to build again, and her body grew tight as a bow.

Beneath her, Tanner stared at her intently. "Come with me," he ground out.

"I—I don't—" She couldn't get the words out.

He reached between them, pushing a finger inside her before rocking his hips once, then twice. With a silent scream she convulsed around him, a million stars forming behind her eyelids. Tanner rocked his hips one last time before breathing her name with a sigh and pulling her body down to rest against his.

SUNLIGHT BEGAN to make its way across the bed. Tanner was habitually an early riser thanks to years of early tee times. Even after a strenuous night of the best sex of his life, he couldn't get his body to sleep past daybreak. Not surprising, the part of him that got the most exercise last night was up and ready to do it all over again.

And again.

He glanced over at a sleeping Paige. *Bad idea.* She looked like a sexy wanton with one bare leg poking out from the covers. The sheet was scrunched to the side exposing a very pert nipple. Careful not to wake her—he wouldn't want to ruin his view—he checked the clock on his phone trying to gauge if he had enough time for a round four with Paige.

Six-twenty. He was meeting his mum at the club at seven-fifteen. His dick twitched as if to say "more than enough time, buddy."

Except Paige might be feeling a little worn out this morning.

Or worse, have regrets.

Jesus, please don't let her have regrets.

Because he was pretty sure he was falling for Paige Hollister. The stunning schoolteacher was an unexpected breath of fresh air into his life. He'd never known a more compassionate person. Standing up for a child she just met without a second thought. Believing in him—*the real him*—when no one else bothered to scratch the surface.

After losing Tristan, he was doubtful anyone could ever fill up the hole in his heart. He thought he could fill it with his career. With golf. The past week showed him that notion wasn't foolproof. But with Paige—and Whitney—he was beginning to feel as if he was finally healing.

And he didn't want to live without either of them. Whatever that looked like. Paige slashed an arm through the air in her sleep. Tanner ducked to miss being knocked in the head.

Even if she did sleep like the Tasmanian Devil.

Chuckling to himself, he slipped from the bed. He grabbed a pair of joggers from the pile on his dresser and quietly made his way to the kitchen to brew some coffee. If Paige was like most women, she would probably be more grateful to wake to a cup of coffee rather than him cupping her ass, anyway.

Standing at the great room window a few moments later, he watched the sun rise as he sucked down the first few sips of caffeine from his mug. Two arms, clad in his robe, wrapped around him from behind.

"Coffee," she croaked into his shoulder.

He turned and handed her his mug. As expected, she downed half of it with one gulp. She sighed when he untied the robe's sash and spanned her waist with his hands.

"You left me." Her fake pout was yet another thing about her that was adorable.

"I remembered how much you like my coffee," he teased.

She grinned rapturously. "Multiple orgasms *and* coffee? Tanner Gillette you are God's gift to women."

He opened the robe wider, pressing his body flush against hers, skin to skin. "Mmm. Forgive me if I don't add that to my social media profile. I'd prefer we keep that our little secret."

His arousal made its presence known against her stomach.

Paige sucked in a lusty breath. "We may have to table this until later. I promised Kate I'd take the girls to breakfast this morning so she can help Patricia get ready for the baby shower."

"I've got a tee time with my mum in forty minutes," he murmured against her jaw. "But your suggestion of a shower has a lot of merit. Come on."

Thirty minutes later, Tanner was searching for his socks as well as his lost brain cells. Paige going to her knees as soon as the shower spray hit them was unexpected. *And so fucking hot.* He was nearly hard again just thinking about what her mouth did to him.

For her part, Paige was serenely sipping coffee while she sat wrapped up in his robe. "You'll let me know when you find Whitney's mother, won't you?"

Her words hit him like a driver to the head. *Shit.* Was she actually serious about their time together only being one night? Something twisted painfully in his chest. He couldn't lose her, too.

"Stay." He hadn't meant to ever say the word. Instead hoping she'd choose him first. But that didn't matter to him any longer.

Her mug was poised before her mouth. "What did you say?"

He scrambled to come up with the right words. Words that wouldn't make it sound like he was paying her to stay with him. Except he would be. He just hoped the idea wouldn't insult her.

Whatever it took.

Tanner walked over to the chair and sank to his haunches in front of her. "Stay here with Whitney until I find her mum. She needs you. If you leave now, who knows how much it will set her back."

Look at that. I do know how to negotiate dirty. Guess I'm a true Gillette after all.

"I—"

"I know you have your job and your students to return to. And it wouldn't be fair to leave them before the year is out. But the school can find a substitute, can't they? I'll pay you your entire year's salary if you stay here until this is resolved."

Her eyes went wide.

"Hell, I'll even make an endowment to the school to make up for the inconvenience to them."

She pursed her mouth in what looked like disgust. "That won't be necessary."

It didn't escape him that he was on his knees begging, but he didn't care. He wanted her more than he wanted his golf game back. Hell, if he never got rid of the yips but still had Paige, he could be happy.

"Tanner, I—"

"Yo, Tan-Man!" Sonny's voice echoed down the hall. "Get your ass in gear. I don't want to hear it from Blythe if we're late."

"Think about it," he said before leaning in and kissing her soundly.

He grabbed his shoes and headed out the door praying that he hadn't scared her off.

CHAPTER SEVENTEEN

Tanner's softly uttered plea continued to ricochet between Paige's ears for most of the morning. His offer was tempting. Not just because last night had been darn near a religious experience. The man knew his way around a woman's body, that was for sure. More nights like that could easily become addictive.

The question of what happens when Whitney's situation is resolved continued to nag at her, though. She trusted that he wouldn't deceive her like Jon did. But would he get bored with her once he didn't need Paige to look after his niece? By all accounts, Tanner was used to a lot of variety among his partners.

Complicating matters, there was Whitney herself. When Paige arrived to pick her and Emily up for breakfast, Whitney greeted her with her biggest smile yet and a bear hug. Tanner was right that it might not be fair to the little girl to force another change on her. It might even do her harm. Paige already knew her own heart would suffer yet another blow leaving Whitney behind.

"Paige?"

Her father's voice interrupted her musings. He crossed the inn's lawn toward where she was pushing Whitney in a wooden swing hanging from one of the stunning live oak trees. The first day she stayed at the B & B, she noticed a small carriage house tucked behind the gazebo. His Bronco was parked out front.

"You and Patricia don't live at the inn?" she asked once he was beside her.

His lips turned up into a sheepish grin. "We like our privacy."

Now there was an image Paige didn't need in her head.

Her dad was out of uniform today, dressed in khaki-colored jeans and a cream-colored golf shirt. His sunglasses shielded his eyes, but the set of his jaw told her that his outfit might be the only thing casual about him right now. She wondered if, like her, he felt as if he was walking on eggshells whenever they were alone together.

"Hey there, Whitney," he said, offering the girl a soft smile. "Are you ready for the party?"

Whitney nodded enthusiastically.

He turned his attention to Paige. "How 'bout you?"

She shrugged. "It's a beautiful day. I'm just happy to be outside in the sunshine."

He scoffed. "You say that now, but there's something I think you should know about the McAlisters." He leaned in as if he was sharing a secret. "They are insane."

Paige stared at him, surprised he would say such a thing about a family he seemed keen on.

"Insanely competitive," he clarified with a laugh. "You would not believe the mundane things they compete over. And if there are party games this afternoon—and there always are— be prepared for Patricia's brood to be cutthroat."

"I grew up with two older stepbrothers who made burping

the loudest into a competition." She rolled her eyes. "I'm sure the McAlisters aren't that bad."

He shook his head. "Don't say I didn't warn you."

They stood in silence for a few moments as Paige gently pushed Whitney. A car door slammed off in the distance. People were beginning to arrive. Judging from the amount of food in the inn's kitchen, the entire town of Chances Inlet was invited to the shower.

"So how is your family?" her father surprised her by asking.

More than likely, he was just trying to make polite conversation. Except Paige felt uncomfortable talking about her mom with him. Especially since his second marriage appeared to be a happy one.

When Paige was five, her mother married a widower twelve years older. She suspected the marriage was merely a means to an end for her mother. Once again, it got her out of her father's house and off the farm. Even if the move was only twenty miles away, it was in town.

Jim Franks was a good man, a loving dad, and a hard worker. He was kind and generous to both Paige and her mom. The fact that the couple never had any children of their own gave Paige pause, though. She wondered if her mom simply settled for the path of least resistance.

"Everyone is well. Mom and Jim are still holding out hopes one of my stepbrothers will make them grandparents soon. They're looking forward to a cruise they're taking this summer."

Her dad shoved his hands into his pockets. "That's nice. I'm glad she's happy. When you speak to Heather, please tell her I said hello."

Wait, what?

Paige nearly missed Whitney when the swing propelled her back.

"You haven't spoken to her?"

"Why would I need to?" He was studying her quizzically behind his sunglasses. She could practically feel his eyes boring into her.

"Oh, um, I don't know. I figured you'd call and let her know I was here."

"She doesn't know you're here?"

This was getting awkward. Why did she think her father would pick up the phone and immediately call her mom once Paige arrived? *Paranoia?* She was so raw when she arrived a week ago, she suspected everyone of being out to get her. Even her father.

"Oh, yeah, of course she knows," Paige backpedaled. "I don't know why I thought you two still talked."

"Once you became an adult, there really was no reason for us to remain in contact. She's settled into a new life and so have I." He cleared his throat. "Paige, you aren't harboring some fantasy about your mom and I getting back together, are you?"

She barked out a laugh. "God, no!"

Was he kidding?

Nothing could be further from the truth. Oddly, she didn't even dream about that when she was younger. And now, seeing her dad with Patricia, she was glad he followed his own path. They seemed much better suited for one another than he and her mom. Although, she didn't want him to think she never wished for him to be a part of *her* life. That would be cruel.

Paige smiled at him. "I realized the futility of that dream a longtime ago," she told him.

The corners of his mouth relaxed again. "I never got a chance to know you as a little girl," he said. "But I'm still holding out hope of getting to know you now."

A boulder lodged itself in her throat.

He picked up Gladys from her perch against the tree trunk. "I'm here whenever you need me, Paige. I always have been."

"Aunt Paige!" Emily shrieked.

Paige still jumped whenever she heard that moniker in front of her name.

Emily raced across the grass, a beautiful Australian sheepdog trotting beside her.

"You have to meet Tessa." Emily paused to suck in two big breaths. "She's Aunt Lori's dog, and she's much better behaved than Midas. Watch." She turned to the dog. "Tessa, sit."

The dog did as it was told, one blue and one brown eye alertly trained on Emily.

Emily helped Whitney from the swing. "Hold out your hand," she instructed the younger girl.

Whitney hesitated fleetingly before placing her palm out flat.

"Tessa, shake," Emily commanded.

As if sensing Whitney's trepidation, the dog lifted its paw and gently placed it in Whitney's hand. They were all rewarded with a giggle from the little girl. Paige gasped and looked over at her dad. He smiled broadly before crouching down and calling the dog to him.

"How's our best girl enjoying living in Washington?" He rubbed the dog's ears, earning him a lick to the chin for his efforts.

"Come on, y'all." Emily tucked one hand into Paige's and with the other took Whitney's. "Mom wants to introduce you to Uncle Miles and Aunt Lori."

Tessa ran ahead, announcing their impending arrival with a series of shrill barks.

"Remember what I said about the games, Paige," her father warned with a smile when he fell into step beside them.

Paige grinned back at him. After all, the man had just removed one of the major stumbling blocks to her remaining in Chances Inlet. He and the McAlisters would be none the wiser to her epic failure. Maybe she could consider Tanner's offer. She skipped along with the two little girls.

TANNER SCANNED the inn's veranda looking for Paige. Melinda waved to him from the porch swing where she was juggling both boys. He was surprised to see her at the baby shower until he realized Patricia likely invited all her guests to celebrate alongside family and friends. It was a very "Patricia" thing to do.

He started to head toward his sister-in-law when the sight of Whitney and Paige skipping across the lawn had his heart doing its own skipping. Paige was practically glowing. Her hair was styled into soft waves that made her appear as if she'd just come from the beach. She wore a long-sleeved, jersey dress in navy that hugged her curves at the top and flared out at the hips. A soft sheen of pink lip gloss made her sassy mouth look even more delectable. He groaned thinking about the pleasure those lips gave him.

Whitney spotted him first. She tugged free of Emily's hand and ran toward him. The delight on her face brought a huge smile to his own face. As soon as she reached him, he grabbed her in his arms and swung her around.

"Hi ya, Whit. Don't you look pretty."

She was wearing a pink and white dress with bunnies outlined in puffy cotton circling its hem. Her hair was held back with a big pink bow.

Tanner almost melted when Whitney looped her arms around his neck and leaned in for a tight hug. Over the girl's shoulder, he locked eyes with Paige. She grinned back at him.

"Whitney, Henry is here." Emily tugged on Whitney's leg. "Let's go show him where the secret cupcakes are."

"Secret cupcakes?" he whispered to Whitney. "Make sure you save one for me."

She rubbed her nose against his before shimmying down and taking Gladys from the sheriff. His throat was tight with awe as he watched her link arms with Emily and race away, the sheriff following in their wake.

"She missed you," Paige said quietly.

"What about you?"

"Oh, she missed me, too." She shot him a sly smile.

Saucy wench.

Christ, he wanted to touch her. To lay her down in the grass and taste her sweet skin from head to toe. Too many prying eyes kept him from doing the first. Decorum kept him from doing the second.

"I meant did *you* miss me?"

She swayed so the skirt on her dress swished from side-to-side. "Hmm. Let me think about that."

The hell what anyone else in this town thought. He took her elbow, quickly guiding her around the inn toward the gazebo. Luckily it was empty. Lucky for Paige it was still fully exposed to the gossips of the town—not to mention both their families—and would prevent him from thoroughly ravaging her.

At least for right now.

"They're gone," he announced as soon as they climbed the steps.

"Who's gone?"

"The yips. I shot a seventy today. Four under par."

"Oh my gosh!" She threw her arms around his neck. "That's wonderful."

His hands automatically went to her waist. They stood like that for several long heartbeats, the inches separating their bodies feeling like miles. She sank her teeth into her bottom lip. He groaned when she slowly dragged her hands from his shoulders.

"Too many people," she whispered.

"Mmhmm," was all he could manage.

His hands lingered on her waist until she started to step

back. He slid his fingers down her arms and took her hands in his.

"Your mom must be delighted," she said.

He snorted. Of course his mother was taking full credit for the achievement. Sonny was busy finalizing arrangements for Augusta next week. If his putter didn't desert him tomorrow, he was back on track to achieve his goal of winning the cup this season.

Tanner knew that nothing his mother did scared the tremors away. Maybe Janey was right, and it was the sex. Somehow, he doubted that, too. He suspected it was sharing his secret burden with someone who believed in him. Who believed he was doing the right thing. Hell, maybe it was Tristan spreading some good juju from wherever was. He'd like to think his brother was grateful to him for stepping up.

"My mother is already arguing with Sonny about who will be on the bag in Augusta next week." He rubbed the pad of his thumb back and forth against her palm.

Her shoulders sank ever so slightly. "You'll be leaving on Monday, then?"

"Yes. Almeda can come back, but—"

"I'll do it. I'll stay and help with Whitney."

A wave of relief rolled over him at her words. He didn't realize how badly he wanted to hear her say them until she did. He closed his eyes for a second, letting out a thankful sigh.

"I have conditions, though," she said.

That doesn't bode well.

He snapped his eyelids up.

"I can't accept a full year's salary from you. A weekly wage equal to what I would have earned at Preston is fair."

That was not what he expected her to say. Though he was grateful for her practicality. It made the relationship between the two of them much less complicated. Unless she took that off the table, too.

"I'm paying you to look after Whitney. Not for sex."

Her eyes narrowed. "I never thought you were."

He dropped her hands to run his fingers through his hair.

"That came out wrong. What I meant to say is there's no pressure for you to do anything you don't want to do. With me. I mean, I'd like you to want to do everything with me but—" He couldn't decipher her expression. Was she going to laugh at him or knee him in the balls? "Argh. What I'm trying to say is I want you, Paige. I've wanted you since the first moment I laid eyes on you. What I won't do is take advantage of you while you're working for me. Unless you want me to."

Her lips twitched. "Let me put you out of your misery. You are definitely going to get lucky tonight, Tanner Gillette. And if it makes you feel better, I'll leave a twenty on your nightstand when we're done."

He didn't realize their bodies had drifted back together until he felt the warmth of her words on his neck. "Surely I'm worth at least fifty," he teased.

She laughed as she leaned into him.

"I don't blame you, girly-pop," Bernice Reed's voice rang out. "Gotta love the way that man fills out his golf pants."

Paige jumped back, her face flushing crimson.

"Save the hanky-panky for later, you two. I've been sent to bring you back to the party," Bernice announced. "The games are about to begin."

Tanner groaned. "This family and their games."

"My dad had the same reaction as you. What's the big deal with this family and games?"

"You'll see," he chuckled. "But don't worry. I won't let them intimidate you." He intertwined his fingers with hers and gave her hand a squeeze. "We're a team now."

CHAPTER EIGHTEEN

THE MCALISTERS KNEW how to put on a party, not to mention how to enjoy it. Paige smiled graciously as she was introduced to half the residents of Chances Inlet. All of them indulging her with a different tale of how her father and Patricia made life in their favorite place on earth better. She was surprised to see her reserved dad actually blush a few times.

The only other person pressing the flesh as much as Paige was the oldest of Patricia's sons, Miles McAlister.

"Paige." He offered his hand to her when their paths finally crossed. "It's a pleasure to meet you at last."

"You, too, Congressman."

Kate cackled from a few feet away. "Don't you dare 'congressman' him," she said.

Gavin came up behind Miles and slapped his brother on the back. "Yeah, we don't stand on ceremony in this family. We simply refer to him as asshole or uptight. His wife's personal favorite is Dudley Do Right. Isn't that right, Lori?" Gavin winked at the dark-haired woman threading her arm through Miles'.

"If we want the poor woman to come visit her father ever again, maybe we shouldn't show her this family's warts just yet," Lori said.

The McAlister siblings responded with a resounding "why not?"

A young woman who Paige met earlier in the day edged her way into their circle. She was carrying several baby dolls in her arms. Patricia fostered Cassidy Burroughs for several months before the girl left for college last fall. Based on the ferocity of the teasing and ribbing between Cassidy and Patricia's children, the young woman was an honorary member of the family. Cassidy, in turn, obviously considered the inn her home.

"The course is all set," Cassidy announced. "Kyle is ready for the first heat."

Gavin whistled loudly. "We're ready for the stroller races everyone! Grab a partner and head to the starting line back by the garden shed."

"Stroller races?" Paige looked down at her wedge sandals. "Nobody mentioned we would be racing. I would have worn different shoes."

"Of course we didn't tell you," Kate said. "You look like a runner. I needed some sort of advantage over you." She pointed to the sleek white sneakers on her feet.

"You're welcome to sit this one out, Paige," Miles suggested. Something about the challenge in his eyes told her she'd endure all kinds of humiliation for not racing as opposed to at least trying. "We don't expect you to be able to keep up with us."

Her father wasn't exaggerating about the competitive nature of the McAlisters.

She squared her shoulders and smiled at Miles. "I'm in."

He arched an eyebrow at her. "You're sure?"

"She's sure," Tanner replied, coming up behind her and planting his fingers on either side of her waist.

The congressman's eyes narrowed briefly, taking in Tanner's possessive posture. "And you already have your partner, I see."

Paige nodded.

Miles' face relaxed into a broad grin. "That works."

"You can use my sneakers if you want," Jane offered. "My partner is still at spring training so I'm not participating."

"You're not getting out of it that easily. Ryan would be ashamed of you," Kate told her best friend. "Deputy Lovell needs a partner. Team up with him."

The deputy looked at Kate like he'd just been drafted to dig ditches. "Doesn't Elle need a partner?"

The youngest McAlister, Elinor, or Elle as she was called, was also the runt of the McAlister litter, it appeared. Her petite, lithe build was very similar to her mother, Patricia's. The rest of her siblings towered over her.

Elle's eyes were grayer than her mom's. But it was the red hair that really differentiated her from her brothers and sister. Paige suspected Patricia must have had hair the same color at one time. Elle sidled up next to Gavin.

"Elle is filling in for Ginger." Gavin glared at his siblings, seeming to dare them to argue. "My wife is *not* racing while seven months pregnant."

"Ryan is going to be paying dearly for this when I get to New York next week," Jane mumbled as she took her place at the starting line.

"Make him pay double," Bernice said with a wink as she pushed her stroller into the lane next to Jane. "What's the use of dating a younger man if you're not going to tap into all that delicious stamina."

With a deep belly laugh, Elle positioned her stroller in the lane all the way at the end.

Kate scowled at Bernice. "Ick. That image is not nearly as sexy when you consider the younger man is *my baby brother!*"

"Take your marks," Cassidy called out. "Ladies will go around the course first. When they get back here to the starting line, they have to unstrap the baby, burp it, and return it to the stroller before their partner can take off for the final lap."

Lori steered her stroller into the lane beside Paige.

"Everybody set?" Cassidy asked.

"Hold on." Paige bent down to unclip her wedge sandals. She gingerly stepped out of them before handing the shoes to Tanner.

He looked at her warily. "You sure?" he whispered.

"Summers on a farm make for tough feet," she replied with a sly grin.

Everyone else stared at her.

"Paige, I'm not sure that's wise," Alden warned.

"Can we get a ruling on running barefoot?" Miles said to no one in particular.

"Wait, are there actual rules for this?" Paige asked. "Because if there are, I'd like to see them."

Tanner chuckled behind her.

"Cassidy went over the only rules to the game," Patricia interjected. "The runners are allowed to wear whatever they want on their feet."

Paige smiled smugly at both men.

Kate grinned at Paige. Her eyes brimming with respect. "It's on, girl."

Cassidy blew the whistle. Lori took off so quickly that Gavin was shouting something about a false start. Elle was close on Lori's heels. Jane, on the other hand, was barely putting any effort in, despite Henry's cries for her to hurry up. Bernice was remarkably spry for someone her age, but no match for Paige.

Paige used the same strategy she used during her competitive swimming days. She maintained a distance of a stroller length behind Elle and Lori, confident she could overtake either woman in the last ten yards of the race based on the longer length of her legs. Kate, on the other hand, was the wild card. Running neck and neck with Paige, it looked as though she was employing the same strategy.

Just then, Kate seemed to trip. "Ow," she cried.

But when Paige peeked over her shoulder to check to see if she was okay, Kate sprinted past triumphantly.

"Made you look," Kate shouted.

Gavin and Miles hollered with laughter. Ignoring the sharp pine straw digging into her feet, Paige moved into another gear. The heck with waiting until the final five yards. She was making her move now. She could hear Tanner whooping at the finish line as she turned the corner toward home. One-by-one she overtook Kate, Elle, then Lori.

Whitney jumped up and down when Paige crossed the finish line first. Paige snatched the baby from the stroller and threw it over her shoulder. She strapped the doll back as Tanner gripped the handles. Beside them, Lori was laying a kiss on her husband's mouth. Tanner moved in as if to do the same, but Paige smacked him on the bottom.

"Go!" she cried. "While they're dawdling."

No sooner had Tanner raced off when Elle and Kate each draped an arm over Paige's shoulders.

"You'll do," Elle said.

"Yeah," Kate added. "I knew you were one of us the moment I met you."

Tanner was no match for Miles, who was apparently a triathlete when he wasn't representing his hometown in Washington. Gavin finished second, while Tanner was a respectable third. Paige didn't mind, though. She was too busy reveling in the newfound friendship she found with the McAlisters. It was a relief not to have to worry they'd find out about Jon and her firing at any moment. After months of hiding behind her anger and shame, she could enjoy herself once more.

The next game they were forced to play involved the baby dolls yet again. Each team had to change their baby's diaper—using cloth diapers and pins. The couple finishing first would be the winner. Everyone was surprised when Bernice and her significant other, Gus, beat Kate and Alden. Not that Tanner and Paige really tried.

"It's a good thing I didn't have to look after Whit when she was an infant. She would have bled to death," Tanner said after stabbing himself in the thumb with the diaper pin.

Paige chuckled. "I don't think parents use diaper pins any longer. Your fingers and any future children you have are safe from harm."

Based on his interactions with Whitney, Paige knew immediately he'd be an amazing dad. Her mouth was suddenly dry at the thought.

Holding the diaper firmly against this thumb, he aimed a thoughtful look her way. "I never thought kids would be part of my future."

That surprised her. "Never?"

His amber gaze grew heated while he slowly shook his head. "But I'm beginning to wonder if the future I imagined is the one I really want."

She'd heard that line before. Jon claimed to be married to his work. But upon meeting Paige, he insisted she was responsible for him rethinking his priorities. She sucked in a ragged breath. How could she have been so foolish to believe him?

Tanner isn't Jon, she reminded herself. She crossed her fingers on both hands for added reassurance.

"What about you?"

His question brought her back to the present, scattering the doubts that were constantly on the periphery of her thoughts. For now.

"Do you want kids?" he asked when she didn't immediately reply.

"I'm a teacher. My answer should be obvious."

"Any child would be lucky to have you as its mother."

She blinked at the moisture threatening behind her eyes. She could feel his stare trained on her. Fortunately, Patricia arrived to save her.

"Who's ready for cake and the gender reveal?" Patricia announced.

The kids all shrieked in agreement, a mob of them racing to the veranda. Tanner's sister-in-law was pushing a double stroller with her twin boys up the long drive.

"We should invite her to join us," Paige said. "I'm sure her little ones would enjoy some cake. And they need to get to know Whitney."

Tanner's expression grew solemn. "Whitney will always be my responsibility."

"I understand that. But we don't know if she has any other family. The fact that her mother left her with you seems to indicate she might not. She'll enjoy having cousins one day."

He jammed his hands in his pocket with a sigh. "I know. And I would kiss you right now for your invaluable wisdom, but I can feel your father's eyes boring into my back."

Paige laughed. "He's not the boss of me."

"Mmhmm. Just in case, I'm going to leave you alone so I can go say hello to my nephews. Save us some cake. We'll be up in a minute."

She smiled softly watching him walk toward his sister-in-law. When Paige turned to join the others on the veranda, it was to find that Tanner was telling the truth. Her father was intently focused on Tanner's movements.

"Aren't you curious about whether it's a boy or a girl?" she asked him once she'd climbed the steps.

"Doesn't matter as long as the baby is healthy."

She wanted to ask whether he cared one way or the other about her sex before she was born. Based on her grandfather's tales of a shotgun wedding between him and her mom, he wasn't excited about being a father at all, initially. She wondered if he might have returned home more often if she were his son instead of his daughter.

Before she could dig up the courage to ask, Whitney appeared at her side. She slid her hand into Paige's, pulling her to where Ginger and Gavin were about to cut into the cake. Her father smiled when the little girl grabbed his hand, too. When he lifted her up onto his shoulders so she could see over the crowd, something shifted inside Paige.

Not jealousy. Something on the other side of the spectrum. Something she was afraid to quantify.

"The video is rolling," Cassidy announced. "Cut the thing already."

Ginger grinned nervously at her husband. Gavin picked up the knife and hovered above the cake. It was a shame to cut into it. The three-tiered creation featured ballerinas and architecture tools surrounding the bottom two layers. The top layer was decorated with baby things. The inside would either be pink or blue. The crowd counted down until Gavin dug the knife through the fondant, revealing a layer of bright pink cake.

"Yes!" Emily shouted. "Girls rule!"

Gavin handed the knife to his mother before wrapping his arms around Ginger and bending her over his arm for a lusty kiss. The guests all cheered. Bernice took over the cutting of the cake while Patricia wiped tears from her eyes. Paige's dad bent down to kiss his wife. Whitney leaned in to give Patricia a hug, as well.

Moments later, Paige was finally able to congratulate the happy couple.

"I'm so glad you were here for this," Gavin said as he wrapped her in a hug.

"Me, too," Ginger added when it was her turn to embrace Paige. "I can't believe you're leaving tomorrow. This week went too quickly. I hope you'll come back this summer to meet our daughter."

"I've already got dibs on her for nannying," Kate interrupted.

"Actually…" Paige looked around to make sure only McAlisters and her father were within hearing. "I'm going to stay a little bit longer."

Her announcement was greeted with stunned silence.

"Uh, just until Tanner can locate Whitney's mom. I—we feel it would be best for Whitney. To provide come continuity for her right now."

"Continuity?" Miles mumbled beside her. "Is that what they're calling it now?"

She jerked her gaze over to him. He wore a sly smile as he placed his arm around her shoulders. "That's a magnanimous gesture you're making for Whitney," he said a bit louder. "And I'm selfishly glad because it means I'll have more than one day to get to know you."

"Hear, hear," Gavin called out just as Kate and Ginger enveloped her in a hug.

"Oh my gosh! This is fantastic news," Ginger said.

"I'm so excited to hear this," Kate whispered. "And I heard that 'we.' I knew there was something going on between you and Tanner. I'll expect all the details over wine later."

Kate would be waiting a while before Paige started dishing. She wasn't even sure if she could tell Summer. Sure, the arrangement with Tanner solved her employment problem. But only for the time being. The sticking point in the plan?

Managing the intense physical attraction between her and Tanner without letting her emotions get out of control. Paige was determined to keep it light and fun. No way was she putting her heart all the way out there to get stomped on again.

Patricia was next for a hug. Paige met her father's eyes over his wife's shoulder.

"What about your job?" he asked.

"Oh, um, I've asked for a sabbatical." She hated the way the lie rolled off her tongue so easily. Except it was too late to tell them the truth. She'd already been lying to everyone for a week. "It being a private school, the principal has a lot of flexibility."

Another lie.

The truth was, her principal went to battle for Paige, only to be overruled by the board.

"Oh, my goodness," Patricia said. "We have so many things to celebrate today."

Patricia began to hand out the cake to her family. Paige's father made his way over to where she was hemmed in against the railing. The back of her neck began to tingle when he gave her a pointed look.

"I'm not going to lie. I'm glad you'll be staying in town a while longer," was all he said.

Paige got the feeling he was waiting for her to say something. Or spill her guts. The man could be damned intimidating when he wanted to be.

"Me, too," she replied quickly. "I've enjoyed spending time with your family."

She thought he might have growled low in his throat, but no words came out. All he did was continue his heated stare, as if he was boring into her skull and reading her mind.

"I would love some cake. Thank you," Paige said enthusiastically when Patricia offered her a piece. Her father hesitated a long moment before taking his own.

"I'm just going to check on Whitney," Paige said. "Excuse me."

Tanner was right. It was possible to feel her father's eyes burning into her back.

CHAPTER NINETEEN

Tanner wiped the frosting off Liam's hands while Melinda wrestled with Luca to clean his chubby cheeks.

"Wow," Melinda said. "Look at you being all domestic."

He looked over at her, caught off guard by her words. "What do you mean?"

Melinda shrugged. "I don't know. I just never pictured you being attentive to children. Wiping hands. Changing diapers. From what Tristan told me, your father never was."

"I don't think it was because my father never wanted to." Tanner couldn't believe he was defending his dad. Some of his earliest memories, though, were of his father reading to him and Tristan. All three of them snuggled in a chair while his dad patiently read and reread the same book. Hell, he distinctly remembered his dad feeding one of the twins a bottle while his mum fed the other so Melinda could get some sleep those first weeks the boys were born. "He just wasn't around all that much when we were growing up, that's all."

She made a tsking sound. "If you say so."

"Hold up." Tanner was getting agitated now. "Are you saying you don't think Tristan would have been an involved father?"

"We'll never know, will we?"

Something fierce and painful unfurled inside of Tanner. "He was already one hundred percent invested before these two were born. Tristan commandeered my helicopter because he was desperate to get home to *you*. And to these boys."

"I'm carrying around enough guilt without you having to point that out," she snapped.

Jesus.

Melinda felt responsible for Tristan's death? How had he missed that?

"You have nothing to feel guilty about, Mel," he reassured her. "No one forced him to get on that chopper."

"I did," she said quietly. "I was miserable. And lonely. I begged him repeatedly to come home."

Tanner swore beneath his breath. Knowing Melinda the way he did, he could easily imagine she was telling the truth about demanding Tristan come home. But the accident that followed was not her fault. He wouldn't let her take the blame.

"What happened was an accident, Mel. It's no one's fault but Mother Nature's. Certainly not yours." He rested his hand on her arm. "And I'm happy to fill in for Tristan wherever I can."

"No!"

The sharpness of her tone made him recoil. He sucked in an astonished breath.

Melinda squeezed her temple. "Don't you get it? I can't look at you and not see him. God, I can't hear your voice and not hear Tristan's. Every time I do, it's a painful reminder of what I lost." She gestured to the boys. "Of what they'll never have."

Tanner felt as if he'd been bludgeoned. His jaw ached from being clenched so tightly. Taking a breath was suddenly painful.

"It hurts too much," she whispered. "Maybe someday when the ache dies down, I can tolerate you playing more of a role in their lives. But not now."

He sat in stunned silence, knowing the unbearable pain she felt losing Tristan. He still felt it, too. How could he have been so selfish not to recognize the agony he caused Melinda whenever he was around?

The sound of Emily and Henry's laughter floated through the air. They were on the lawn chasing a balloon with Whitney. Liam began to pump his legs wildly with excitement watching them with the balloon.

"Me play," he cried.

Melinda sighed before rescuing her son from the stroller. "You'll have your hands full with Whitney, anyway," she said. "I still can't wrap my head around you being a father. Tristan would be proud of you for doing the right thing."

Tanner bit back a caustic laugh. Irony was a bitter pill to swallow.

"She looks like her mother," Melinda said.

A heavy coldness unexpectedly enveloped him, and the world seemed to stop spinning. "What did you say?"

Melinda looked at him like he was daft. "Whitney has her mother's eyes. Surely, you've noticed?"

"You've—you've met Whitney's mum?" He was gripping the sides of the Adirondack chair so tightly that he wouldn't be surprised if he walked away with splinters embedded in his palms. "When? Where?"

"She came to the office. The one at the Silver Canyon development. In Las Vegas." She enunciated the words as if he'd never heard of either place. "She was looking for you."

Tanner was having difficulty drawing air through his lungs. His lips felt numb. "When? When did she come to the office?"

"I don't remember exactly," she replied testily. "I was pregnant with the boys. Tristan was supposed to meet me there for lunch because the doctor had just told us bedrest was imminent. As usual, his board meeting was running late."

"Did Tristan speak with her? With Whitney's mother?"

"No. She left before he arrived. I told him about her though. We joked about your lovers being so desperate to find you, they had to track you down at Gillette Industries. He never mentioned it to you? He said he would."

He knew. Tristan knew.

The chair began to tilt. Tanner felt like he might vomit.

"I'm sure he would have gotten around to it," Melinda added softly. "Had he not died the following week."

"Is it bath time for these two?" Tanner's mother joined them on the veranda. Her voice sounded as if she was speaking through a long tunnel.

She and Melinda gathered up the fussy toddlers. Tanner sat still trying to force his body to digest what Melinda just told him.

Damn you, Tristan.

He didn't realize he'd uttered the words aloud until Melinda chastised him.

"Don't be angry at him," she said sharply. "It all worked out in the end. She obviously found you."

She snatched up the diaper bag and carried Luca into the inn. Tanner's mother remained standing over him. Liam squirmed in her arms.

"Is everything okay, Tanner?"

Fuck, no!

He heaved a sigh. "The yips are gone. Nothing more for you to worry about."

When his mother didn't budge, he risked a glance at her. Liam reached down to tug on Tanner's hair.

"I wasn't talking about your golf game, Tanner," she replied softly. "I'm asking if you are okay?"

He gently extracted the toddler's fingers from his hair. "Just missing Tristan."

It was the truth. Of course, if his brother was standing on this veranda right now, Tanner wouldn't hesitate to go lights out on him.

His mother leaned down and pressed a kiss to his head. "I know you probably miss him more than all of us. He was part of you. But at least he left two pieces of him behind for us to treasure."

Make that three.

Tanner felt like his body was moving on autopilot. He wandered around the inn to the wooden steps leading to the beach. Slipping off his shoes and socks, he headed down. The tide was high, leaving little sand between the surf and the berm. He rolled up his pant legs and stepped into the chilly water. Oddly, the ocean felt warmer than the blood running through his veins right now. He picked up a rock and tossed it into the tide, releasing a primal scream as a send-off.

"Tanner?"

He glanced back over his shoulder. Paige was standing at the top of the stairs wearing a tentative expression. Not that he blamed her. He didn't know who he was right now. Only, he did know that he needed her. Needed the one person who understood him and his situation. He held out his hand.

Paige didn't hesitate, stepping out of her shoes and setting them next to his. She hurried down the steps and into his arms. Tanner couldn't resist any longer. He sealed his mouth over hers with a demanding kiss. She responded to his kiss with a gentle fervor. The tide swirled around their ankles while his mouth ate at hers. The kiss wasn't doing anything to calm the restless ache within, however.

Little soothing sounds emanated from the back of her throat as if she knew how troubled he was. Her hands traced calming circles on his back.

"Shh," she whispered when he broke the kiss and buried his face in her neck. "It's okay."

"He knew," Tanner said against her warm skin. "He fucking knew."

Paige's hands stilled on his back. "Tristan knew about Whitney?"

Yet another thing he adored about the woman in his arms. She knew what he was thinking without him having to explain. "Yeah."

Sighing, she wrapped her arms more tightly around him.

"I don't want to hate him, Paige." The words were difficult to push out of his raw throat.

"You can be angry at someone and still not hate them." She brushed her lips over his ear. "That's what unconditional love is all about."

They stood like that, her giving him comfort and him selfishly soaking it all up, until voices drifted down from the yard above them.

"Let's go home," Paige whispered, unwrapping her arms from around him. Taking his hand, she led them up the wooden steps. Tanner realized he'd follow this woman to the ends of the earth if she led him there.

Two hours later, Tanner sat in his study staring at the cotton candy sky the setting sun left behind. He'd gone over all the details for next week's tournament with Sonny. His swing coach texted with a schedule for practice sessions.

Golf.

It was crazy to be defined by a game, but dammit, Tanner loved the skill and science involved in outwitting the individual who designed the course. He thrived on making a name and a fortune for himself and not living in the shadow of either of his parents. The damn yips weren't ever coming back. He wouldn't give his brother the satisfaction.

Paige ambled into the room, her hair in a ponytail, her face scrubbed clean of makeup and a Milwaukee Growlers football jersey covering up all the parts Tanner wanted to lick right now.

"What's with the Milwaukee Growlers? I thought you lived in Chicago?"

She moved around the desk to where he sat and rested her backside against it. The position put her bare thigh within striking distance. Tanner shifted painfully in his chair.

"My best friend, Summer, is dating Luke Kessler." She helped herself to his glass of scotch.

"No kidding? I had him on my fantasy football team last season. For a little guy, he scores a lot of points."

"Mmhmm." Her tongue darted out to capture a drop of whiskey on her lip.

Tanner gave up fighting it. He reached over and lightly trailed his finger along the sleek skin tempting him. "Where's Whit?"

"Asleep," she whispered.

He could feel her shiver when he pressed his finger a little higher. "Paige. I'm not myself tonight. I know you mentioned something about getting lucky earlier, but I can't promise you I won't just take from you. So, if that's not what you want, you'd be smart to leave. Now."

Paige didn't hesitate. Her gaze locked with his, she wrapped her fingers around his wrist and slowly guided his hand higher up her thigh. When she pulled it beneath the jersey, he nearly exploded on the spot. The woman wasn't wearing anything underneath.

It was barely a matter of minutes before he shucked his clothes and bent her over the desk. She responded with lusty moans of encouragement, sprinkling in a few raunchy words here and there to egg him on.

He leaned over her back. "Don't you dare scream," he taunted her. "You'll wake Whitney."

It was his turn to swear when she clenched her internal muscles around him, bringing him in deeper.

"Now, Paige," he ordered.

She flung her head side-to-side. Tanner reached around her belly and pressed a finger to the tender nub driving her. She came immediately, throwing her head back with wild abandon, nearly knocking him unconscious. Tanner pressed an open-mouthed kiss to her neck as he pumped into her twice more, nipping at her skin when the blinding release overtook him.

Neither of them moved for what felt like hours. His pulse still pounded in his ears. They both struggled to regain normal breathing.

"I'm not done with you," he warned her.

She chuckled softly. "Good. Because I've got plans for you, too."

Paige reached around and smacked him on the ass.

A few hours later, they lay tangled together in his bed relaxed and sated. The musky smell of sex mingled with the sweet scent of whiskey he'd licked off her body minutes before. The only light in the room was the glow the moon cast over the bedspread.

"Tanner," she said softly.

He fingered a strand of her hair. "Hmm?"

"How did you find out Tristan knew about Whitney?"

He didn't want to talk about his brother. Not when he was still high from the most mind-blowing orgasms he'd ever experienced. But it wasn't fair to use her to take the edge off and not fill her in.

"Melinda met Whitney's mother."

Paige shot up to a sitting position. "*What?*"

Tanner sighed. "Apparently Whitney's mother has the same unique eyes."

"But where did they meet? How? I don't understand."

He patted the mattress. She lay back down on her side, propping her head up with her hand.

"Donella—that's the name on the note that was left with Whitney—came to the site office at a development in Las Vegas that Tristan was overseeing at the time. Melinda was there waiting to have lunch with him. Donella was asking for me, obviously. She likely didn't know I was a twin. Or that it was Tristan she really wanted to see."

Paige placed a hand on his chest. Her touch calmed his escalating heart rate right away.

"Anyway, Melinda said she left before Tristan arrived. Apparently, my brother and his wife had a good laugh at my expense. Something about spurned lovers trying to track me down. Tristan was supposed to mention it to me. Of course, he never did."

The sour taste was back in his throat.

"That's . . . incredible." She rolled over on her back, pressing their palms together and lacing her fingers with his. "It's a shame the site office isn't like a military base or some place where people have to sign in. You might be able to track down Donella that way."

Tanner jerked his head toward her. "What did you say?"

She tilted her gaze sideways. "If she had to sign in to visit Tristan, surely they'd ask for I.D. There would be a record of her name. Her full name."

That was it. Tristan was a stickler for security. Theft was a big issue while the developments were under construction. He was also paranoid the Gillette name made him a target. Donella most definitely had to sign in. Best of all, his father owned those records. Tanner wouldn't need a court order to access them.

He leaped out of bed.

"Where are you going?"

"To call the head of security at Gillette Industries. And then your dad's P.I. friend in Las Vegas." He bent back down to plant a hot kiss on her mouth. "You stay right where you are. I'll be back in fifteen minutes. I'm going to spend the rest of the night thanking you for your brilliance."

CHAPTER TWENTY

WHITNEY PLAYED out on the screened porch, swinging the plastic golf club with enthusiasm as she attempted to putt the ball into a plastic cup tilted over on its side. Paige kept an eye on her from the sofa in Tanner's study. Other than his bedroom, this room reminded her of him the most. She was surprised at how much she missed his presence in the house.

Tanner, his parents, and Sonny left for Augusta two days earlier. There was still no word from the private investigator, but Tanner was upbeat and hopeful Donella would be located soon.

"You look different." Summer scrutinized Paige via the cellphone camera.

"Just relaxed, that's all," Paige replied.

A weekend of earth-shattering orgasms will do that to a girl.

Not that she was sharing that snippet of info with her best friend. Paige hated hiding things from Summer, but her friend would be disappointed if she thought Paige was burning up the sheets with a man who couldn't remember the name of the woman he'd fathered a child with. Explaining things to Summer would mean revealing Tanner's brother's secret. She wouldn't do that to him. For now, it was better to leave her friend in the dark about whatever it was that was happening between Paige and Tanner.

"It's been nice not having to watch my step everywhere I go," Paige continued. "There aren't any parents of Preston students in Chances Inlet making my life miserable. It was pretty isolating not being able to leave the apartment for weeks on end."

Summer nodded. "I wish you would have confided in me about how bad it was. You could have come to Milwaukee and stayed with Luke and me."

"No offense, but the weather here is much nicer."

"You do have a sun-kissed glow. How was the baby shower?"

Paige smiled in spite of herself. "It was fun. This town is home to quite a few celebrities. Did you know Will Connelly, a pro football player with the Baltimore Blaze, lives here? He and Gavin are best friends."

"No way! His wife designs the most gorgeous wedding gowns."

"Been thinking of wedding dresses, have we?"

A week ago, Paige would have been devastated by the thought of Summer marrying. After all, she'd been fantasizing about a double wedding for her and Summer a few short months ago. The sting wasn't nearly as brutal today.

Not because she was planning a wedding to Tanner Gillette. Far from it. But the man did a lot to massage her badly flagging confidence. When this thing between them fizzled out—and it would because she never fell for the monogamous ones—Paige would walk away with her heart intact. Because she was determined not to give him more than a sliver of it.

The trick, she learned, was to go into a relationship with her eyes wide open. Tanner wasn't hiding anything from her. And she wasn't hiding anything from him. Well, except for the

"I've been fired from my job for being an adulteress" thing. But she wasn't sharing that with anybody in Chances Inlet. Period. It was way too humiliating. Besides, like she told Summer, she liked not being judged everywhere she went.

"The only wedding dress I'm thinking of is the one Luke's grandmother is going to wear when she and Papa Harry take their vows in June," Summer replied.

Luke's grandmother and Summer's grandfather met and fell in love while both were residents at the same senior community last fall.

"I still can't believe they are waiting until June," Paige said. "They're not getting any younger."

"Papa Harry wants to make sure he observes a proper mourning period for Grandma Bonnie."

"Oh, jeez, Sum, I'm sorry," Paige said, feeling like a terrible friend for not considering Summer's grandmother, who only recently passed away from Alzheimer's. "I totally get that. It's sweet. Leave it to your grandfather to always do the honorable thing."

"You'll be home by then, right?"

"Yeah, of course. This gig is only until Whitney's mother is located."

"Hopefully it doesn't take much longer. Although, it gives you more time to get to know your dad and his new family," Summer, the eternal optimist, said. "Please tell me you're at least giving them a chance."

Paige thought back to the baby shower and the good time she had with the McAlisters. Their joyous reaction when she announced she'd be staying longer in Chances Inlet was unexpected. And kinder than she deserved. Even the tension between Paige and her dad had begun to thaw.

"I'm giving them more than a chance," she admitted to Summer. "In fact, Whitney and I are headed to a ballet class shortly that's being taught by Gavin's wife. Kate and her daughter will be there, too. Later, we are all going out for the weekly family dinner."

Just as Paige expected, her friend's face melted into a goofy smile. "I'm so glad. You need to be surrounded by nice people right now. I can tell it has already done you some good. You deserve it."

Whitney wandered into the study, her ballet shoes in her hand.

"I guess someone is ready to put her dancing shoes on." Paige pulled Whitney in for a hug. "Whitney, can you say hi to my friend, Summer?"

The little girl gave Summer a shy wave.

"I'm so happy to meet you, Whitney," Summer said. "Are you taking good care of Paige? Is she eating all her veggies? Is she going to bed on time?"

Another one of those precious giggles escaped Whitney's lips. They were becoming more and more frequent lately.

"You girls have a great time at ballet." Summer blew them both a kiss. "Talk to you tomorrow."

***

"No word on Whitney's mom?" Ginger asked later that evening.

Paige, Ginger, and Kate were seated at a picnic table near the town square. Gavin and Alden were waiting in line for ice cream with Whitney and Emily. Patricia and Paige's dad were taking a stroll along the city pier.

"Nothing definite," Paige replied. "He called me on the way over. The private investigator told him she has a credible lead she's tracking down, but she wasn't ready to share details with Tanner until she had more information. He's pretty optimistic they'll locate her this week."

Ginger sighed. "Darn. I really want to give Whitney a part

in the spring recital. It's not for another six weeks and these girls have been working on it for months now. But Whitney is so talented, she'd be able to learn any dance quickly."

"Is there a small part you can put her in?" Kate asked. "One that wouldn't take away from the final performance if Whitney isn't there?"

"That's a good idea." Ginger seemed to mull it over. "And it wouldn't leave me open to complaints from the other moms if I suddenly gave a newcomer a primo part."

"I guess the real question is, will Tanner give her up once mom reappears?" Kate aimed a pointed look at Paige.

She shrugged. "I don't think he knows what his plan is." She knew he would always have a role in Whitney's life. What type and how much of a role depended on Whitney's AWOL mother.

"Given his touring schedule, it would be very hard to keep things as is," Ginger said.

"Why not?" Kate gestured toward Paige. "He's got the perfect nanny. And they do make an adorable little threesome."

Ginger smacked Kate on the arm. "Ignore her. She want's everyone to find their happy ever after here in Chances Inlet."

"Hello? It's the town of second chances, remember?" Kate countered. "And if it means Paige sticks around here forever, then why not?"

Paige took a sip of her wine. She was well aware this little peaceful interlude in her life was temporary. Soon, she'll need to figure out what comes next. What her career path should be. She did know her new life wasn't waiting for her back in Chicago. Or Iowa. As much as she belittled Chances Inlet, the place—and its residents—was beginning to grow on her.

"The public schools are always looking for teachers," Ginger suggested. "Perhaps there are openings in Chances Inlet."

"That's a great idea," Kate agreed.

It was a great idea. One Paige considered only yesterday. If not for that pesky part about the school district checking her employment record, she'd pursue it.

Summer insisted Paige give up teaching altogether and look in a whole new direction. It was the best way to keep her past buried. It irked Paige that her friend was right. That she'd been the one punished while Jon got off scot-free. By giving her heart to that scumbag, she'd derailed the only career she ever envisioned for herself. For Paige, nurturing children to discover their love of books, of writing, and learning brought her a great sense of satisfaction. She couldn't imagine doing anything else.

"Evening, ladies."

The three women waved to Denise who was locking up the bookstore.

"Are you and Lou taking a day off tomorrow?" Kate tilted her chin to the sign in the door announcing the shop would be closed the following day.

"Yes." Denise didn't look too excited about it. "We've got an appointment in Raleigh we both need to be at."

"Something fun, I hope." Ginger smiled at the older woman. Denise didn't return it.

"You don't have anyone who can keep the store open for you?" Paige asked even though she already knew the answer. Last week, she'd been pressed into service to help with customers when Lou and Denise became overrun after the reading.

"It's just the two of us." Denise cleared her throat. "We are all each other has."

Based on things Denise said the first day Paige visited the store, she knew they couldn't afford to hire anyone else, much less shut down their business for a day.

"I worked for an indie bookstore in college. They used the same software for their register. I'd be happy to help you out tomorrow. If you're okay with Whitney coming, too."

What was she doing? But it was too late to take back her offer because Denise's eyes were already brimming with tears.

"You'd do that?" the other woman asked.

Paige shrugged. "The weather looks like a washout for the pool or beach tomorrow. What better way to spend a rainy day than surrounded by books?"

Denise threw her arms around Paige's neck. "I'll leave the keys and instructions with Bernice. She'll meet you back here at ten tomorrow, if that's okay?"

"That's perfect. Whitney and I will be here. Don't you worry about a thing."

"Thank you, Paige. You're a lifesaver." Denise wiped her eyes. "I better get home and let Lou know the good news. She'll appreciate it."

"I'll walk with you," Kate said, her tone not allowing for argument.

"That was sweet of you," Ginger said. She rubbed her hand along her belly. "Any chance you're qualified to teach ballet?"

Paige laughed. "Not a one. Why? Are you worried the baby will arrive before classes end for the year?"

"No. Audra's got things covered. And if this little girl inside me has any ballet chops at all, she'll know to stay inside until after the spring performance. But Tiny Dancers has become so popular that we are turning potential students away. We need to hire another instructor to fulfill all the requests for our summer dance camp. Not to mention before the fall session."

"I'm sure you'll find someone. I mean who wouldn't want to dance with the villainous Destiny Upchurch from *Saints and Sinners*," Paige teased.

"Aunt Ginger," Emily said when she and the others arrived back at the picnic table. "Mom says sticking out your tongue at another person is undignified."

TANNER FINISHED up his second round of the tournament with a seventy-two, putting him four shots under par and in third place. He was confident in his game going into the weekend.

"Excellent round today, Tanner." His mother fell into step beside him as they headed to the clubhouse. "You didn't let that bogey on the front nine rattle you."

"I'll say," Sonny said from behind them. "He rattled off birdies on the three holes after that."

The caddy and Blythe Gillette had been busting each other's chops all week now, and Tanner was tired of listening to it.

Of course, his mother had to get in the last word. "I'm not sure I would have used the five-iron—"

Tanner turned to both of them and held up his hands. "Enough. Mum, I appreciate the support, I really do. I select my own clubs based on Sonny's excellent advice and that's not going to change. If you have notes or suggestions on the course, I'm happy to go over them with you later." She'd been leaving detailed strategy notes under his door all week. "Right now, though, I'm going to grab a hot shower and a cold beer. I'll see you at dinner." He kissed his mum on the cheek.

Sonny followed him into the men's locker room.

"She might have been right about the five-iron," the caddy shocked him by admitting.

Tanner shook his head and opened his locker. The screen of his mobile phone was lit up with multiple messages. All of them from the P.I. in Las Vegas. *Call me, ASAP,* the last one read.

He sank down on the bench. "Sonny, I think I'm going to need that beer before my shower."

The P.I. picked up before the phone even rang.

"Tell me everything," Tanner demanded.

"Her name is Donella Barber. At the time Whitney was conceived she was a dancer in a Broadway review show at one of the casinos here in Las Vegas. She and your brother were involved for at least five months, as far as I can tell."

Tanner pinched the bridge of his nose. There went his theory of Whitney being the result of a weekend fling.

"He rented an apartment for her shortly before the relationship ended," the P.I. continued. "She left before the lease ran out, however."

"Left for where?"

"It's hard to hide a pregnancy in a skimpy showgirl costume, so she returned to L.A. She took a job at a dance studio there. By all accounts, things were going well. Donella and Whitney lived in a garage apartment in Burbank until she lost her job several months ago."

"How did she lose her job?"

"The studio director wasn't very forthcoming with information other than she was fired for cause. He did say it was a hard decision for him because she was well-liked among the students."

"Where did they go from there?" Tanner was almost afraid to ask.

"Unfortunately, where most homeless people end up, living in their cars."

Tanner's stomach began to roll.

"She worked several jobs at various fast-food chains. The manager of the last place told me he let her go because she had a drug problem."

"What?" Tanner leaned his head back against his locker.

"Her former landlady told me she kept Donella on as long as she could. But the landlady needed the income to support herself. She's still storing Donella's stuff in her garage for free. Last month, Donella came to pick up some things—mostly for Whitney. Donella told the landlady she was going to do whatever it took to get her life back on track."

"All addicts say that," Tanner said with disappointment.

He'd hoped Donella could play a role in Whitney's life. Now he wasn't so sure.

"The thing is, Tanner, I think she's trying to do just that."

"What do you mean?"

"Mail was still being delivered to her apartment. There are multiple letters from various in-patient treatment centers. It looks like she checked herself into a drug rehab program after she left Whitney with you."

As soon as I get my life together, I'll be back for her.

Could that be what she meant in the note she left with Whitney? She was getting her life together in rehab?

"Can you track her down?" Tanner asked.

"I've got inquiries at all the centers she received mail from. They all have strict patient confidentiality policies, though. It's going to be hard to get anyone to go on the record and admit she's there."

Tanner huffed out a breath. "Those places aren't free," he said. "How does a homeless woman with no income pay for that kind of treatment?"

The P.I. hesitated before answering. "The week before she dropped Whitney off with you, she cashed in one hundred thousand dollars in stock."

"Stock? What the hell kind of stock would she have?"

"It was Gillette Industry stock, Tanner."

Well, fuck.

CHAPTER TWENTY-ONE

THE BELL above the door jingled cheerily as a family left the bookstore with a puzzle and several books. Paige re-stacked the books they left behind while Denise worked on the computer. After their appointment in Raleigh, Lou hadn't been back to the bookstore. Paige had taken to dropping in each morning under the pretext of picking up a book for Whitney. She ended up staying several hours, helping Denise out.

"It looks like I'll need you to fill out a W-9," Denise said.

"Not a chance," Paige replied. "I should be paying *you* for letting Whitney and me hang out here." She peered at Whitney who was quietly coloring at the little table in the children's section. Gladys sat in the chair next to her.

"Good thing then, I guess," Denise said. "Because I don't know how long I'll be able to keep the doors to this place open."

Paige feared as much. The little bookstore had been a balm to her soul since arriving in Chances Inlet. She'd been tossing ideas around in her head for the past several days. "You don't have to throw in the towel just yet. There are tons of small business loans out there—especially for female-owned businesses."

The bell jingled again when Kate entered. It was odd seeing carefree, fun-loving Kate wearing a white medical coat. She seemed to adopt a whole new personality when she stepped into her medical director's shoes. Kate had been stopping by the bookstore every day this week, disappearing with Denise for a walk around the square.

"There are also lots of celebrities who are well-off in Chances Inlet," Paige continued. "Maybe one of them would be happy to invest?"

Denise exchanged a look with Kate. "It's not the money," she said. "I was married before Lou. To a very generous man who kept me safe and accepted me for who I was. He left me with enough money to maintain four bookstores."

"But you said you couldn't open one in Manhattan because of the high rents?"

"Yeah, I didn't want to pay rent to anyone else." Denise scoffed. "I wanted to own. Lou isn't aware of the scope of my trust fund. She loves the idea of her and I growing old running this place together. Just the two of us." Denise cleared her throat. "Of leaving behind a legacy, which would be impossible in New York City. She fell in love with this town the first hour we visited. I thought, what better spot to open a bookstore than a welcoming place like Chances Inlet? This shop is a labor of love from me to her. I wanted to make all her dreams come true for as long as possible."

Denise's words were starting to trigger alarm bells for Paige. "But?"

Reaching for a tissue to wipe up her sudden onslaught of tears, Denise nodded at Kate.

"Lou has brain cancer," Kate said matter-of-factly. "It's been in remission for over two years. The doctors were hopeful that a new drug regimen they prescribed for her was shrinking the tumors." Kate left the rest unsaid.

Whitney suddenly appeared at the counter, wrapping her arms around Denise's legs.

"You are a little angel, you know that?" Denise managed between sniffles. She lifted Whitney up for a fierce hug. "I want to spend as much time with Lou as we have left. There isn't any time to hire and train a manager, much less additional employees."

"No need to do that. You already have one." Paige arched an eyebrow at the woman.

"B-but you are only in Chance's Inlet temporarily. Until—" she leaned her head toward Whitney.

"I haven't got anything lined up for the summer yet," Paige said. It was only a matter of time before they located Donella.

Kate opened her mouth, presumably to protest that Paige was nannying for her, before quickly closing it when Paige aimed a scathing look her way.

"Lou would love knowing her baby was in the hands of someone who reveres books as much as she does," Denise said with a watery smile. "And, frankly, I was worried about being closed during tourist season. Of course, I might not be away that long." She hiccupped a sob. "It's a big commitment, Paige. Think about it overnight and let me know tomorrow."

"I'm not going to change my mind. Take as long as you want. Tell Lou her legacy is safe with me."

"WELL, that explains Whitney's mad dance skills." Paige was curled up on the sofa in the study staring at Tanner's image on her cellphone. Despite the crazy news about Whitney's mother, he looked relaxed and ready for the final round of the tournament the next day where he would be starting in second place.

"Ginger was right. She probably did learn to dance as soon as she learned to walk."

"Mmhmm. I just hope that's all she learned from her mother."

"Hopefully the P.I. is correct, and she's getting help. Based on Whitney's behavior and demeanor, everything points to Donella being a decent mother."

"Still, I'm having my lawyers petition the court to give me sole custody."

What?

Paige's breathing hitched. Was he serious? Did he realize what he was doing? He said he'd always be a part of Whitney's life. She took that to mean he'd be supporting her. Not actively raising her.

"But what will happen if Donella resurfaces? And she reveals you're not Whitney's father?"

"My name is on the birth certificate. Legally, the only person who can dispute that is dead."

Paige wasn't so sure. A mother's love for her child was a force to be reckoned with. Donella might have a thing or two to say when she returned. *If she returned.* Either way, Tanner was taking on more than he realized.

"You've got tournaments scheduled for nearly every week this summer. How can you possibly fit Whitney into your life?"

"That's where you come in. I was hoping I could convince you to stay in Chances Inlet for a few months longer until I can work out something permanent."

Continue hiding in sleepy Chances Inlet where no one knows her shame? Keep playing house with the sexy golfer? *Yes, please.*

She ignored the alarm bells clanging in her head.

"Actually, you don't need to convince me. I'm already staying for the summer. But I took another job in town."

"Another job?"

She explained about Lou and Denise.

He shook his head. "Life is precious. And none of us has any idea how long we have in this world." He smiled softly at her. "That's an incredible gift you're giving two people you barely know. I have to say, for a woman who was hell-bent on getting out of Chances Inlet, you sure keep finding reasons to stay. Not that I'm complaining." He winked at her.

"Whitney can come to the shop with me these next few weeks," she replied, ignoring his flirting. "Cassidy Burroughs is going to help out when she returns to Chances Inlet at the end of the semester. It will all work out. You won't have to worry about Whitney at all this summer. You can concentrate on what's most important to you, playing golf."

When he didn't respond immediately, Paige couldn't help but feel as if she'd said something wrong.

"I better get to sleep," he said, eventually. "Will you make sure Whitney watches tomorrow?"

"Of course. Patricia is having a viewing party at the inn. Everyone will be there cheering you on."

"That's great. Night, Paige."

The abrupt end to their conversation had Paige feeling off-balance and restless. She wasn't going to lie to herself by nurturing the belief that her relationship with Tanner was anything more than it was: a fun fling while they shared a house. He was a man, after all. The lessons of her past relationships were seared into her brain.

And the pieces of her heart.

The out-of-this-world sex was simply an added benefit for both of them. She may as well enjoy it while she can. Besides, she reasoned, she can't be taken advantage of if she knows the expected outcome up front. And a guy like Tanner Gillette wasn't going to be interested in a woman like Paige for long.

No matter how desperately she wished it so.

Pouring herself a sip of his scotch, she carried the glass back to her bedroom. She quickly realized it was probably not the best idea. Its taste and smell reminded her so much of him that she'd likely toss and turn half the night.

She peeked in on Whitney. It had been several nights since the little girl called out for her mother in her sleep. Knowing what she now knew, Paige tried to imagine the fear Whitney must have felt living in a car for months. Had that been the trauma that stole her voice? Or was it her mother leaving her behind with a total stranger? She shivered. Or was it something worse she and Tanner didn't know about yet?

Paige tucked the covers snugly around Whitney and Gladys. "Your mom did what she thought was best for you," she whispered. "And she made the right choice. Tanner will keep you safe. And loved. He'll also find your mom for you. And then the words will come back to you."

"Why would you need more than one green jacket, anyway? How often would you wear it?"

Tanner laughed at Paige's inane question. She looked so innocent lying on top of him, her silky skin warming his. Her swollen lips turned up in a saucy grin. She rested her chin on top of her hands where she'd placed them on his chest. He knew her words were meant to distract him from being annoyed at finishing second at Augusta. Ironically, weeks ago, he would have been pissed at himself for not seizing the win. Except it was hoping he'd be able to lose himself inside of her once he got home that lessened the sting of not finishing first.

He arrived back in Chance's Inlet close to midnight. Their phone conversation from yesterday was still lingering in the back of his mind. He was ecstatic she was staying the summer in Chances Inlet. And not just because she'd be there for Whitney.

Every time he and Paige made love, he felt the connection between them grow stronger. The very idea should have scared him shitless. Only it didn't. Instead, he could feel the peace he'd been seeking since Tristan's death steadily grow within him.

There was a lick of dread nagging at him too, however. He couldn't get a read on whether Paige felt the same way. She seemed skittish about discussing their relationship. It was so unlike any woman he'd ever met. Tanner was confused where he stood with her.

Despite the late hour, she was waiting up for him in his study when he arrived home. No words were exchanged when she saw him. Instead, she wrapped her arms around his neck and kissed him soundly. The alluring woman tasted like scotch and sin and he damn near took her on the desk again.

They made it to his bed where they both poured all their unspoken feelings into worshiping the other. He realized he was worried for nothing. He didn't need to hash things out with Paige. She let him know her true feelings through her hands, her mouth, and her body. He'd never felt surer about anything in his life.

"You don't get a second green jacket," he explained. "The jacket stays at the club in Augusta and that's the only place you get to wear it. Unless you win and then you get to take it home with you for that year."

"Seriously?" She scrunched up her face. "That hardly seems fair. It's your prize for winning. You should get to keep it."

"Mmm." He kissed her nose. "Some people have a replica made, but it's not the same. There's something mystical and almost holy about the actual jacket, you know?"

"It comes with magic powers?"

He smacked her lightly on the ass.

"Or—" She placed her palms on the mattress above her shoulders and pushed herself up so her lips hovered over his.

"Is the jacket like an old lover you can't wait to get wrapped around your body?"

"There's no one else I'd want wrapped around my body besides you."

The words were out before he could stop them. He meant to keep things light. To not pressure her. To not scare her off.

Astonishment lit her blue eyes before a flash of something chased it away and she quickly shuttered her expression. She seemed unsure what to do next, so he wrapped his arms around her and gently curled her in against him. He was relieved when she settled her cheek against his chest again.

They were quiet for several long heartbeats.

"There's no shame in finishing second," she eventually said, effectively closing the door to any further elaboration on his comment.

He smoothed a hand over her hair. "Not as long as I'm still ranked number one in the world. That's all that matters to my father. For him, there's no point in doing something unless you are the best."

"The only way to impress your dad is to be number one?"

"I'm not sure I'll ever impress my father. But I would like him to take me seriously. If I finish the season at the top and win the cup, maybe he'll understand that my life choices weren't made just to embarrass him."

She stiffened beneath his palm. "Why would he think you just want to embarrass him?"

"Because at one time, I did just that. Not on purpose, mind you." He drew in a deep breath. "When I won at Augusta the first time, I was a twenty-four-year-old cocky jacksnipe who didn't bother to think before he spoke. Why should I? I was on top of the world. I was so excited to have the big magazines clamoring for interviews that I didn't consider the implications of the answers I gave."

She laid her hand over his heart. "Like what?"

The ugly memories flooded back making his stomach roll. "One particular interview veered off into subjects I wasn't well versed in. Like the effects on the environment caused by rapid development of large-scale communities."

"Like the ones your father develops?"

"Exactly like those. I naively spouted off what I thought the interviewer and readers wanted to hear." He groaned. "Big developers should do more to preserve our planet."

She rolled back onto his chest so she could look at him. "I doubt your father took that well."

"His first reaction was fairly tame until the protestors started picketing his development sites. One entire community had to be relocated. The loss of income was substantial. But it was the hit to my dad's reputation that caused the most damage. Up until I opened my big mouth, Gillette Industries never had a blemish on its record. If there's one thing my father hates more than anything, it's being caught off guard."

"Oh, Tanner. You were young, though. And you didn't have the years of experience your father did at the time. He should have cut you some slack."

He smiled at her. "You sound like Tristan. He spent three years acting as a buffer between my dad and me. It didn't help with my father's opinion when my golf game failed to live up to my early success."

She pressed a kiss to his neck. "And now you don't have your brother to run interference with your dad."

An uncomfortable lump formed in his throat. "I wonder sometimes if things would have been better for my family if it had been me in that chopper. Melinda would still have her husband. The boys would have their dad. My father would still have the son who made him proud."

Her eyes glistened with unshed tears. "Don't you dare talk like that, Tanner Gillette. You and I both know Tristan wasn't perfect, either. Far from it."

"To my parents, he always will be." He rubbed her arms with his palms. "Donella cashed a hundred grand worth of Gillette stock right before she disappeared."

She blinked in surprise. "Really? Do you think she got that from Tristan?"

"I don't know where else she would get it."

"Wow. That's even more damning evidence that he knew about Whitney, isn't it?" Her voice sounded as disappointed as he felt.

"Yeah. All indications are that he did. And he paid Donella off with stock."

She curled against his chest once again. "Don't you dare ever think the wrong brother died in that crash."

The fierceness of her words both surprised and delighted him. He brushed a kiss to the crown of her head. He and Whitney were going to be all right. As long as they both had Paige in their lives.

CHAPTER TWENTY-TWO

THE DAYS WERE GETTING LONGER and warmer as spring sped into summer. Denise moved Lou to a beach house across the Intercoastal Waterway in Magnolia Bay. It had a private beach and view of the lighthouse beside the Coast Guard station. Paige and Whitney visited once a week bringing with them food prepared by Patricia and tales from the bookstore.

Tanner crisscrossed the country playing in a tournament nearly every week in order to maintain his number one ranking. The P.I. continued her search for Donella, but she hadn't turned up yet. In the meantime, Tanner's lawyers got a judge to grant him full custody of Whitney. Donella paid a huge price for abandoning her child. Whitney seemed happy enough with Paige and Tanner, but the child still had not spoken a single word.

Summer wasn't nearly as disappointed as expected when Paige didn't return for her concert. "Chances Inlet looks good on you. You seem more and more like the old Paige every time we talk. I'm happy you're doing something you love and reconnecting with your dad."

Paige wanted to argue that the old Paige—the one who was

used and abused routinely—no longer existed. New Paige was here to stay. And she was enjoying a new career she never imagined, a man who made her feel valued and life in a place far from her past mistakes.

As for her relationship with her father, it remained pretty much status quo. Neither of them wanted to ruin things by actually talking, so they didn't. Still, he stopped by the store nearly every day, either to take Whitney to tea at the inn or to rehearsals for the big Founder's Day show. Most mornings he popped in with coffee for Paige and a donut for Whitney.

The streets in town were bustling as tourists flocked in for the long holiday weekend and the Founder's Day celebrations. Bernice somehow talked Tanner into being the Grand Marshal of the parade, which meant he was in town for the weekend. It was his first weekend home this month, and he wanted to spend as much of it with Paige and Whitney as he could. Cassidy was minding the bookstore while Tanner and Paige took in Whitney's dress rehearsal at the ballet studio.

"Whit, you are going to be the prettiest butterfly ever to grace the skies of Chances Inlet." Tanner gave her a fist bump.

"I think this calls for tea and cookies." Paige helped Whitney put her backpack on. Tanner gently settled Gladys inside. They each took one of the little girl's hands as they strolled the crowded sidewalks. Every five steps, they'd raise their hands, lifting a giggling Whitney up into the air. Passersby smiled at her adorable laughter.

"Baby girl!" a woman shrieked from across the town square.

"Momma!"

Paige nearly tripped, she was so startled by the sound of Whitney's voice. The little girl tugged her hands free of Paige and Tanner's grip before racing across the lawn of the square straight into the arms of a slight woman with impeccable posture. Beside Paige, Tanner stood so still, it was as if he was in a trance. Slipping her arm through his, she gave him an encouraging squeeze. The move propelled him into motion until he was practically dragging Paige across the green.

"Go easy on her, Tanner," Paige pleaded. "Especially in front of Whitney."

Donella was sloppily kissing Whitney's cheeks by the time Tanner and Paige stopped in front of them. Whitney giggled when her mother pulled Gladys from the backpack and kissed her, too. There was no mistaking their relationship. Whitney had her mother's unique eyes. And if her mom's beauty was any indication, the little girl was destined to be a knockout in a few short years.

The love between the two was abundantly apparent, as well. Not that Tanner noticed. He was too busy shooting stony glares at the woman before shoving his hands in his pockets.

Whitney reached an arm toward them. "This is Paige," she told her mother.

Paige was still a little shellshocked hearing the child speak in complete sentences.

"She's my friend," Whitney continued.

The smile Donella gave Paige was equal parts wary and embarrassed. "Thank you," she said. "Thank you for taking care of my baby girl. I hope she didn't give you any trouble."

"No trouble at all," Paige replied with a reassuring smile. "She's a sweetheart."

Paige nudged Tanner, hoping he would keep things pleasant.

"She missed her mother, though," he added. "How do I even know you're her?"

Whitney's eyes went wide. The unfamiliar anger in Tanner's tone startled the poor child, causing her to cling tightly to her mother's neck. For her part, Donella lifted her shoulders and straightened her spine, a momma bear prepared to do battle.

"I deserve that," she told Tanner. "But I did what I had to do. I don't expect you to understand right now, because frankly, there are parts of this story I don't even understand. I'd like an opportunity to tell my side of things before we go home."

"Home? Whitney *is* home," Tanner practically growled. "Her home is in Chances Inlet. With her father."

Donella blanched. "You're not—"

"You should have thought of that before you put my name on the birth certificate and abandoned her on my doorstep. The court granted me full custody weeks ago."

Tears pooled in Whitney's eyes and her chin began to wobble. Paige was furious at Tanner's tactless assault. She put her hand beneath Donella's elbow when the woman began to wobble. Tanner stood resolute with his arms crossed over his chest, the asshat.

Paige rolled her eyes at him.

"Why don't we take this discussion somewhere private." She gestured to the tourists strolling through town, several of whom were gawking at Tanner. "We were on our way to have tea at the inn," Paige said to Donella. She gave Whitney's arm a comforting pat. "Please join us. Whitney loves Miss Patricia's cookies."

She steered mother and daughter in the direction of the inn, not really caring if Tanner followed or not. He was letting his ego and his emotions about Tristan get the better of him. As much as he thought he was protecting Whitney, he wasn't. He couldn't simply cut Donella out of her daughter's life. Like she said, there were two sides to this story. And Paige, for one, really wanted to hear Donella's version of events. She suspected the other woman might be as much a victim as she was with Jon.

"Whitney is an incredible little dancer." When she peeked back, Paige couldn't decide if she was relieved or not to see Tanner following along behind them. She tried to distract Whitney from the tension surrounding them by filling the air with chatter. "She has a part in the performance this weekend at Founder's Day."

Donella's face lit up. "Do you, baby girl? What part are you dancing?"

Paige was surprised when Whitney looked to her for encouragement before answering.

"A butterfly," Whitney replied softly.

"Ooo," Donella cooed. "I'll bet you're the prettiest butterfly in the corps."

Wanting to hear more of Whitney's voice, Paige encouraged her to keep talking. "Tell your mom how you're a working girl now."

She was rewarded with a giggle from Whitney who went on to tell her mother about the bookstore and how she and Gladys "worked" there. By the time they reached the inn ten minutes later, both mother and daughter appeared to be more relaxed.

Tanner clearly was not, however. He stomped up the steps of the veranda behind them. Patricia's eyebrows curved up slightly when she caught sight of Whitney in Donella's arms. To her credit, she sized up the situation immediately.

"The music room is open if you'd like to enjoy your tea in there," she offered.

Paige donned a grateful smile before mouthing "thank you."

"Whitney, how about you come to the kitchen with me and pick out some cookies for everyone?" Patricia held her hand out.

The little girl hesitated until Donella pressed a kiss to her forehead. "Go on now. Momma is not going anywhere. I'll never leave you again, baby girl."

Her tone was a clear warning to Tanner. Paige followed him and Donella into the music room and firmly closed the door. Donella circled to the other side of the grand piano, effectively putting it between her and a brooding Tanner.

Paige sighed wearily. "Look, this is a conversation the two

of you need to have in private. Before I slip out, though, both of you need to remember you were taken advantage of by the same man."

Tanner pinned her with a flinty stare.

"A man you both loved," she continued with a softer tone. "And lost. But who left you with a precious gift in that little girl. You need to work together to do the right thing by Whitney. She's depending on you. On both of you."

She moved to leave the room when Tanner reached out and locked his fingers around her arm. Despite his firm grip, he was trembling. He slowly slid his fingers down her arm until he'd laced them through hers. When she glanced up into his eyes, she saw something she didn't expect.

Fear.

Her heart ached so badly for him, it felt like someone was reaching in and wringing it out. He'd lost his twin. Now, he was determined to do everything in his power not to lose Whitney, too. She got that. He simply needed to approach this meeting with the same finesse he employed on the green. Not as if he were driving the ball off the tee.

She leaned in to brush a kiss along his cheek. "Hear her out. You're not giving up Whitney by allowing her mother to have a role in her life."

He swallowed harshly before jerking his head up and down once. Paige pulled her hand free and quietly left the room.

TANNER IMMEDIATELY RECOGNIZED what attracted his twin to Donella Barber. It wasn't just her exotic eyes or her fascinating beauty. It was Donella's backbone.

The muscle his twin exercised the most was always his brain. No one loved a good debate more than Tristan. He didn't have time for the vapid socialites who didn't dare offer up a differing opinion. Tristan was always seeking a verbal sparring partner. Someone who could dish it out and take it just as easily. It certainly didn't hurt if she was sexy as sin. The woman standing in front of Tanner with her spine ramrod straight and challenge in her provocative eyes fit the bill perfectly.

Tanner was still trying to wrap his head around why Tristan never mentioned this woman. He and Tristan told each other everything. Or so he thought. Her humble life or the color of her skin wouldn't have mattered to Tanner or his parents. Blythe and Marcus had not raised their boys to be elitists. The only thing that would have mattered was Tristan's love for her.

If Tristan had in fact loved Donella.

His temples began to throb with the beginnings of a migraine. He slumped down in the nearest chair. "Where have you been?"

"Wow. You want to start at the end?" Donella shrugged. "Okay. I'll do it your way. I was at the Everwell Substance Abuse Center on Black Mountain."

For fucks sake.

"All this time you were barely two hours away?"

She pursed her lips. "I wasn't going any farther away from my baby."

He shook his head. "Was there no one else you could have left Whitney with? No other family?"

"My family is not the sort that you unexpectedly drop off another mouth to feed."

Lovely.

"I've been on my own since I was seventeen," she explained, her tone implying it was none of his business, but she was humoring him anyway. "I won a scholarship to a college dance program in Las Vegas where I made my own way."

"How old are you?"

"Twenty-four."

Jesus. She was young.

"Can we circle back to the rehab? What were you doing there?"

"Well, I wasn't dancing the tango," she quipped. "I was getting sober."

"And are you?" Even to his own ears, he sounded like a dick.

"Seventy-two days." She came out from behind the piano she'd been using as a shield and took a seat on the bench. "This might be easier if we started at the beginning."

Tanner lurched forward. "Did he know? Did my brother know about Whitney?"

Her eyes were suddenly glassy. "I never told him."

He slammed his eyes shut against the painful light, resting the back of his head against the wall. It hurt him deeply to know that all these weeks he'd been accusing his brother of abandoning Whitney.

"We met at one of the elite poker games the casino held for high rollers," she began.

Tanner jerked his lids up. "Tristan didn't gamble." At least, not the Tristan he knew.

She smiled fondly. "I know. He was there with friends and bored to tears. I was dancing in the Broadway review, but I would sometimes pick up shifts as a cocktail waitress for extra money. My tuition was covered, but things like food, books, gas, and car insurance were not."

He nodded.

"He wasn't exactly flirting with me, yet somehow, we got to talking and the next thing we knew were discussing the big libel trial that was all over the crime podcasts. I was surprised a successful businessman like him paid any attention to those sorts of things."

Tanner leaned forward again. "Is that when he introduced himself as me? As Tanner Gillette?"

Her forehead pleated. "No. We didn't exchange names. I

knew him as Mister Gillette only from the name on the bar tab. Honestly, I never expected to see him again after that evening."

"But you did."

"He came back the next night. And again, the night after that. He took me to a late dinner." She smiled softly.

"And that's when he told you his name was Tanner."

"I guess so," she replied testily. "Does it really matter what name he used? He was lying to me the entire time we were together!"

"I'm just trying to figure out why he did it!" he fired back.

"That makes two of us."

A tense silence followed. Tanner felt like the biggest ass for upsetting her. What Tristan did to this woman was much more egregious than impersonating his twin brother. Why couldn't he let it go?

"We were together for five months," she eventually continued. "Each one better than the last."

"He set you up in an apartment."

She arched a delicate eyebrow at him. "He signed the lease. *I* paid the rent. I was living in a group house with no privacy before then."

Tanner recalled the P.I. reporting the apartment she shared with Tristan was nothing lavish.

"Why did you two split?"

"I didn't realize we had 'split.'" She used her fingers to make air quotes. "He said he had business back in Australia. That he'd be gone for a month. Except he didn't come back. He'd been ghosting me for three weeks when I discovered I was pregnant. A month later, I discreetly asked one of the poker players where your brother was hiding. I got my answer when the guy showed me his engagement photo." She made a tsking sound. "So much for believing in fairy tales."

Disgusted by his brother's behavior, Tanner went to stand in front of the French doors leading out to the veranda. In fairness, if she was telling the truth, Tristan never knew about the baby, so he couldn't be faulted for not doing the right thing. Except—

He spun around to face her. "Where did you get the hundred grand in Gillette stock?"

Donella sighed. "Would you believe me if I said it simply showed up in the mail?"

"No."

Her laugh lacked any humor. "A year and a half ago, about four months after the accident—"

"Accident? What accident?"

She sighed. "A slip and fall at the studio. I herniated a disk in my back. For months, I could barely walk without discomfort much less dance."

"The owners of the dance studio should have compensated you."

"Yeah, they compensated me by showing me the door."

"Bastards!"

This time her laugh was genuine. "My thoughts exactly. Anyway, the doctors told me surgery would help alleviate the pain. Except government insurance only covers the bare minimum. My out-of-pocket expenses would be ten times what I had in my bank account."

The pieces of the puzzle began to fall into place. "So, you went back to Las Vegas to ask Tristan for help?"

"I thought at the very least we were friends," she said quietly. "I would have paid him back. And I wasn't planning on using Whitney as leverage, either. I never intended to tell him about her. He'd moved on. At that point I was too scared he might take her away from me."

She shot him an ugly look. Tanner refused to cringe. He would do what was best for his brother's daughter.

"Imagine my surprise when I found out Tanner Gillette was some hotshot golfer while the developer of Silver Canyon was his twin, Tristan. And oh, by the way, I had the pleasure of meeting his gorgeous and very pregnant wife."

Tanner dropped back down into the chair he vacated minutes before and dragged his hands through his hair. "And then you ran."

"Yep. All the way back to L.A. where I filled the prescription for opioids that the doctor insisted were the next best thing to surgery."

"You became addicted to them."

"Believe it or not, it's relatively easy to do."

He swore violently. "You shouldn't have been forced into that situation."

"Not all of us get to live the charmed life you do."

Her acerbic response made him angry again. "You still haven't explained the stock."

"Yeah, the stock." She puffed out a breath. "It came in the mail about a month after I returned from Las Vegas. There wasn't a note accompanying it. The only thing on the envelope was the return address for Silver Canyon. I honestly didn't think it was real. When I called there and asked for your brother, they told me he had died." She swallowed roughly. "I kept thinking of his wife and her unborn baby."

"Babies," Tanner said. "Melinda had twins."

Donella gasped. "God bless her." She wiped her brow. "I never intended to use the stock until Whitney went to college. But then I realized she'd likely never get to college living in a car with a mom who was fast becoming a junkie. I told myself that getting clean was the most important use of Whitney's money."

Tanner snapped his gaze up to stare dumbfounded at Donella. "Whitney's money?"

She nodded. "The stock was in her name."

He slumped back against the wall. "How can that be?"

Donella shrugged.

Could Tristan have somehow found out about Whitney? If he hadn't been killed, would his brother have done more for his daughter? Or was it hush money as he suspected? A one-time payment for his sins? He clenched his fists. Tanner wanted to believe with all his heart his brother would have acknowledged Whitney. Provided for her. And he would expect Tanner to do the same.

"Why bring her to me?" he asked, genuinely curious.

"As you so eloquently pointed out when we first met, your name is on her birth certificate. It made the most sense. If something happened to me, she'd be with her other legal guardian."

"That was a huge risk," he said. "How did you know I'd keep her?"

That soft smile was back on her lips. "Because despite how things turned out between us, your brother was a good man. A decent man. You share his DNA. It wasn't a risk to believe you would be a good and decent man, too."

CHAPTER TWENTY-THREE

"How do you think it's going in there?" Paige whispered to Patricia after twenty minutes of stalling in the kitchen.

"I couldn't say." Patricia glanced over at Whitney who was carefully arranging cookies on a plate while chatting with Gladys. "But for her sake, I hope they can work things out. Did her mother say where she's been?"

"She had a medical issue, I believe." Paige avoided the other woman's perceptive gaze.

"Something tells me there is a lot more to that story," Patricia said.

Paige nodded but didn't elaborate further. She wasn't sure how Tanner wanted to spin Donella's reappearance. And she certainly would never reveal any of his secrets.

"How will this impact you?"

Patricia's question caught Paige off guard. "What do you mean?"

"Well, Whitney isn't going to need a nanny any longer. Will you go back to Chicago?"

Everything happened so fast earlier, Paige hadn't given a thought to how Donella's return would affect her. Patricia was right, though. Her reason for living at Tanner's was out the proverbial window. At least the reason she presented to everyone.

Would Tanner want her to stay when he no longer needed her to look after Whitney? Would she be foolish to stay if he asked? Or was their relationship one of those "right time, right place" deals? If she was smart, she'd hightail it back to Chicago and spare her heart any further damage.

A summa cum laude degree from Northwestern didn't make her smart enough, apparently. "I made a commitment to Denise and Lou to keep the bookstore going for them this summer."

"Well, you know you always have a place to stay here." The corners of Patricia's mouth twitched. "Unless you have different reasons for staying with Tanner?"

Paige could feel her cheeks burning. *Great.* The entire town was likely gossiping about them. Could she survive being the subject of another round of disdain and ridicule when the relationship fell apart? Fortunately, Paige's father entered through the screen door, saving her from any further discussion.

"Who is the adorable little magpie?" He lifted Whitney up into his arms, clucking her under the chin. "Why have you been depriving us of your beautiful voice all these months?"

Whitney giggled. "Momma is back."

Astonishment flashed briefly in his eyes. "That so?"

All three nodded.

"We're putting together a welcome platter of cookies while she and Tanner talk," Patricia said, pointedly.

"Ah," he replied.

Donella appeared in the doorway. "You called the cops on me?"

"Momma!" Whitney practically jumped from Paige's father's arms into Donella's.

"Heavens no," Patricia laughed. "This is my husband."

"This is Sheriff," Whitney added. "He's funny."

Paige swallowed a surprised laugh of her own. She'd never heard her father referred to as funny.

"Donella Barber, this is Patricia McAlister-Hollister. She's the innkeeper here," Paige explained. "And this is her husband, my father, Sheriff Lamar Hollister."

Her dad held out his hand. "Pleasure to meet you, Donella. And it has been a pleasure getting to know your beautiful daughter."

"You didn't have to lock her up for anything?" Donella teased.

Whitney giggled.

"Not even for littering," he replied with a wide grin.

"You always make Momma proud, baby girl." Donella kissed her daughter.

"Come, sit and have some tea." Patricia gestured to the kitchen table. "You're welcome to join the guests in the salon, but family takes tea in here. And, well, Whitney is practically family."

Donella looked at them incredulously. "Gladys, we're not in California anymore." She lowered Whitney into one of the chairs at the table. "Seriously, this town and you people aren't like anything I've ever known before. I thought places like this only existed in the movies."

Patricia set the plate of cookies Whitney put together on the table. "Nonsense. You've just been living in the wrong places."

"Indeed," Donella replied.

Whitney held out another plate of cookies. "These are for Tanner." She turned to Paige with a questioning look on her face.

"He was on his way to the gazebo when I came in," her dad said.

Paige took the plate from Whitney. "I'll take them to him, honey. You catch up with your mommy."

Tanner was sitting on the steps of the gazebo, elbows on his knees as he stared off toward the bluff above the ocean. Midas ran back and forth dropping a tennis ball at his feet. Tanner absently chucked it into the yard for the dog to chase.

When Paige approached, Tanner slid over to make room for her on the step. He took a peanut butter cookie off the plate and munched on it. Paige settled for a lemon bar. Midas lost interest in fetch after a few tosses, disappearing toward the cool shade of the garage.

"She never told him about Whitney." The relief she expected to hear in his voice wasn't there. "But the stock was in Whitney's name."

Talk about mic drops.

"How can that be?"

He shrugged before reaching for a chocolate chip cookie. "Beats the hell out of me."

"Do you think she's telling the truth?" Paige hated herself for having to ask, but her ability to trust was a little faulty.

"My gut says yes." He swallowed roughly. "Someone knows the truth about Whitney, though. Or knew."

She leaned her cheek against his shoulder. "What happens now?"

Tanner sighed. "We're still fine-tuning what Whitney's future will look like. I'll remain her legal father, providing for her just as Tristan would have done had he gotten the chance. We decided that no one needs to know any differently for now. If Whitney asks when she's older, we'll tell her the truth."

Paige couldn't help the ridiculous grin that formed. "Look at you going all Daddy Warbucks."

"Who would have figured, right? Obviously, with my career, I can't be a full-time, hands-on dad. But I'm not handing her back completely into Donella's care until I know more. She's agreed to stick around Chances Inlet while we settle things. Best-case scenario, she can find a job nearby while she's here. That would be the easiest solution to me remaining a part of Whitney's life."

"Hm. I just might be able to help out with that."

He chuckled. "You already have Cassidy working at the bookstore. How many people are you going to put on Denise's payroll while she's not looking?"

"*I'm* not going to hire her. But Ginger and Audra are on the hunt for someone to teach at Tiny Dancers. Preferably in time for summer camp next month."

He jostled the shoulder she was leaning on. "Look at you going all fairy godmother on us." He leaned down and kissed the top of her head. "I'll go by the studio later and speak with Audra."

"Whitney needs her mother."

"Mmhmm." He threaded his fingers through hers.

"She needs you, too. I'm glad things finally worked out."

"Nothing is final yet. They'll both stay at my place for the time being. Donella refuses to be more than fifty feet from her child."

They both grew quiet, letting the lazy afternoon settle in around them like a comfortable blanket. The sound of a car door slamming, followed by Emily calling Whitney's name, brought them both back to reality.

"Didn't take long for word to get around," he said.

Paige untangled herself from Tanner, dusting off the seat of her shorts when she stood up. "I should go and grab my stuff from your place."

"Yeah." He stood, too. "Donella will want the room closest to Whit. I'll help you move your stuff into my room."

He took a few steps, turning back when Paige didn't follow.

"I'm not moving into your room, Tanner." The confusion and hurt in his eyes made it difficult to continue, but she was determined. "Sneaking around with a four-year-old in the house is relatively easy. But with another adult living there it will be sort of obvious."

"So? Who says we're sneaking around, anyway?"

"Then what are we doing?"

"What every grown-ass couple who are attracted to one another does!"

She chewed on her bottom lip. This was a lot easier when she'd been playing it out in her mind on the walk over. Mainly because he didn't get angry. He'd been like every other guy she dated and moved on to the next woman.

He shoved his hands into his pockets. She recognized it as his signature tell when he was anxious. "What's this about, Paige?"

"You don't need me anymore," she whispered.

"The hell I don't." He took a step closer.

She pinched her forehead. "I meant as a nanny for Whitney."

"Spit it out, Paige, before I pull you in my arms and prove to you how much *you* need *me* right here in full view of your father and his family."

"That's just it!" She stomped her foot. "I don't want them to know!"

He looked confused before the hurt settled back into his eyes. "You don't want them to know about us?"

"No! Yes!" She was messing this up royally. "I want my private life to be private. I don't want to be the subject of everyone's gossip in this town. And I certainly don't want you to be with me because I'm convenient. Because that is what everyone will think when you move on to someone else."

He shook his head as if to clear it. "Whoa! We'll circle back to the first part later." He drew his hands from his pockets as he closed the distance between them, cupping her face with his palms. "Paige Hollister, I'm not with you because you're 'convenient,' dammit. I'm with you because from the moment I met you, I've been drawn to you. And every moment I've been with you has only made me want you more. Why would I want anyone else?"

But do you mean it? The voices in her head were screaming at her.

The screen door slammed, followed by the shrieks of the two young girls racing across the lawn. Tanner swore. Paige backed out of his embrace.

"I think it might be best if I stay here. At the inn," she said.

He growled something unintelligible before holding up his hands. "You win. I will respect your wishes on this one. Stay at the inn. But know this, Paige. This is not a convenient fling for me. This is more. A hell of a lot more. And if it's the last thing I do, I intend to prove it to you."

The intensity of his words had her rocking back on her heels. He turned and grabbed a giggling Emily and Whitney under each of his arms and carried them to the swing.

AUDRA GREAVES GRINNED ear-to-ear as she shook Tanner's hand.

"Thank you, Audra," he said. "For giving her a chance. You're doing me a huge favor."

"Are you kidding? You're the one doing me a favor," the dance instructor replied. "I was beginning to fear I'd have to scale back on dance camp this year. On behalf of all the little girls of this town, thank you."

"I'm no dance expert. And I have only her word to go on with regard to her skills and her work ethic. Hopefully, she won't betray our trust."

"Having seen Whitney dance, I'm not worried about Donella's skill. And don't forget where we live. This is the home of second chances. We'll give Donella one and see what happens." Audra patted him on the shoulder. "I have a good feeling about this, though."

Tanner hoped she was right. He was headed out of the torpedo factory that housed the dance studio when Gavin poked his head out of the entry for McAlister Construction and Engineering.

"Hey, man. You look like a guy who could use a beer." Gavin opened the door wider to reveal his brother Miles and their friend, Will Connelly. They were sitting with their feet up on the coffee table watching baseball on TV.

"You just missed Ryan smoke a double into right," Will said as he handed Tanner a bottle of beer from a mini fridge in the corner.

"It this the new hide-out?" Tanner asked before unscrewing the top and taking a refreshing pull from the bottle.

"This weekend it is," Miles answered. "Every year, it seems more and more people flock to this event. There won't be a barstool open at Pier Pressure for the next five days."

"Which also means you won't have to be there kissing random babies and smiling for selfies," Gavin teased. "Because most of the patrons don't vote in this district."

Miles saluted his brother with his beer. "Here's to a night off."

"Don't let these two bullshit you," Will interjected. "Gavin is gonna be a dad any day now. He's got the jitters, so we're keeping him company."

"More like his hormonal wife kicked him out," Miles added. "He's been hovering over Ginger like a mother hen. Even when she tries to take a nap."

Gavin smirked at his brother. "I was simply checking to see if she was still breathing."

"And that's why she's up there now cuddling with Midas and not you," Miles joked.

Tanner and Will laughed while Gavin chugged from his bottle of water. He pointed at Will then Tanner. "Be glad neither of you had to go through this ridiculous stress the first time you became fathers."

The mood in the room was suddenly less lighthearted. Will Connelly had no idea he fathered a son until his now wife, Julianne, showed up looking for a transfusion to save Owen. Judging by the look on his face now, he would have preferred worrying over his pregnant wife than not knowing about being a dad. Luckily for him, he got a second chance when their daughter was born a few months ago.

Gavin groaned. "That was a dumbass thing to say. I'm sorry guys. I didn't mean it. I'm beginning to think I'm the one who is hormonal."

Will suddenly barked out a laugh. "Haven't I always said Gavin was more in touch with his feminine side?" He fist-bumped Miles before his expression sobered. "Becoming a dad is scary shit. No matter how it happens." He looked Tanner's way. "But I wouldn't trade it for anything else in the world."

Would Tanner? What the other men in the room didn't know was Whitney was not fully his flesh and blood. Will was right, though. As upending as it was to have a four-year-old dumped in his lap unexpectedly, he wouldn't go back and change anything.

Unless it would bring Tristan back.

Chances are, though, if Tristan had lived, Tanner would never have met Whitney. Never heard her infectious giggles or felt her small hand wrapped inside his. She was a part of him now. Forever.

The room grew quiet again and Tanner realized they were expecting him to comment.

"Sorry, mates. It's been a day." He raised his beer bottle in the air. "To fatherhood."

Will eyed him shrewdly. "I heard Whitney's mom showed

up today. I hope she had a good explanation for deserting her child."

Tanner tried not to flinch. He really needed to come up with some rote explanation for his situation with Whitney and Donella.

"Very similar to your experience, except she was the one with the medical emergency." It was the truth without revealing the whole truth.

"So she's sticking around?" Gavin asked.

Tanner nodded. "As a matter of fact, she'll be filling in with Audra while your wife is on maternity leave."

"No shit?" Gavin bumped his water bottle against Tanner's beer. "I swear Ginger planned to hold that child in until Audra found someone."

"Problem solved," Tanner said.

"How's that going to work?" Miles asked. "Having Whitney's mother around? I can imagine that might put a cramp in things with Paige."

Tanner paused with the beer bottle halfway to his lips. "'Things with Paige?'"

"Yeah. You and Paige." Miles wiggled his eyebrows.

The three men all wore knowing smiles. Tanner slammed his beer down on the coffee table before shooting to his feet. "Jesus. She was right. The whole damn town is gossiping about us." He dragged his fingers through his hair, swearing violently. "No wonder she ran."

It was Miles' turn to jump out of his chair. "Ran where exactly?" he demanded.

Tanner didn't like the guy's menacing tone. "To the inn. Not that it's any of your damn business."

"It is my business, Tanner. You do realize she's our sister, right?"

Gavin chuckled. "For someone who didn't want the sheriff

to marry our mother, you sure are quick to adopt his daughter."

"She's just as much a McAlister through marriage as your wife and mine," Miles argued. "And thus, under our protection. Mess her up, Tanner, and you'll answer to us."

Tanner wondered if Paige knew what she had with the McAlister family. He hoped by extending her stay even longer, she'd come to value her new siblings and trust them. Because something was definitely haunting her. He thought back to what the sheriff told him when she first arrived. He believed she'd been hurt. Badly, in his opinion. And her sudden about-face spoke volumes.

Maybe it was better she was at the inn. Their relationship evolved under unusual circumstances. Perhaps that was what was scaring her. He'd give her space. Just not a lot of time. Life was short. Tanner was already on the road away from her for weeks on end. He wasn't sure how long he could stay away knowing she was in the same town as him.

"Come on, bro," Gavin said. "I doubt Tanner did anything to hurt her on purpose. Paige is probably feeling a little jealous now that Whitney's mom is back in the picture."

"She's not 'back in the picture' that way," Tanner snapped. "Never was. Never will be." Let them think what they will, but it was true.

Miles pinned him with a glare the congressman probably thought was intimidating, only it didn't come close to the sheriff's.

"Good," Miles finally said. "Keep it that way."

"You're lucky I don't vote in this country," Tanner told him.

Will roared with laughter. Miles jotted something down on a slip of paper and handed it to Tanner.

"What's this?"

"The code to the clubhouse." Miles gestured to his campaign office. "You've got three females in your life now. You're going to need a place to decompress." He looked Tanner in the eye. "Paige seems like she's got a good head on her shoulders. Give her a chance to process things. You're one of the good guys. Deep down she already knows that." He settled back into his leather chair. "Of course, a good grand gesture never hurt," he added with a wink.

Tanner stuffed the code into his pocket before turning to leave. "I better go deliver the good news to Donella about her new job."

"Give me a shout if you need any pointers about being Grand Marshal of the parade tomorrow," Miles called after him.

Gavin rolled his eyes. "Because smiling and waving is so complicated."

"Hey, Tanner," Will said. "I'm here if you need anything."

Tanner nodded in understanding, grateful for the friends he had in this town. They made the ache of no longer having Tristan to confide in bearable.

"I'll follow you out," Gavin said. "I want to check on Ginger."

Gavin pulled the door closed to drown out the protests of his brother and Will.

"They might be right," Tanner told him. "You should probably let her rest."

"Yeah, I've learned my lesson. That was just a smokescreen. I really came out here because I wanted to let you in on a little secret that you might want to take advantage of while Paige is staying at the inn."

CHAPTER TWENTY-FOUR

PAIGE CLOSED the bookstore later than usual that evening. Chances Inlet was crowded with tourists, all of whom wanted flags to wave during the parade the following day. Kudos to Cassidy for anticipating the need and ordering them earlier that week. Especially since many of the flag-seekers ended up purchasing a book or a magazine to read while soaking up the sun at the beach this weekend. Denise and Lou would be thrilled when she told them.

She waved at Cassidy who was working her second summer gig, manning the Patty Wagon, a tricked-out ice cream truck owned by Patricia. Cassidy was industrious and hardworking, no doubt from spending time under the wing of the innkeeper.

"Headed home?"

Paige jumped at Deputy Lovell's question.

"Sorry," he said. "I didn't mean to startle you. On busy nights like this, I like to stop in and make sure things are locked up tight with my mom's store."

She looked over his shoulder at the shop's window

featuring a fabulous display of red, white, and blue yarn in honor of Founder's Day.

"Yarn is a hot commodity on the black market, I take it?" she teased.

He dipped his chin. When he lifted it back up, his dazzling smile had her rocking back on her heels. "Dude. Where do you think bank robbers get all their knit masks from?"

Paige laughed until tears escaped.

"Okay, that wasn't that funny," he insisted.

She wiped her eyes. "I know. But it was totally unexpected coming from someone as serious as you. And I mean that in the nicest way possible." She patted his shoulder. "I needed a good laugh after the day I've had. Thank you."

He nodded. "Your father mentioned Whitney's mother reappeared."

His reminder sucked the mirth right out of her. "Yep." She sighed. "But it's a good thing. Really. Whitney needs her mom."

"That's a very noble thing to say. You're definitely your father's daughter."

The deputy's words startled her more than his sudden appearance. He had it wrong, though. She carried her father's DNA, but she wasn't her father's daughter. Just like Whitney, the title of father went to the man who raised her. Not that she particularly wanted to discuss their relationship with the man who was her dad's protégé.

He must have sensed her reticence because he quickly changed the subject. "Is your car parked out back?"

"No. It's at the inn," she replied, certain he already knew that.

"You're walking all the way there alone? At night?"

She scoffed at him. "It's barely nine o'clock, and this isn't Chicago. I'll be fine."

"That's what Patricia thought last Founder's Day. She was hit by a drunk driver and left for dead."

His revelation shocked her. "I didn't know that." Her chest grew tight just thinking about the woman she'd come to admire suffering for even a moment.

"Long days in the sun and alcohol don't mix well. Anything could happen out here tonight. Your father would fire me if he knew I let you walk. My cruiser is at the end of the block. I'll run you up to the inn."

The no-nonsense deputy she'd encountered weeks ago when she first found Whitney had returned. Resistance was futile. There would be no arguing with the man. Paige followed without protest as he led her to his cruiser.

He was right about the crowds being a lot more animated than previous evenings. Twice he had to flash his lights to clear a side street. He radioed something cryptic to another deputy.

"It's going to be a long night," he told her.

"You're making my point that I don't need a babysitter to walk home."

He sighed in frustration. "Look, Paige, I want to share something about your dad."

She held up a hand. "Deputy Lovell—"

"Hayden," he interrupted. "Please. Call me Hayden. I have two amazing parents I love more than anything. But your dad, well, he's like a second father to me. It would mean a lot to me if we could be friends."

"At least he was a father to someone," she muttered bitterly.

"That right there. That's the reason I wanted to talk to you. To set you straight."

"I'm not five-years-old, Hayden," she snapped. "Your 'second father' has been my absent father for twenty-eight years."

He steered the car down the long drive leading to the inn.

"Yeah, well, while he was 'absent,'" your dad was busy saving the lives of countless servicemen and women. Including mine."

Given his allegiance to her father, she wasn't surprised.

She'd grown well aware of her father's distinguished career. Whenever her mother spoke of her father, she always mentioned his heroics. She had to admit, though, it was humbling to be sitting next to one of the recipients of her father's selfless actions. It would be rude not to give Hayden his two minutes.

"I didn't just leave bits and pieces of my leg back there in Afghanistan. I left a big chunk of my self-worth. Your dad helped me find it again. He took me under his wing in counseling and he put me on the path to a new career. I'm not exaggerating when I say I wouldn't be here today if it wasn't for him."

"Counseling?"

"No one goes through what we went through without scars. Some of those scars are a result of the sacrifices we all make to serve our country. In your dad's case, his sacrifice was you."

She felt like she'd been punched in the stomach. He pulled up to the steps leading to the inn's veranda and jerked the cruiser into park with a heavy sigh.

"I have no right butting into this. And you can tell me to shove it if you want. I deserve it. I just wanted you to know that you weren't the only one who suffered when your father couldn't be a part of your everyday life."

Paige gnawed on her bottom lip, feeling every bit like the selfish brat Hayden had just accused her of being. She sat in stunned silence until a call came over his radio that he needed to respond to.

"Your father would rip me a new one if I let your ride along while I respond to a drunk and disorderly call."

She reached for the door handle. "Thanks for the ride, Hayden. Be safe out there tonight."

He waved a curt goodbye, heading back toward town as soon as she closed the passenger door. She pondered Hayden's words as she climbed the steps into the inn. In the two months she'd been in Chances Inlet, Paige and her dad managed to avoid any deep discussion of their relationship. In fact, she was surprised her father never brought the subject up. He seemed content to let the subject lie. Perhaps that was the best way to handle things between them.

"Paige?" Patricia stepped out of the library. "Is everything okay?"

"Yeah, sure. Just lost in thought."

"It has been an eventful day, that's for sure," Patricia said. "Would you like to join me in the kitchen for a cup of chamomile tea?"

Any other night, Paige might have enjoyed that. Tonight, though, she didn't feel like the best company. Not only did Hayden's remarks stir up a lot of uncertainty within Paige, but she missed Whitney. And she missed Tanner even more.

"Can I take a raincheck? I've been dreaming of a relaxing bath for the past hour."

"That works, too." Patricia pulled her in for a hug. "Sleep well, Paige."

Paige was headed for the stairs when she turned back. "Patricia?"

The other woman looked up from where she was fanning out a pile of maps of the downtown on the foyer table. "Yes, hon?"

"Is my dad around by any chance?"

Patricia shook her head. "He's got everyone out on patrol tonight. I can call him if it's important."

"No." Paige waved her off. "Nothing that can't wait until tomorrow." She wasn't sure what she would say to her dad, anyway. "Night."

She hurried up the stairs and into her suite. A long soak in the tub would soothe her nerves. After kicking off her shoes, she dropped her bookbag onto the loveseat. A movement by the bed startled her. She swallowed a scream at the sight of Tanner reclining on the mattress.

A very naked Tanner.

"What? How?" The words were hard to push past her panicked throat.

He grinned at her distress, the rat bastard.

"Imagine my surprise when Gavin showed me the secret entrance to this room."

Her pulse jumped up another ten notches. "There's a secret entrance?"

Great.

There went any chance of Paige getting any sleep in this room. She ran to the wall and began tracing her fingers along the wainscoting. Out of the corner of her eye, she saw Tanner lift up one of her beloved paperback books.

"But what really surprised me?" He cocked an eyebrow devilishly. "Reading how naughty those dudes in Victorian England were."

"Oh. My. God!" She jumped on the bed, trying to rescue her book. "Give me that!"

He laughed as he held it out of reach. She sprawled across his bare chest in an effort to retrieve it. Except the minute she came in contact with his warm skin, she lost interest in the book. His familiar scent filled her nostrils making her insides quiver. Her lips found their way to his neck as though following a homing beacon. She tangled her fingers in the coarse hair at his navel. He groaned when her hand traveled lower to wrap around the hard velvet length of him.

Her breath hitched when he reversed their positions. He skimmed his lips along her jaw. His greedy fingers slid beneath her T-shirt to toy with her breasts.

"I really want to try out the position they describe on page one-seventy-three," he whispered. "First, we need to get these clothes off. You're a bit overdressed."

He snapped open the button on her shorts while Paige tried to gather up her scattered wits. She was supposed to be taking some time away from him. Time to figure out if he was worth the risk to her heart. She swatted at his hands. He took his hands from her body immediately. Then he pushed up on his elbows so that he was hovering above her. Her body instantly began complaining about the lack of contact.

"Paige," he groaned.

"Why are you here?"

"Because you're here," he replied solemnly, as though it was the simplest answer in the world.

She slammed her eyes shut.

Why did he have to be so wonderful?

He touched his forehead to hers. "Paige. You don't want people to know about us. Fine. I respect your wish for privacy. Trust me. I know how brutal gossip and the media can be. We'll do this your way. As long as we can still be together, I'll take whatever you'll give me."

She felt his lips trace over her closed eyes.

"Tell me you don't want this." He thrust his hips into hers. "Tell me you want me to go. I will if you ask me to. But you have to use your words, Paige. And you have to do it now."

A moan escaped her lips. She forced her eyes open. The uncertainty in his eyes made her stomach clench.

"This thing between us is like nothing I've ever felt before," he whispered. "Tell me you feel it too."

She did. She was just having trouble making herself believe that the sentiments he professed were true.

"I'm scared," she whispered. The words came out of nowhere. She meant to keep them bottled up with her battered heart. Except Tanner always seemed to be able to unravel all her secrets.

His face relaxed into a stunned grin. "Yeah. This feels pretty damn scary to me, too. I never expected to fall for you. To fall for anyone." He kissed the tip of her nose. "It's a lot to ask you to get involved with a guy who's on the road half the year. But we can make this work. I know we can. We'll figure out a way for you to keep your job in Chicago if you want that, too."

A manic laugh rolled past her lips.

Tell him.

He spoke before she could spill her truth.

"I'm all yours, Paige Hollister. You're the only one who knows all my secrets. You're the only one I trust with them. I've got nothing to hide from you. Do you trust me?"

His softly uttered question nearly destroyed her. She thought back to all the ridiculous things Jon had once said to her. Lies about her being the only one in his life. About him seeing them together forever. Tanner was saying the same thing. But with one exception.

Trust.

In the past two months the man leaning over her had demonstrated countless times that he was a man of character. A man she could trust. He wasn't hiding anything from her. Suddenly, she knew that to be true with every fiber of her being. Without hesitation, she took a leap of faith and gently pressed her lips to his.

"Yes," she murmured against his mouth.

With a low growl, he stripped her naked and proceeded to act out the scene from page one-seventy-three.

CHAPTER TWENTY-FIVE

THE FOLLOWING MORNING, Paige snatched up a scone from the inn's crowded breakfast room and filled a to-go cup with coffee before heading out to the bookstore.

"That must have been some bath last night," Patricia announced from where she was watering the hanging baskets on the veranda. "You certainly have more pep in your step this morning."

Paige's cheeks burned. Of course the woman must know about all the secret entrances to her inn. Did she also know what she and Tanner were up to the night before? That her bath was actually for two? *Great.* Now the rest of her was burning just thinking about all the things Tanner did to her in that bathtub.

Pasting on a bright smile, she risked a glance over at Patricia. "It's amazing what a good night's sleep will do for you, right?"

Not that there had been much sleeping last night. Still, she felt energized in a whole new way. For the first time in her life, someone was choosing her. Tanner wasn't going anywhere. And she was pretty sure it could last forever.

"Mmhmm. A good night's sleep is always amazing," Patricia replied. "See you at the parade."

Paige wasn't sure, but she thought the other woman might have winked at her before she disappeared back into the inn.

Hayden was setting up a table outside his mother's store, Knotical, when Paige arrived at the bookstore.

"Mornin', Paige," he said a bit sheepishly.

He looked a lot younger out of uniform. His titanium leg was on full display beneath his golf shorts. Her throat clogged up thinking about all that he'd gone through at such a young age. She impetuously threw her arms around his neck and hugged him. He hesitated before returning her embrace.

"What's this about?" he asked.

Paige unwrapped her arms, patting his rock-solid chest when she stepped back. "Law enforcement should always be celebrated when they return home safely from a shift."

"Amen to that," Claire Lovell added from her perch in the doorway of her shop.

Paige met Claire and her sister Kitty, Knotical's co-owner, when she first took over for Denise and Lou weeks ago. Hayden's mom won Paige over immediately with a welcoming smile, and her perky demeanor. Kitty went a step further with a slice of hummingbird cake that was to-die-for. While Kitty was more earth mother, Claire was one of those southern ladies who knew how to expertly apply her makeup to always look fresh and camera-ready. Her sassy short hair held its volume, even in the face of smothering humidity, without ever having a hair out of place. Silver bracelets snaked up her forearm, giving Claire her own personal soundtrack wherever she went.

Her son definitely did not get his height from his mother. Even with her hair teased high on her head, she barely reached his shoulder. What she lacked in height, though, she made up for in mother's intuition. Given the way her eyes were darting between Paige and her son, that intuition was picking up the wrong vibe.

"I've adopted your son as my little brother," Paige explained.

Claire tried hard to disguise her look of relief, but Paige saw it anyway. She almost laughed. Hayden's mother likely had her future daughter-in-law picked out for him and he didn't know it yet.

Hayden rolled his eyes. "One sister is enough," he said.

"Too late. You're stuck with me, too."

"Paige! Deputy!" Whitney called from down the block.

Hayden grinned. "There's a sound I never thought I'd hear."

Whitney pulled free of Donella and Sonny's hands and raced down the sidewalk toward them.

He lifted her up and spun her around. "Now you're flying like a butterfly," he said.

"Not without her wings," Donella said. "We are on our way to the studio to get her into her costume." She placed her hand on Paige's arm. "I don't know how I'll ever be able to thank you."

"Seeing—and hearing—Whitney so happy is thanks enough."

Donella looked around the town square all dressed up for the weekend's festivities. "I never pictured myself in a place like this."

"Give it time," Paige said. "In a few weeks you'll never imagine being anywhere else."

Hayden lifted an eyebrow. Paige ignored him.

"I better get the store open." She crouched down to hug Whitney. "You enjoy the parade. I'll be in the front row of the gazebo for your recital."

Whitney placed her palms on Paige's cheeks. "I missed you last night," she whispered.

Paige felt the sudden sting of tears at the back of her eyes. "I missed you, too. But aren't you a lucky girl to have your momma back? And a whole town of new friends."

"You're not gonna leave, are you?"

"No." Paige shook her head. "I believe I'll stick around."

Whitney kissed both Paige's cheeks. "Sonny, you stay here and keep Gladys company." She plopped the rabbit into the golf chair the caddy set up. "Make sure you put her on your shoulders when Tanner goes by so she can see him."

Sonny bowed to the little girl. "As you wish."

As EXPECTED, Whitney, Emily, and the rest of Audra and Ginger's Tiny Dancers were a big hit. What wasn't expected was Ginger going into labor as their encore. The McAlisters—and half of the residents of Chances Inlet—were already crowded into the labor and delivery waiting room by the time Paige and Cassidy arrived. Kyle, Cassidy's boyfriend, stayed behind to manage the store.

Bernice was entertaining the children with a movie on her cellphone. Lois, from the Java Jolt, set up a pot of her specialty coffee in the corner. Tatum Fisk brought over cookies and cupcakes from her bakery. Even Tony from the Slice and Sip pitched in with enough pizza to feed the entire hospital.

"This town is better than Disneyland," Donella remarked.

"Just wait until you see it at Christmastime," Cassidy said, helping herself to a slice of pizza.

Donella and Whitney exchanged a delighted smile.

"How is it going?" Paige asked her father. He looked a little peaked.

"Just suffering a little PTSD from when we were all here last year," he said. He twined his fingers through his wife's. "Although this time it's for a much happier event."

"Last year wasn't so bad," Patricia said.

"That's because they gave you the good drugs and a bed while the rest of us suffered out here," Miles joked.

Lori swatted his arm. Tanner entered the room along with Will Connelly and his wife Julianne.

"Did we miss it?" Will asked.

"She's pushing now," Patricia said. "Kate and Alden are back there with Gavin."

Jane held up her cellphone so Ryan could join in. Emily, Henry, and Miles made funny faces into the phone's screen.

Tanner stepped up beside Paige. "What are the rules here?" he whispered. "Am I allowed to stand by you in public?"

She grabbed his hand with hers and gave it a squeeze.

"I love it when you push the envelope, Hollister," he teased, moving a little closer to her.

Kate came through the hydraulic doors wearing a huge smile. Gavin followed her out carrying a baby swaddled in a pink blanket. A collective "aw" went up from those gathered in the room. Emily, Henry, and Whitney silently crept forward to get a better look.

"Here she is," he said, his voice shaky. "Hazel Patricia McAlister."

Patricia moved toward her son and his daughter while Jane trailed her with the cell phone.

"She's beautiful," Patricia and Ryan said at the same time.

Everyone laughed as they all began to circle around Gavin and the newborn.

"Paige!" Summer suddenly burst into the waiting room, Luke Kessler breathing hard behind her. "Thank goodness you're okay."

Everyone turned at once to stare at the newcomers.

"Summer! What are you doing here?" Paige couldn't believe her best friend was standing in front of her.

"I—we came to surprise you. But we went to the inn, and you weren't there. Then we tried the bookstore, and the guy there said you were at the hospital and I was so scared something had happened to you." Summer hugged Paige tightly. "But you're okay. You're really okay."

Paige laughed. "I'm fine. Ginger had her baby."

"Oh my gosh." Summer glanced around the room. "She's gorgeous. I'm so sorry for intruding."

"You're not intruding," Patricia said. "Any and all friends of Paige are welcome in our family."

"Um, everyone. This is my best friend Summer Pearson and her boyfriend, Luke Kessler."

"Summer Pearson the cellist?" Jane asked.

Julianne clapped her hands together. "I've been dying to meet you."

Her husband nodded at Luke. "Kessler."

Luke grinned at Will. "My ribs thank you for retiring, Connelly."

"I'm so glad you're okay," Summer said before swatting her. "Ow!"

"Why aren't you answering Mrs. Kliphuis' calls?" Summer demanded.

"Mrs. Kliphuis?" What could Preston's principal possibly want with her? "I blocked her weeks ago."

"You shouldn't have done that, silly." Summer took both Paige's hands in hers. "She's got great news. You can have your job back. The board decided to un-fire you."

The room suddenly grew quiet. The only sounds were Hazel's soft baby snuffles.

"Oh, and here's the best part," Summer continued, oblivious to Paige's impending heart attack. "That snake Jon was two-timing his wife with multiple women. Not just you. One of them went to his wife with proof and she's kicking him out and taking all his money. The board got wind of it and they are reinstating you with back pay and a written apology."

"Sum." Luke put his hand on Summer's shoulder.

"Well, they haven't agreed to the written apology yet, but my brother is insisting on it. You know how he . . ." Summer's voice trailed off.

"You were fired?" Of course her father would speak up first.

"You're the other woman?" Bernice tsked.

"Was this documented in the media?" Miles asked.

"Paige?" Summer whispered. "Please tell me they knew about this already."

Paige risked a peek around the room. Everyone was focused on her with varying degrees of shock. Even Tanner. Her chest began to constrict so fiercely she wasn't sure she could pull in another breath.

"Who the hell is Jon?" Tanner wanted to know. "And why is this the first I'm hearing about all this?"

The disappointment in his eyes gutted her. Paige jerked her hands from Summer's grasp. "I'm sorry," she choked out before bolting from the room.

THE DOGS WERE FEELING NEGLECTED after being deserted at the inn while everyone else in the family was at the hospital. Paige took pity on them, inviting Tessa and Midas up to her suite so she'd have company as she packed. Tessa anxiously shadowed her around while Midas investigated every nook and cranny of the room with his snout.

"Your family will be back soon enough," she told the dogs. "They'll have lots to celebrate. Midas?" The dog looked over at her. "You are going to have to learn to share." The dog grunted and went back to exploring. "Oh, who am I kidding, that baby will have you wrapped around her finger in less than a week."

"I'd say that's highly likely."

She looked up from the duffel bag she was hastily filling. Her father was leaning against the doorjamb, arms crossed over his chest. She hated the disappointment she felt that it wasn't Tanner standing there. Not that she blamed him for being angry at her. Less than twenty-four hours ago, they lay together on this very bed, his legs wrapped around her and she'd told him she trusted him.

Just not enough to tell him the whole truth about her life. About her mistakes. Her embarrassment. Because she was too scared to give him everything.

The irony was they both had trust issues. Tristan burned Tanner just as badly as Jon burned her. By withholding the truth. And she'd gone and done it to Tanner again. She deserved his disappointment. Not to mention the disgust he likely felt.

Her hands were shaking as she tried to stuff her flip flops into the overflowing bag. One fell to the floor. When she reached down to pick it up, her father's hand closed over hers. Paige froze. She had no memory of him ever touching her before this moment. His palm was warm against her skin. His grip was sure and steady.

Comforting.

Before she could stop herself, she leaned into him. He pulled her into a hug, holding her with the same gentleness one might hold a valuable piece of crystal. Paige once vowed never to cry in front of her father, but it was soothing to let it all out while wrapped in his secure embrace.

"Hush, child," he murmured while his palm stroked her back. "I've got you."

He led her over to the loveseat. They both sat while Paige tried to get control of her emotions.

"I wish you would have told me what was troubling you when you first arrived," he said.

"I figured you would call mom, and she'd tell you everything."

"Ah. So that's what that conversation was about at the baby shower."

She brushed her hair off her face. "You knew something was up when I first got here?"

He arched an eyebrow. "It's part of my skill set."

"But—"

"I was hoping you'd tell me when you were good and ready," he interjected.

"Instead, I embarrassed you in front of your new family." She hung her head. "I'm so sorry."

He looked askance at her. "What exactly did you do to embarrass me?"

She brushed the tears from her cheeks. "Well, I was a gullible fool, for starters."

Her father actually chuckled. "Welcome to the human race, Paige. We all make mistakes. If you're not making them, you're not really living."

"Not on the grand scale I did. I wrecked a family, Dad. People I don't even know crucified me on social media. I was fired from the job I love. For cause! They actually put the word 'adulteress' in my file." She shivered.

"You have a big heart, Paige. Someone ugly took advantage of that. You did nothing wrong."

"Except for not being smart enough to know better." She smacked her head. "I was so desperate for attention that I didn't even realize I was being used. I ignored all the signs just so I wouldn't be alone. How pathetic is that?"

"You are not at fault here. There's no crime in opening yourself to someone."

"There is if you get burned," she argued.

He made a growling noise. "For crying out loud, Paige. If you weren't a grown woman, I'd take you over my knee. Hell, I have a good mind to march you down to the office and lock you into a jail cell until you come to your senses. You did nothing wrong. Summer said it's all worked out. You can go back to your job and resume your life."

She groaned. "Except now my colleagues and the kids' parents won't be whispering about me with condemnation. It will be pity, instead."

"You can always stay here," he offered.

"Are you kidding? Everyone in this town knows my humiliation now, too." She shook her head. "You saw how they looked at me! It was obvious what they were all thinking. I'm not going to saddle Patricia and her family with my toxic reputation."

"I think you're jumping to the wrong conclusions, Paige."

"Am I? You heard Miles ask if there's any media coverage." She buried her face in her hands. "Oh, God, I hope not."

Her father gently pried Paige's hands from her face. "There aren't many things Miles and I see eye-to-eye on, with the exception of his mother's happiness. Today, though, he and I are on the same page. We both want to punish this Jon guy. I hate to break it to you, but Miles now considers you his sister to protect. Sure, he's abrasive and obnoxious about it most times. But I've learned it's his way of caring." He sighed. "Miles and Summer's brother are already in cahoots making plans about your legal strategy. I wouldn't put it past the congressman to subpoena the guy before a congressional committee if he could pull it off."

"Seriously?"

He nodded. "Gavin, Ryan, Will, and Summer's friend, Luke, are advocating bodily harm. Kate was spouting off about the misogynistic hierarchy within school systems. She offered to apply her skills with a scalpel to unman every male member of the Preston Board of Directors. As a member of law enforcement, I can't condone that kind of violence. But believe me, if that guy Jon or any of those board members ever step foot in this county, God help them."

She gave him a watery smile. "But—"

"No buts, Paige." He pulled her back into a hug, this one tighter than before. "We all have skeletons in our closets. Even the McAlisters. Stick around and they'll tell you all about them."

She buried her face in his shirt. "Am I one of your skeletons?"

He pulled back. "What kind of question is that?"

Paige forged on. The thought had been circulating in the back of her mind for years. Her conversation with Hayden last night only made the question more important. "Do you regret getting involved with my mom? Having me?"

"Whatever gave you that idea?" He looked like she had physically struck him.

"My grandfather always told me your wedding was a shotgun wedding."

"Yeah, the shotgun was for your mother." He leaned forward, resting his elbows on his knees. "Have you never wondered why you only have one set of grandparents?"

She sank her teeth into her bottom lip knowing what she was about to say would likely hurt him. "I figured they didn't want me, either."

He whipped his head around to stare at her, a thunderstruck expression on his face. "Is that what you thought? That I didn't want you?"

The only response she could manage was a nod.

Mumbling something that sounded violent, he got to his feet and began to pace. It took him several trips back and forth before he was composed enough to speak. Still, his voice was edgy with emotion.

"Nothing could be further from the truth. I grew up in foster care. The only thing I ever wanted was a family. Believe it or not, I was excited when your mom told me she was pregnant. Still, it was one hundred percent her choice what we did about it." He shook his head. "Of course, your grandfather had other ideas. He saw a good excuse to yank her back to Iowa, and he took full advantage of it."

"But if it weren't for me, you and mom wouldn't have married." It was a statement of fact. Not a question.

He stopped in front of her. "No."

She sighed. "Thank you for being honest with me. Mom constantly dances around the subject like she wants me to believe my conception was some big love story. Honestly, I always felt like were it not for me, she would have had the life she dreamed of."

"That's not the way it went down." Sighing heavily, he returned to the loveseat. "Circumstances got in the way of your mom realizing the dreams she thought she wanted. First it was me getting deployed overseas. Then your grandmother died. Both things sending her back to the farm. But know this, she never once felt like *you* killed her dreams. Her dreams changed when you were born, yes." He took her hand. "They became all about you. She always told me you were the gift she got to keep forever."

"She said that?" Could that be why her mother resisted Paige's leaving so much? She wanted Paige all to herself?

He crossed his heart with his finger. "She assured me she was content in her life as long as she had you beside her. And you were pretty attached to her, too. I was deployed so often you hardly knew me. And when I came back..." He swallowed. "I wasn't exactly in a good place mentally. Your mom and I believed it might be upsetting to suddenly interject a grizzly army veteran into your life while I was still...adjusting."

Her heart formed a knot in her chest. Hayden was telling the truth. He had sacrificed her. And she paid him back by rebuffing every one of his gestures of love over the years. Suddenly, she was more ashamed of her behavior as a teenager than falling for Jon's lies.

"By the time I got my head right, you wanted nothing to do with me," he said quietly.

She leaned her head onto her father's shoulder. "I'm sorry I was such a brat growing up. I should have tried to see things from another point of view besides my own stubborn one."

Paige felt his chest rumble with laughter. "With age comes wisdom. Besides, I can't really hold it against you. One of my foster moms used to threaten that the universe would pay me back for my stubbornness one day. Karma and all that."

"I'm glad you finally got your big family."

He laced his fingers through hers. "I'm glad you have two families who love you and want to see you happy."

"I was sort of hoping to make it three families," she whispered. "Do you think I blew it with Tanner?"

"Well, the poor guy is getting a bad case of whiplash from the number of times he's been blindsided these past few months."

Her heart sank at the truth in her father's words.

He pressed a kiss to the top of her head. "Lucky for you, he's made out of sterner stuff. I had to threaten to arrest him if he didn't let me come up and speak to you first. Hayden is keeping him company out in the gazebo."

A wave of optimism and profound relief washed over her. She jumped to her feet and raced to the door before turning around and throwing her arms around her father's neck. "Karma may have had the last laugh on both of us when my car broke down in this town. Thank you, Dad."

Summer was sitting at the bottom of the stairs with Luke beside her. Her friend's eyes were red rimmed and puffy. "I'm so, so sorry."

"She didn't know, Paige," Luke added.

"I know." Paige gave her friend a firm hug. "It's okay. Really."

"Based on Tanner Gillette's reaction, you've been keeping a lot from me," Summer accused.

Her friend had every right to be angry. Paige would be, too, if the roles were reversed.

She took both of Summer's hands in hers.

"I'm sorry. We were keeping it from everyone."

The hurt in Summer's eyes was painful to see. Her friend tried to pull her hands free, but Paige held fast.

"I didn't realize I was lumped in with everyone else. But Tanner Gillette? Paige, I thought he was another jerk like Jon?"

"That's just it. He's not who either of us thought he was." She squeezed Summer's fingers. "The situation with Whitney is complicated, but it's not my story to tell. You have to trust me on this. It's—he's—"

"You're in love with him," Summer whispered.

Paige nodded. "Against all odds, yes."

A slow smile grew on Summer's lips. "Well, then that's all that matters." She leaned into Paige's embrace.

"Except I probably screwed it all up," Paige told her. "He doesn't like secrets."

"Well, if he can't get past this then he doesn't deserve you. But something tells me you two will be okay." She turned Paige by the shoulders and pointed her in the direction of the kitchen. "Go put my theory to the test."

The lobby and breakfast room were blessedly empty with most people enjoying dinner in town. When Paige reached the kitchen, it was a different story. It seemed everyone who'd been in the hospital waiting room was crammed into the kitchen, all of them staring out the windows at the gazebo. Tanner was pacing in a circle like an animal in a pen. Hayden was standing on the steps.

"Oh my God! Is Hayden holding him at gunpoint?" Paige cried.

"It's not a real gun," Cassidy explained.

"It's Henry's squirt gun," Miles said around a mouthful of cookie.

"I told y'all that toy was too realistic," Jane protested. "It better disappear after this is over."

"I'll have Midas bury it in the yard somewhere," Gavin suggested.

Paige spun around, the shock piling on. "Why are you not at the hospital with your wife?"

"Just getting some grub. And neither of us wanted to miss this." He held up his cellphone. Ginger was visible on the screen, Hazel sleeping in her arms.

"Oh, Paige, honey," she said quietly. "I hate that you had to go through that thanks to that jerk. I wish I was there to give you a hug."

"I've got it covered," Kate said before wrapping her arms around Paige. "You can't get rid of us that easily," she whispered. "You're one of us whether you want it or not. Still, I hope you want us. Because we want you in our family."

Paige's father slipped into the kitchen. He grinned at her.

"It's probably too much to ask for privacy?" Paige said.

"We were all just on our way to the front porch." Patricia made shooing motions with her hands.

A chorus of groans went up, mostly from Miles and Cassidy, before they all began to file out. Summer blew her a kiss. Donella gave her arm a squeeze as she passed.

"You're right about this place sucking you in." Donella's lips twitched. "I'm looking forward to living here."

Worried her courage might fail her, Paige hurried across the lawn. When Hayden spun around to greet her, she yanked the squirt gun from his hands.

"Give me that!"

She sprayed the water at the deputy.

"Hey!"

"Go!" she ordered. "Everyone is around front."

He looked like he wanted to protest, before changing his mind and stomping off. Paige placed the squirt gun on the bottom step of the gazebo. She risked a glance in Tanner's direction. He was seated on the bench, his face intense with an emotion she was having trouble defining.

Slowly, she made her way toward him.

"I'm sorry my father and Hayden were being so ridiculous. You don't have to stay here. I'm sure there are other places you'd rather be."

"Are you kidding right now? You expect me to just walk away?"

She wrung her hands together. "I wasn't totally open with you. And I know you value that."

He jumped up from his seat. "Yeah, I do. So why then must the people I love most in this world keep secrets from me?"

Her heart skipped. "Wait? Did you just say you love me?"

"Oh for the love of . . . you're just now figuring that out? Did you hear anything I said last night? Or has that asshole damaged you so badly you can't tell what's real anymore?"

"Something like that," she murmured.

He mumbled something ugly about Jon. "The issue is not *me* loving *you*. It's *you* loving *me* and trusting me with *your* secrets."

"I didn't tell you because I was mortified!" she shouted. "I let someone take advantage of me. I let someone ruin my reputation. Make a fool of me. He took away my livelihood and my identity. You have no idea how humiliating that was for me." She choked on her words. "I didn't want you to see me that way."

His face softened. "Sweetheart, those are the kinds of things you're supposed to share with me. So I can make you feel better. So I can make things right for you."

"You have made me feel better. I didn't lie last night when I said I trust you. I do. Tanner, I lov—"

"Oh no." He held a hand up. "You don't get to say it back to me. Not yet. Not until I know you're all in. With me. With Whitney. With this freaking town. Because this isn't just for the time being, Paige. For me, this—" he gestured between them "—is forever."

He whistled loudly. She heard the crunch of footsteps on the gravel path followed by the sounds of voices as everyone made their way onto the lawn.

"Get your camera ready, Cassidy," Tanner called out.

There were a few catcalls when Tanner took both Paige's hands in his. The fact that his were trembling as much as hers was the first sign that he wasn't as sure of himself as he let on. Paige loved him even more.

He pulled her closer.

"I didn't think I would survive without Tristan. He was literally a part of me. But I did survive. And then on a New Year's Eve when all I wished was for the powers that be to bring him back to me, I ended up crossing paths with you." He touched his forehead to hers. "I truly believe he sent you to me. And me to you. I love you, Paige Hollister. You filled the hole my brother left inside of me and now it's overflowing. Please say you'll spend your life with me."

She ignored the chorus of sighs and gasps from the spectators, concentrating only on the sincerity in Tanner's eyes. The knowledge that he meant what he said melted the last bits of her anxiety and replaced it with profound joy.

"I love you, Tanner Gillette," she promised him. "Now and forever."

He swept her up in a dizzying kiss as her friends and family swarmed the gazebo. Paige was engulfed in a sea of love and acceptance. She had finally reached her destination.

EPILOGUE

A WARM JULY breeze blew in off the ocean, ruffling the petals of the pansies hanging above the porch swing on the Tide Me Over's veranda. Guests mingled on the lawn, soaking up the late afternoon sunshine. Paige and Summer sat side-by-side, swinging, ever so slowly, back, and forth.

Summer sighed. "This really is an amazing place. I'm trying to convince Luke we need a vacation house here."

"Seriously? I would love having you in Chances Inlet. Even if it's only for a few months of the year. We could have beach days and you could take golf lessons with me. You could even put on little impromptu concerts on the square."

Summer nudged her friend. "As long as I drive foot traffic into the Whale of a Tale Bookstore, right?"

Paige laughed. "Of course. The shop is doing well without any gimmicks, though." She glanced up to the sky. "I hope Lou is proud of me."

They said goodbye to Lou three days before with a beautiful memorial service. Summer performed while friends and family read passages from some of Lou's favorite books. Denise offered fifty-one percent of the store to Paige. Thanks to a small settlement Sterling insisted the board at Preston award her, Paige was able to take the leap and invest. The irony that she was sinking her roots deeper in the "backwater town" she'd resolved never to see again wasn't lost on her.

This afternoon, they were celebrating little Hazel's baptism. It was even better attended than the baby shower months earlier. Ryan McAlister skipped the All-Star game to meet his new niece and spend time with his family. Not to mention the family he seemed to be creating with Jane and Henry. Ginger's friend Diesel Gold was also in town, currently strumming a lullaby on his guitar.

Then there were the guests no one expected.

"I can't believe your mom and Jim are so chummy with the sheriff and Patricia," Summer said with an astonished chuckle.

Sure enough, Heather and Jim Franks were playing a rousing game of cornhole against Paige's dad and Patricia.

"I know," Paige replied. "I really thought it would be weird having them here. Especially staying at the inn where they were sure to run into my dad and Patricia often." Her mother laughed at something her father said. "I guess I'm the only one who felt uncomfortable about it. And my mom seems happier for some reason. Maybe she felt bad about how things went down with my dad."

"She could have felt guilty your grandfather made him marry her."

Paige shrugged. "Who knows? Besides, as soon as my mom found out about Whitney, there was no keeping her away. Did I tell you that both my stepbrothers sent me texts thanking me for providing a grandchild for our parents to dote on?"

They both watched as a laughing Whitney raced across the lawn, Midas and Henry on her heels.

"She's the biggest winner in all of this," Summer said of Whitney. "Growing up in this place, surrounded by so many people who love her."

"I miss having her at the house every day."

Denise insisted Donella and Whitney move in to the two-bedroom cottage she and Lou had been renting in town. It turned out Denise liked living on the ocean, so she kept the lease on the house she'd rented for Lou's last couple of months. Donella was a hit with the dancers at summer camp. As a result, Audra put her in charge of the competition dance team the studio was forming. The group already had a wait-list for dancers, much to Audra and Donella's delight. Donella was also teaching a hip-hop exercise class at the Ship's Iron gym. It was so popular, they often had to turn people away.

"Ah. Poor you. All alone in that big house with just Tanner for company." Summer smirked.

Paige's cheeks burned at the memory of how Tanner kept her "company" last night. And again this morning. He'd been in Scotland for a week and Ohio the week before that. She missed him when he was away. But his homecomings definitely made up for his absences. Especially when he insisted on re-enacting the steamy scenes from her favorite books.

"Where is Tanner, by the way?" Summer asked.

"Someone from Gillette Industries is in the area finalizing a project near Myrtle Beach. He insisted he needed to speak with Tanner before he left tonight." She checked her watch. "I expected him back by now, though."

Emily stormed up the front steps. "Miss Summer! Miss Summer! You have to come play your cello. Diesel wants to do a duet with you."

Summer laughed as Emily practically dragged her off the swing. "Why does it feel like I don't have a choice?"

"It's easy to get swept up in things in this town," Paige told her friend. "It's better to just go with the flow. I'm going to see if Patricia needs any help in the kitchen while you set up."

She slipped inside the quiet inn, making her way toward the

kitchen, only to stop short at the entrance to the music room. Tanner was sitting at the piano lost in thought.

"Hey you," she said softly.

He looked up at her. The warm grin that spread over his face gave her the same thrill every time he gifted it to her. He reached a hand out. Seconds later she was in his lap, his lips blanketing her mouth. She sank her fingers into his thick hair, letting her tongue parry with his. He trailed his palm along her thigh beneath her skirt. A groan rumbled from his chest when his fingers came in contact with the string of her thong under-wear. He tore his mouth away with a muttered curse.

"I'm glad I didn't know you were wearing that earlier. We never would have made it out of the car and into the church."

She traced the line of his jaw with her finger. Despite his playful demeanor, his eyes still looked pensive. "Is everything okay?"

"It is now." He nipped at her bottom lip.

"Tanner," she insisted. "Tell me."

With a sigh, he set her next to him on the piano bench. "You are far too tempting."

"You're stalling. Did something happen with the guy from Gillette Industries?"

"Jared Hoffman," he said. "He's my dad's executive assistant. It seems my dad wants me to go to Paris to accept an award on behalf of the company."

"Wow. That's . . .unexpected. Also exciting."

He grinned. "It will be because you're coming with me." His voice suddenly was filled with wonder. "Gillette Industries is being presented a global award for its work in environmental preservation."

She gaped at him.

"I know," he said with an amused shake of his head. "Apparently Tristan took all my crazy comments in that long ago interview to heart. He immediately set up a committee within the company to address all the issues I spouted off on. Jared used to be Tristan's assistant. He said my brother wanted my dad to respect my ideas. Who knew?"

"Oh, Tanner. I wish I could have met Tristan," she whispered.

He nodded. "Me, too. But I still believe he sent you to me."

Something fluttered in her belly. She wasn't very fanciful with her beliefs, yet she liked the idea that Tristan was still watching over his brother. That they were still connected spirits somehow. And that he was looking out for Whitney and Donella. That he'd brought them all together for a reason.

"My dad called to thank me," Tanner continued. "He said that ever since I gave that interview, he's scrutinized every environmental impact statement with clearer eyes." He cleared his throat. "He actually said the words 'I'm proud of you.'"

She wrapped her arms around his neck. "Of course he is. All this time, you thought you had to be the world's best golfer to prove your worthiness to him. To everyone. Except you've already proven it. You've kept your brother's secret. You've loved Whitney as your own. You've protected Melinda from further grief. No one asked you to do that. You just did." She leaned her shoulder against his. "You're the best man I know, Tanner Gillette."

He gave her a bashful smile. "Jared sent the stock to Donella."

"What?"

"Yeah. He knew about their relationship because he was working so closely with Tristan at the time. When Melinda told Tristan about Donella's visit, Tristan asked Jared to try to locate her. He wanted to make sure she was okay." He cleared his throat. "Of course, he died a week later."

Paige brushed a kiss against his cheek.

"Jared kept looking, though. When he found her, he learned about Whitney. He told me Tristan had no idea Donella had his baby. Jared knew Tristan would want his daughter provided for somehow. He set up a trust in her name. She's supposed to get shares every year. Except Donella went off the grid, so she only got the first installment. Whitney won't ever have to worry about living in a car again."

"I think that was a foregone conclusion even without the stock." She kissed him, softly at first until desire took over.

The sound of tennis shoes squeaking on the tigerwood floor forced them apart.

"Yuck." Henry made a face. "Everywhere we go people are kissing. It's disgusting."

Paige bit back a smile at his revulsion.

Emily rolled her eyes. "That's because it was your mom kissing Uncle Ryan."

"And Aunt Elle kissing Deputy Lovell!" Henry argued.

Whoa! Hayden and Elle?

Paige did not see that coming. From what she'd observed, those two couldn't stand one another.

"Shh!" Emily slapped a hand over Henry's mouth. "We're not supposed to tell that, or Aunt Elle won't take us to see the turtles tomorrow. Besides, she said they weren't kissing. It was an accident."

Tanner coughed out a laugh. "An accident?" he mouthed at Paige.

She shrugged, barely able to contain her own giggle.

Whitney put her hands on her hips, donning a look like a Sunday school teacher about to take her pupils to task. "Come on you two. Summer and Diesel are putting on a concert. Miss Patricia says everybody has to come outside to listen."

"And then Summer is going to teach me to play the cello," Emily announced before scampering down the hallway.

"You're too little to play the cello," Henry called after her.

"Am not!"

"Are too!"

Their shouts echoed back into the music room through the open window.

Whitney extended a hand to Tanner and one to Paige. "You guys have the rest of your lives to kiss each other."

Tanner leaned over to kiss Paige above Whitney's head. "I'm not sure that's long enough for me, Whit, but it's a good start."

I hope you enjoyed Paige and Tanner's story. It's always hard to leave Chance's Inlet and all its quirky residents. Well, how about a free novella featuring the town? It's yours for subscribing to my newsletter. Simply scan the QR code:

If you want more day to day details about my books, my crazy writing life, and opportunities to name places and characters in my books, come hang out with my reader group, the X's and O's, on Facebook. Scan the code below to join.

Are you curious about the rest of the McAlister family? Read Ginger and Gavin's story in **Back to Before**. Then catch up with all their shenanigans in **All They Ever Wanted** featuring Miles McAlister and more with Patricia and Lamar. Then, join the McAlisters for a very special **Second Chance Christmas** when Ryan finally returns to Chances Inlet.

And please, don't forget to tell other readers how much you enjoyed **It Had to Be You** by leaving a review on the site where you purchased it, as well as, Goodreads and BookBub. It's the best way to show an author some love and I ALWAYS appreciate it!

Are you curious about Summer and Luke's love story? You'll find it in **Double Dog Dare**, a romantic comedy featuring the Milwaukee Growlers football team. Luke was introduced in the first book in the Milwaukee Growlers sports romance series, **_Just for Kicks_,** featuring a kilt-wearing placekicker who needs to marry or be deported.
And how about Will and Julianne's second chance love story? Click here to add **Foolish Games** to your TBR pile.

Catch up with Will's Baltimore Blaze teammates, too:

Game On – a grumpy hero sports romance
Risky Game – a fake relationship sports romance
Sleeping with the Enemy – an enemies-to-lovers second chance
sports romance

How about a little suspense with your romance?
Recipe for Disaster – a mistaken identity Secret Service
romance
Shot in the Dark – a forced proximity Secret Service romance
Between Love and Honor – a second chance Secret Service
romance

ACKNOWLEDGMENTS

As always, it takes a village to get a book out to readers. Thank you to Melanie, Ann, Gina, and Kim for the beta reads. Thank you to Jeannie Moon for the editorial feedback. Thanks also go to Kate Foley for making sure all the i's were dotted and t's were crossed. And without a doubt this book wouldn't be possible without my assistant, Rachael, who keeps me on task and makes me look good, even when I mess up!

A huge thank you to Billy Ellison for putting up with my stalking and allowing me to purchase his gorgeous photo for my cover. His photography is amazing. Be sure to check him out at billyellison.com.

Finally, I'm humbled and grateful to all of you for taking the time to read my books. I absolutely love what I do. You're the best!

ABOUT THE AUTHOR

After years of writing reports and testimony for Congress, **Tracy Solheim** decided to put her creative talents to better use. The recipient of the 2020 Georgia Author of the Year Award, she's the *USA Today* best-selling author of contemporary sports romance, romantic suspense, and small-town second chance novels. Tracy lives in the heart of SEC country, also known as the suburbs of Atlanta, with her husband, two adult children who frequently show up at dinner time, and a neurotic Labrador retriever who keeps her company while she writes. See what she's up to by subscribing to her newsletter at Tracy Solheim.com.